A DAY IN THE LIFE

T0315624

BLACK SWAN

A DAY IN THE LIFE
A BLACK SWAN BOOK : 0 552 77127 9

First publication in Great Britain

PRINTING HISTORY
Black Swan edition published 2003

1 3 5 7 9 10 8 6 4 2

Compilation copyright © Transworld Publishers 2003
For copyright details of individual stories, see opposite page.

The line from 'Musèe des Beaux Arts' by W. H. Auden on
page 312 is reproduced by kind permission of Faber & Faber Ltd,
3 Queen Square, London WC1N 3AU.

Set in 11½/14pt Electra by
Kestrel Data, Exeter, Devon.

Black Swan Books are published by Transworld Publishers,
61–63 Uxbridge Road, London W5 5SA,
a division of The Random House Group Ltd,
in Australia by Random House Australia (Pty) Ltd,
20 Alfred Street, Milsons Point, Sydney, NSW 2061, Australia,
in New Zealand by Random House New Zealand Ltd,
18 Poland Road, Glenfield, Auckland 10, New Zealand
and in South Africa by Random House (Pty) Ltd,
Endulini, 5a Jubilee Road, Parktown 2193, South Africa.

Printed and bound in Great Britain by Clays Ltd, St Ives PLC

www.**booksattransworld**.co.uk

The Random House Group Limited supports The Forest Stewardship
Council (FSC®), the leading international forest certification organisation.
Our books carrying the FSC label are printed on FSC® certified paper.
FSC is the only forest certification scheme endorsed by the leading
environmental organisations, including Greenpeace. Our
paper procurement policy can be found at
www.randomhouse.co.uk/environment

MIX
Paper | Supporting
responsible forestry
FSC® C018179

Contents

Foreword

As Patron of leading national charity Breast Cancer Care, I am delighted to be writing the foreword for this book. It is wonderful that so many female authors have united to support the issue and contributed their powerful and entertaining stories. I am equally delighted that at least £1 from the sale of each book will go towards the valuable work that Breast Cancer Care does.

In the UK almost 40,000 women are diagnosed with breast cancer every year, making it the most common form of cancer in women. With statistics like this it's no surprise that so many of us have been affected in some way. I personally have lost a close friend and a beloved aunt to the disease, so I know at first hand how it turns lives upside down in the most unimaginable way, often leaving people feeling frightened, overwhelmed and powerless. And of course it doesn't stop there because the impact of that diagnosis extends to their families, friends and colleagues.

By being with my friend and aunt during their illness, I realized a very important thing – that good quality practical and emotional support, like that provided by Breast Cancer Care, makes a huge difference in coping with this complex and bewildering disease. At Breast Cancer Care we have contact with over 500,000 people a year who are affected by breast cancer in some way. We offer them information and support, mainly through a helpline, website, publications and peer support on a one-to-one or group basis. The services are free and confidential and delivered not only by health professionals but also by trained volunteers who have themselves experienced breast cancer.

All of these vital services need funds to continue, so the donation from this book will be put to good use.

For more information or to talk in complete confidence about any breast cancer concern call the Breast Cancer Care's free helpline on 0808 800 6000 (textphone 0808 800 6001) or visit www.breastcancercare.org.uk

Cherie Booth QC
Patron
Breast Cancer Care

Kate Atkinson was born in York and now lives in Edinburgh. She has won several prizes for her short stories. Her first novel *Behind the Scenes at the Museum*, which won the Whitbread First Novel Award and was then chosen as the overall 1995 Whitbread Book of the Year, is published by Black Swan and Doubleday, as are her critically acclaimed second and third novels, *Human Croquet* and *Emotionally Weird*, and her collection of short stories, *Not the End of the World*.

I am not a Joan

For one thing, I am too beautiful to be a Joan. Joans are soft and round and brown. Owlish, even. Joan of Arc was probably an exception but then she was French, which doesn't really count. There is a continent of difference between a Joan and a *Jeanne*. English Joans are tidy and punctual. They frequently wear spectacles that don't flatter their faces and take jobs as part-time librarians. When they have their colours done they are 'autumn'. 'Having their colours done' is the kind of thing that Joans do. They are always looking to change their lives in the details when it's the bigger picture they should be attending to. That's why they go to evening classes, every year a new one – French conversation, cordon bleu cookery, yoga for beginners, and so on.

They're also 'hoping to meet new people' at these evening classes and in their innermost secret heart they dream that a 'wonderful' man will discover them – in the manner of *The Bridges of Madison County* (which is the favourite book of many Joans). Most Joans, by the way, are either married or in the process of getting a divorce. Many are aged between forty-five and fifty-five.

Unfortunately, the only people they meet in evening classes are other Joans with whom they start 'reading groups' or spend afternoons in the sauna, covertly checking out each other's cellulite and operation scars. In the sauna they state they are 'having some quality time for themselves'. In their reading groups the Joans gather and pretend to discuss the latest literary novel when really all they want to do is eat cake and talk about *The Bridges of Madison County*.

This year, my own Joan is going to belly-dancing classes (where it seems unlikely that she'll meet a man, wonderful or otherwise). She thinks it will make her 'feel more positive' about her body. There was a time when Joan fitted her body. She was once (and it's hard to believe, I know) a schools county netball player, but now her middle-aged, baggy body has a waist as thick as the trunk of the ash tree in her garden. The ash tree that shouldn't be there, its seed having floated in one breezy morning ten years ago from a wood a mile away, a tree which now casts a great branching shadow across her garden, draining the life out of her Dutch irises and Asiatic lilies.

Joan went on marches once (a very long time ago), with her first child in a pushchair, and signed petitions demanding free contraceptives and sanitary wear and 'wages for housework'. That was when her body still fitted, more or less, and when she still needed contraceptives and sanitary wear and thought housework wasn't a suitable job for a woman. A time when she bought postcards produced by women's cooperatives to send to female friends, postcards that said things like 'A house doesn't need a wife' and 'A woman needs a man like a fish needs a bicycle'. Now she buys postcards produced by commercial profit-making companies to send to her daughter and these postcards say 'Women fly when men aren't watching' – which is entirely wishful thinking on Joan's part.

The Joan that went on the marches and bought the postcards got married when she was still a student because she fell pregnant with the child in the push-chair who was called 'Matthew' then and is now called 'Matt'. Matt is a software designer in California and gets on very well with Joan ('Mum') as long as he stays on the other side of the globe.

The husband Joan married was a fellow student who was called 'Doug' at the time but now prefers 'Douglas'. When he graduated he went to teacher-training college and he is now 'Head of English' in a large northern comprehensive. He used to say it was a good thing that Joan went on the marches and bought the postcards although really he wanted her to be the same kind of wife that his mother was because that would have made his life much easier. Now that Joan has become the kind of wife that his mother was Douglas has lost interest in her. He is much more taken with 'Miss Carter' who is Deputy Head of Modern Studies and talks to him about gender politics and school funding and the latest production at the West Yorkshire Playhouse as well as giving him 'incredible' oral sex although never, never on school premises, sometimes in his car, but usually in her canalside apartment.

When Douglas was in his probationary year of

teaching, 'Doug and Joan' had another baby because they didn't want the first one to be an only child. This second child was 'Eleanor' but they always called her 'Ellie'. Now she won't answer to anything but 'Storm' even though she's nearer thirty than twenty. Storm's entire body is punctured with metal rings and bolts and studs and she has a tattoo of a green dragon that curls up the length of her spine. In the dark watches of the night Joan imagines the dragon is breathing fire, scorching the soft, vulnerable nape of her daughter. Storm hasn't been home for over a year.

Joan used to believe that every woman should have a room of her own. She gained an MA on Virginia Woolf somewhere between Matthew and Ellie and laughs with the Joans in the reading group about this because she says she 'cannot remember the first thing about Virginia Woolf!' Which isn't entirely true, of course, although most of the things that she can remember about Virginia Woolf are to do with her depression – Virginia Woolf's, not Joan's. Now Joan has several rooms of her own, in fact she has an entire four-bedroom, two-bathroom Edwardian house to herself most of the time because Douglas works such long hours that she is always surprised when he walks in the front door as if he were someone she had almost forgotten about. Douglas seems equally surprised to find himself standing on the tessellated floor of the hallway or next to the marble fireplace in the living room where a fire is never lit any more, not even at Christmas, because their children don't come home for Christmas any more. Joan has noticed that other people's children still come home for Christmas and thinking about what this means makes Joan so upset that she almost stops breathing.

Joan supposes that having the house to herself most of the time is a way of rehearsing for being a widow because any man that works such long hours in such a stressful job is bound to drop down dead suddenly at an inappropriately early age. Joan refuses to entertain the possibility that Douglas is enjoying extra-curricular activities with anyone else because 'trust is the basis of a good marriage'. This does not stop her fantasizing about her own wonderful *Bridges of Madison County*-type lover and sometimes she feels guilty because she knows if the *Bridges of Madison County* lover turned up unexpectedly on the doorstep of her four-bedroom, two-bathroom Edwardian house wanting to photograph bridges or anything else she would pull him inside and have 'really filthy' sex with him.

She does not have really filthy sex with Douglas. The last time she had any kind of sex with him was on holiday last year after they had sat for a whole evening drinking in an open-air café in San Gimignano and the Chianti-fuelled orgasm that they struggled – against all the odds – to share was disappointingly low-key and left them both feeling sad and old.

I, on the other hand, have no husband, nor would I take one. Being beautiful I have my choice of lovers. I prefer sex in the late afternoon, when the sun pierces the blinds at a certain languid angle and the day folds in on itself. On a bed carved from French walnut in the style of Louis XV, with a quilted silk eiderdown and a throw made from the pelts of wolves, and mounds of Hungarian goose-down pillows as soft as clouds that have been captured inside starched white linen. And afterwards I like to wrap myself in the wolf pelts and drink a glass of *chocolat chaud* with a slice of plum torte and watch my lover sleeping, his black curls on the white linen, his skin smelling of mine. Then I stretch like a contented cat and contemplate the classical Arcadian scene that is painted on the ceiling above my head. Later, when the light has gone, when my lover has gone, I will get up and drink sweet white wine, dressed in a blue silk peignoir embroidered with plum blossoms. My hound, also beautiful, will lie faithfully at my feet.

I do not have children. My skin has not been stretched, my brain has not been harried. All of my time is quality time, all of my time is for myself. Joan would never be able to understand what that feels like. She cannot remember a time when she felt like herself. She thinks it must have been back when her body fitted, back when she was goal shooter in the netball team and she could jump so high that all she had to do was drop the ball into the net, jump so high that she thought she might take off and fly. Then she had a thick fringe and long straight hair that fell almost to her waist, except when she was playing netball when she wore it in two plaits or sometimes a high ponytail that bounced in time with the ball and boys stood on the sidelines and watched the muscles in her thighs and calves and tried to get a glimpse of her navy-blue knickers under her navy-blue pleated sports skirt. In the days when she tried to get people to call her 'Joni' and maybe if she had succeeded she wouldn't be the spent person she is now.

Joan used to believe that a woman needed her own source of income, that financial independence was the key to a woman's freedom, and yet Douglas has always been the breadwinner. The wages of a part-time librarian barely cover the dog's food. Douglas is the one with the fully paid-up stamp and the pension, he is the one with his name on the mortgage, he is the one who drives the good car. He even gets the best piece of meat at dinner – a strange atavistic habit of Joan's that comes directly from her working-class grandmother.

Joan also does her husband's washing and ironing, sews the buttons on his shirts, makes the bed when he's left it and then encourages him in his early morning jog around the block by laying out a bowl of muesli and low-fat milk for him on his return. She reminds Douglas when his car's MOT is due, turns mattresses, cleans toilet bowls and depilates the bathroom plugholes. She buys his favourite brand of malt whisky, his underpants and his deodorant. She writes all the Christmas cards, visits his senile mother in her nursing home once a week and cleans up after the dog. Douglas's senile mother is no longer the wife he wanted his own wife to be, she is like an uninhabited shell, a husk of the woman she was. Joan is afraid that one day she too will be husked, that she will sit all day in a room that smells of Jeyes Fluid and no-one will visit her. Or that they will visit her and she will no longer know who they are. That Storm will take the metal rings and bolts and studs out of her body and the light will stream out from the holes that have left her porous and she will put her arms around her and say, 'Hi, Mum, how are you today?' and Joan won't know a damn thing about it.

Joan is an excellent wife. If I were to need a wife then I would like one like Joan. I do not need a wife, however. I have silent, invisible servants who glide throughout my mansion bringing me whatever I desire. In the evening they light candles and lay a table with Crown Derby china in the 'Royal Antoinette' pattern and silver that gleams and flashes in the candlelight. There are always flowers on the table, fresh every day, and the food is always exactly what I want at that particular moment, whether it be a ripe white peach cut into neat slices, or a fat black fig or a plump slice of pink lamb. And a single glass of champagne at six o'clock every evening, served in an engraved Bohemian glass flute.

When I drop my clothes on the floor at night they are returned to me the next morning, laundered, pressed and folded. My clothes are beautiful – long dresses in velvets and silks, trimmed with sable and fox fur, day dresses for the finer weather in organza and muslin and some crisp starched poplin. My nightgowns are fine lawn, trimmed with ribbons. The furniture in my house is rubbed with lavender-scented beeswax, the stone floors washed with lemon soap, the house is aired every day and, in winter, fires of apple wood are laid in all the hearths.

In the division of labour between them, Douglas does have his own role – he changes the batteries in the smoke alarm (when prompted), clears the gutters and deals with sash windows that have stuck fast. He also (although mostly in theory) deals with the removal of heavy, unwanted objects. As far as Joan is concerned the ash tree in the garden comes under this heading. The ash tree with a waist as thick as Joan's trunk. The ash tree that Joan really wants rid of from her life. It isn't that Joan can't deal with the tree, she's as capable as the next person of looking up 'tree surgeon' in the *Yellow Pages*, it's just that it comes within Douglas's domain and she's determined that he's going to fulfil his responsibilities.

The tree is the last thing on Douglas's mind. He has a school inspection coming up and although he keeps asking Miss Carter to 'fuck' him she says she has 'serious issues' about affairs with married men and won't give him anything beyond 'a blow job'. Douglas thinks this is 'the kind of specious argument indulged in by American presidents and prick-teasing whores' but he doesn't actually say this to Miss Carter because he can see it could be counter-productive to his goal. He is careful not to beg her to fuck him because he knows this can also be very off-putting to a woman.

Joan does not know this and yet she senses there is something dark moving in her life. In the long watches of the night she feels it coming, suffocating, like a black veil that will cling to her mouth, her nose, her eyes. Then she falls asleep and has a (ridiculous) dream that she has turned into Virginia Woolf. If it weren't for the dreams she has Joan would be sure that she never sleeps at all. She used to be a good sleeper, when she was the goal shooter, when she had hair down to her waist and the boys watched the sway of her hips as she walked down the street, then she spent every night in the sweetest, deepest sleep where all her future rolled out ahead of her like a magic carpet. She wishes now that she had known that all the boys had been watching the sway of her hips, watching the muscles in her calves and in her thighs as she jumped for the net. She wished she could go back and have filthy sex with every one of them. How surprised they would be.

Sometimes Joan pulls down the fold-away ladder and climbs up to the attic of her four-bedroom, two-bathroom house. The attic smells of dust and has a skylight in the roof and is lit by a 40-watt light bulb. The attic is full of boxes, boxes that are labelled 'Ellie's first drawings' and 'Matt's baby clothes', 'Ellie's books', 'Matt's student stuff'. Boxes that no-one but Joan will look through again until Douglas and Joan are dead and then Matt and Storm – who may be called Ellie again by then – will sit on the attic floor and go through the boxes and say things like 'Oh God, look at that!' or 'Fucking hell, I'd forgotten all about that,' and then, because neither of them will have an attic and one of them lives in America anyway and neither of them are sentimental, they will get rid of most of the contents of the boxes. Then they will get rid of most of the contents of the house and then they will get rid of the house. The only thing you can see in the skylight is sky and light. Sometimes Joan looks through the contents of the boxes, sometimes she just stares at the sky and the light.

In the dream where she was Virginia Woolf, she was

at a party being given by Lady Ottoline Morrell and all of the Bloomsbury set were there, drinking pink gins and whisky sours, and she turned to her sister Vanessa and said, 'I must go the lighthouse,' and then she was on a beach and she was walking in the water and the waves were getting higher but she couldn't swim because of the stones in her cardigan pockets. Joan wakes up drowning, unable to breathe, clutching at Douglas's pyjama sleeve, and he pats her vaguely and mumbles 's' all right' without waking up and Joan wonders if that's better than waking from a nightmare and being alone and decides that it is. She would like to tell him about her absurd Woolfian dream (why no 'Orlando', why no 'Mrs Dalloway'? Or was Mrs Dalloway somehow implicit – in the party, or in the character that Joan had in the dream, which wasn't really her own character, but then what was her own character?) but Douglas is already in the bathroom when she wakes and then he is jogging and then he is at school, only he says, 'I'll jog to school and change there,' and Joan wonders if he'll use the boys' showers in the gym (which she doubts very much because probably he would get arrested) or simply be sweaty all day, never thinking that he jogs only as far as Miss Carter's canal-side flat where he strips off in her shower and where she joins him and gives him a blow job and still refuses to fuck him even though they're naked in the shower together, 'for heaven's sake', so that he's beginning to wonder if she's playing some kind of game. And Joan wonders when it was they stopped sleeping naked and started wearing nightclothes bought from Marks and

Spencer's and she supposes it must have been when they had children. When he comes home that night Douglas doesn't smell of sweat, he smells of someone else's soap.

To recap. Joan believes that:
  Every woman should have a room of her own.
  A fish does not need a bicycle.
  Economic independence is the key to personal free-
    dom.
  Her colours are autumnal.
  She will stop breathing in the street one day and die
    alone or surrounded by strangers.
  Women can fly.

There are many Joans in the belly-dancing class. They are all shapes and sizes and they agree that it's 'marvellous' to be able to do something so sensual with their bodies, that it's 'fantastic' that women with big hips and thighs and arses and bellies can do something that makes them feel good, and the one or two slim women in the class (who aren't Joans) are made to feel deficient. They all dress up in costumes for the class, swishy skirts and fancy bra tops made from cheap materials in bright colours and they tie belts around their hips and the belts have imitation gold coins sewn on them and when the women do their hip clicks and their camel walks and their turns, the coins jingle and all the women smile at the noise the coins make. Joan wonders if the coins were sewn on by small Turkish children for a pittance.

*　　*　　*

Sometimes I dance in my room which is carpeted, floor and walls, with silk rugs from Isfahan and Tabriz, and where against one wall rests a huge gilt mirror. The room is perfumed with attar of roses and sandalwood and I dance in front of the mirror and sometimes I dance with a veil and sometimes I dance with little cymbals on my fingers and sometimes I dance naked but I only dance for myself, never for my lover. Not the old lover with the black curls, but a new one, antipodean and carelessly strong. I have a new lover every day.

Miss Carter is indeed playing a game. She calls it 'Miss Carter's Rules' and she is very strict. She decided (long ago, she is already thirty-nine years old) that 'all the good men are taken' and if they're not taken then they are gay, which 'is fine for shopping' but nothing else and that the only way to snare a heterosexual one is either to 'grab him' when he is in-between marriages (quite tricky) or to winklepick a ripe one out of an existing relationship. Miss Carter has no intention of being a mistress, as easily discarded as a used tissue. She wishes to be married, to answer to 'Mrs', to move out of her canalside apartment and into a house where she will have children born in wedlock and no longer be Deputy Head of Modern Studies. She wishes to shop for a top-of-the-range, family-sized fridge-freezer and Baby Gap clothes and organic apple juice.

To achieve this goal she believes she must drive her chosen victim (Douglas) into a state of priapic frenzy whereby he will agree to anything but, specifically, agree to exchange his old wife for Miss Carter. She believes it is the extreme nature of Miss Carter's Rules – no fucking before marriage – that will drive Douglas crazy. Miss Carter is enchanted by the idea that after many years of 'shagging around' she will walk up the aisle without having been penetrated by the groom. It will almost be like being a virgin. Miss Carter sees a psychiatrist every fortnight as an out-patient but she never tells him the truth about anything. She is under a court order not to go within a hundred yards of her previous boyfriend.

Joan comes shyly into the bedroom. She is barefoot and wearing the swishy skirt and the fancy bra top and the belt sewn with coins by the poor Turkish children. The top is orange and the skirt is a rather lurid pink. Douglas is lying in bed, propped up by pillows, reading some teaching journal. His spectacles are perched on the end of his nose and he looks up when she enters the room and his expression doesn't change. Joan refuses to be discouraged by this. She presumes her husband is stunned by her appearance because he doesn't know about the belly-dancing classes, he thought she was 'improving your bridge skills' every Tuesday evening.

Joan moves in what she hopes is a seductive, eastern way. She snakes her arms and does figure-of-eight shapes with her pelvis. She advances towards Douglas and sways her hips, thinking of all the boys she never had filthy sex with, including Douglas, for they have always been rather sedate in their intimacy. She wiggles and jiggles her soft, sandbaggy breasts and moves her head from side to side, making eyes at Douglas. She has applied her make-up carefully and put kohl around her eyes but the kohl has gone all smudgy and not in a good way. She tries a shoulder shimmy and suspects she looks ridiculous.

When she reaches the bed she does her turns, pushing herself around slowly on one foot while moving her pelvis from side to side, but whereas it's easy to turn on the wooden floor of the Methodist hall where the belly-dancing class takes place, it is much more difficult on the bedroom Axminster. Joan is growing un-comfortably conscious of her size-eighteen, ill-fitting body, of the breadth of her backside, of her clumsiness. She cannot remember how you jump for the net. She wishes Douglas would say something. His expression is enigmatic. She kneels down by the side of the bed and says, 'Oh, master, what can I do for you?' and raises a suggestive eyebrow and licks her lips. She is reminded of the advert for Fry's Turkish Delight.

Douglas can't help himself. He pushes her away and says, 'For fuck's sake, Joan, what do you think you're playing at? Fucking *Carry on up the Kasbah?*' He jumps out of the bed and starts getting dressed while Joan sinks to the floor, her cheap swishy skirt blossoming around her, and she starts to weep in a way that she hasn't done since she was a child and all the little coins on her skirt jingle and jangle every time she sobs but she doesn't smile at the noise. Douglas dresses and leaves the bedroom. Joan is crying so hard she doesn't hear the front door slam.

Joan is weak. I would have killed him. I have killed many men. I kill them when they are rude or annoy me. Or when they're stupid or ignorant. I kill them simply by looking at them. I have a stare that turns them to glass and they have just enough time to understand the error of their ways before they crack and shatter into little shards. I feel no guilt, no remorse.

Douglas walks along the dark, rain-slicked street, the pavement slippery with dead leaves. Douglas always takes the car or jogs, he never walks. He decides he doesn't like walking, especially at night, especially in the rain. He is alarmed to find he is crying. He wishes he hadn't pushed her away, but he finds his wife distasteful in almost every way. He wishes he didn't. He thinks about Miss Carter, snug in her canalside flat, the perfumed candles she lights when it grows dark outside and the bottle of wine she always seems to have open ready. He decides that this is the night he's 'going to give her one' and if she doesn't like it then 'too fucking bad'.

I dance dressed in crimson silks and a belt on which real gold coins have been sewn by happy harem women. There are blood-red garnets at my throat and clasped around my wrists there are turquoises that are the colour of the eggs of the mistle thrush. There is a priceless diamond in my navel. When I shimmy the gold coins on my belt tremble and shiver. I dance to the music of George Abdo and his 'Flames of Araby' orchestra and I am self-absorbed and complete.

Joan is in the garden, in the dark, in the rain, with an axe. She is chopping down the ash tree. The dog sits on the patio and barks urgently. Joan hefts the axe clumsily and thinks to herself how amazing it is that she could be more than half a century old and have never chopped anything with an axe before. She thinks of some of the other things she has never done before. She has never:

been in a canoe
ridden pillion on a motorbike
seen a whale
had filthy sex
sung karaoke
eaten sushi
played bingo
visited China

With each inexpert chop of the axe (flown club class) Joan discovers something else (taken drugs) to put on this list (danced the tango). Lights in the neighbouring houses are turned on. Curtains are twitched and windows are opened as people try to get a better view of the madwoman trying to chop down a tree in the middle of the night. The dog begins to howl. Someone calls the police. Joan is filthy and covered in mud, her pink swishy skirt is stuck to her body like a second, more colourful skin. All the little bells on her belt jingle furiously with every chop. The list of things she has never done has now reached number one hundred and twenty-seven (been to an Ann Summers party). When she reaches number one hundred and thirty-three (drunk Madeira) she sinks to the grass in exhaustion. She feels bruised from top to toe. Her arms are as solid as hammers. She vomits into the autumnal remains of her Dutch irises and Asiatic lilies. She is never going to get the tree chopped down.

I turn up the music of George Abdo and his 'Flames of Araby' orchestra very loud so that I cannot hear the dog howling and the madwoman who is screaming now. It would be good if someone came and took her away. Took her away and strapped her down on a hospital bed and perforated her skin with needles containing soothing amnesiac drugs. If someone held her hand and wiped her brow with a cool cloth and said, 'She'll sleep now.' Sleep would be good. Not waking up again would be good.

My mansion has a tower on one corner of the building. I climb the spiral staircase of the tower, round and round, my beautiful velvet gown trailing on the dusty steps, the cobwebs catching on my lovely long hair which today I am wearing in a high ponytail that bounces with every step I take. My faithful hound follows me. In the room at the top of the tower I rest a while. The lancet windows with their fine tracery let in pale moonlight. I bathe my face in the moonlight. I open one of the windows and squeeze my body through the narrow opening. I am very beautiful. My name is not Joan. I can fly.

Eleanor Bailey is a writer and journalist. She lives in London. She was recently selected as one of twenty-one women writers in the Orange Futures promotion, highlighting the writers to watch in the twenty-first century. Her novels *Idioglossia* and *Marlene Dietrich Lived Here* are published by Black Swan.

Gun

At four in the morning there is a noise outside my room. Fumbling for the clock on the rattan table, I knock the glass of water that has grown warm. It hits the floor. Liquid scatters.

The beach house is still unfamiliar and my feet are tentative on the tessellated floor. I bump against the mahogany dresser, finger its sticky waxed surface. Now silence scares me. Someone is waiting.

I feel but don't find the light switch. The sound of my hands patting impotently against the stone wall gives me away. Feet pause. Cicadas twitch. The blood bangs against my forehead.

I've pictured this a thousand times. The key turns behind me and people can only imagine what happened next, before my dismembered corpse is found in four different places. I knew it. I've expected to die.

A face appears in the darkness. I see a chipped front tooth. I told him he was too old to play rugby months before he fell.

'Christ, Ben, you scared me! Why can't you turn the

light on?' Fear turns to anger. 'And what are you doing prowling around in the dark anyway?'

Ben laughs, lazy, smoke-cured.

'Laura, it's Thursday.'

My hand raises, slowly, fist furled towards his face. He grabs my wrist and I push against him. His nails dig into my skin. We stare at each other, unsure for a moment what's going on. My frown and fingers relax.

'So it is.'

Sure, I'm suspicious.

Standing on the underground platform: over the usual aromatic mix of heat, dust and human effervescence, my nose picked up something darker. The sweetness worried me, tangy, too *nice*. In the trenches, the smell of freshly mown hay, redolent of the uncomplicated past, brought one delighted moment before the poison took effect. When life seems good, it must be extra bad. I'd been waiting for a gas attack. We had been warned. Now. I felt nauseous. My throat constricted. I closed my eyes and waited for the end. Seconds later, still conscious and surprised, I opened one eye and peered right to a squishing sound. Ten metres away a woman was peeling an orange.

Ben smiles at me. A leather string around his neck holds a bead of sea-polished glass.

'It's not funny,' I protested. 'It's not the same any more.'

'You can't live in fear for the rest of your life.' He delivers clichés as fresh as mango.

'I think I can.'

'But nothing *happened* to you.'

'I know that. But if you'd been there . . .'

'Bad things happen to people all over the world all the time, even when you're not there to witness it.'

'Exactly.'

'Laura, you weren't walking around in perpetual terror before this.'

'I was working on it.'

He laughs and I'm glad, although I meant it as well.

I love Ben because he doesn't understand what it is to be afraid. He's a Tollet on his English mother's side and has barely managed to dent the interest of his trust fund in the last twenty years. With this kind of security comes a confidence, a curious absence of need. While we were together, I clung to it. It isn't that Ben thinks he's safe from the myriad threats that torture me, the death, despair and mass destruction, but he does believe in renewal. After his father died, Ben spent two months in Madagascar. He came back happy and an expert on African parrots. A form of emotional stupidity, maybe, but one I envy. I feel cushioned by Ben's insensitivity. His blond teddy bear features, the amiable expression that doesn't question good fortune, even that straight, dull nose. If Ben's laughing at me, everything is all right. It's only when I close my eyes that he disappears.

I take the Lariam every Thursday morning so by nightfall I *am* a little screwy. Ben's been in Africa all of eighteen months but this means he has to take his chances with the older, less effective drug regime for real adventurers. My pale-skinned arrival, five weeks ago, complete with force-ten anti-malarial pills and travel mosquito net underlines his machismo. I make him feel good, he makes me feel good. At dusk, when the guard Joseph drags the gate over the stones and Ben's Jeep rumbles into the drive, I almost run to the kitchen to start slicing the lime. Sometimes I wonder why we broke up.

The following afternoon Ben's latest girl flew in. She had unpacked, showered and changed before climbing up the ladder to my roof retreat. I shielded my eyes as she marched towards me, her hand thrust out.

'You must be Laura. Hi. I'm Rebecca Colt, I'm based in London with CNN as a news trainee.' She added, gratuitously, 'But I'm sure Ben told you that.'

Ben hadn't. She was cute, though she talked like the doctor called in to assess my psychosis. A pale-honey TV bob framed small features on a narrow face, long limbs, pert breasts and a brazen faith in her future that was just asking to be disillusioned.

Somehow Ben found *raspberries* and made delectable smoothies, the scent of which wafted across the garden as he brought them out on a tray. An Egyptian cotton shirt faded to the palest blue opened down his almost smooth chest. He is conspicuously casual.

I devoted the evening to scanning Rebecca Colt for imperfections. Ben stared hungrily, quite revoltingly, at her naked shoulders, the polished, nut-tanned skin. Rebecca Colt looked at her place in the hierarchy and settled on demeaning me.

'Good Lord, Laura, I'm not going to catch anything around you.'

Rebecca Colt stays in shorts all evening, matching Ben, her legs strung across the chair, bare soles playing with the dusty tiles, teasing the scorpion.

Nothing, Rebecca Colt insists, comes near *her*, when I offer my Jungle Fever. Me? Mosquitoes laugh at long-limbed clothing and sink blissfully into my bloodstream. Fag smoke, Rebecca scoffs, lighting a Lucky Strike, is deterrent enough.

'Don't you worry about cancer?'

She looks disdainfully at my anxious face. My hair, neither long nor short, dark nor fair, smacks of hesitancy. Perhaps my eyes, like hers, were certain once.

'I don't worry about anything. Everybody in my family lives to eighty-five at least. They've all smoked and drunk and lived in war zones. My great-great-aunt reported from Gallipoli. My mother was a Vietnam photographer. Not a scratch. I did an undercover assignment for three weeks in the Congo as part of my thesis. I went down the mines and hung out with the militiamen. Even when a stomach virus swept through the camp *I* was fine.'

The lime turned out to be sour. When I went into the kitchen for refills, Rebecca Colt, who clearly knew nothing about Africa, had left the fruit lying on the chopping board and now a hundred-strong troop of ants ran across it in frenzied lines.

Early the next morning, after swimming for an hour, Rebecca Colt stood by the fence looking into the waves.

The wind whipped her turquoise sarong. It flapped translucent and curled up behind her. She is lean and brown and untroubled that the material blew up over her waist, revealing taut arse.

Afterwards, since Ben is never up before ten, the two of us sat in the garden and drank coffee from a silver pot. An unlikely pair, the bright spark and the old flame; it's the kind of thing I used to think Ben would find funny until I realized how little he thought about other people.

His beach house is in the best position, so close the sand blows into his garden. There are two houses in this complex; the other is bigger but further back, adjoining the white road along which low-suspension vehicles bump every now and again.

Officially I was killing time with Ben before my next contract in the spring. Really I was lying low. The explosion had done more than bring an early end to my previous job. It had made the work seem absurd. My arbitrary business projects, tiny neurons in the vast electronic brain, a system within a system, far removed from something one could hold up and say, 'This is what I do.' So complicated no-one understood, least of all the people who paid me. I had lived in euphemisms, like the words of politicians.

Now languid days I boiled on a sunlounger. Pages of my book toasted brown before I turned them over. Plans to walk to the harbour, twenty minutes down a dirt track lined with wilting silver trees, melted away. I hoped that here I could concentrate on something else but destructive images kept returning. Thousands of miles away, fear still consumed me.

I asked her, because it was obvious, if she'd been in London for the bomb. Rebecca Colt sat forward, her little mouth widening in eagerness.

'Three weeks after I'd started! I was at the scene for forty-eight hours solid. It was an amazing opportunity.'

'What do you mean, amazing?'

'Well.' She retreated, aware of how this sounded. 'I mean extraordinary, the human spirit, that is, very inspiring, in such chaos.'

I smiled benignly, a tic on which I increasingly rely.

She inhaled the heat, not yet oppressive, and beamed at the sea, stretched her calves in front of her. The skin was imprinted with the line of the chair. She looked back at me, shielding her eyes.

'Ben says *you* were practically blown up.'

I can't avoid thinking about it, it inhabits me, but I don't want to talk.

'No, not really, I was close by, like thousands of others.'

'And you're staying here while you get over it, right?' She sounded bored, needed to slot me into a pre-confirmed category of her reporter head: neurotic, ex-girlfriend, can't move *on*.

'I did consider cowering in a cave for forty years.'

She frowned. 'You can't run away from fear, Laura, otherwise they've won. You have to stand up to them, like the playground bullies.'

Not a psychiatrist, this is that dying breed of tweed-suited primary-school teacher, all aphorisms and dark consequences delivered with significant eyebrows. (She'll struggle with Ben, the unparalleled ostrich.)

But I was afraid long before the coffee shop blew up. Little girl beware never step out of the pavement square. Swallowed chewing gum can inflate like a balloon and *explode*. One kiss and you will be in the thrall of the male beast *for ever*. Money corrupts (or *worse* lures you into vulgar clothing). Knowledge is dangerous. Floorboards rot. Fat kills. Men leave. Women betray. Statistics lie. Drugs drive you crazy. In the event of a nuclear attack paint windows white. Wrap up warm. Men are put off by intelligent women. Alcohol unveils the truth and *women are particularly vulnerable*.

In the afternoon we drank beer (quickly, lest it overheat). The raw voice of Oum Kalthoum and accompanying qanun wavered from an ancient tape player – Ben had spent time in Egypt and never quite recovered. Quite wrong, of course, for here, but to my ears it is all hot and foreign. Ben cleaned impacted sand from a beaded mat with a Swiss Army knife. Rebecca Colt read Martha Gellhorn, and I endeavoured to turn my pages a little faster than she, whether I'd read the words or not.

An ancient Mercedes pulled into the neighbouring house. A woman sauntered towards us, gold earrings winking in the sun. Her skin seemed brutally dark against her white leather jacket. Underneath, a white halter-neck top pinned down burgeoning curves. Tight dark-blue jeans lengthened her legs with suede ankle-boots. Her hair was subdued and straightened. Her lips were shiny red.

'Who is *that*?' There was no disguising Rebecca's horror.

Ben smiled. 'Grace? Next-door neighbour. The girl-friend of the man who owns this complex. She's local. Reinhard's German, not here most of the time. He has a wife somewhere, but Grace doesn't mind. She does very well out of it.'

Stilettos scraped. I admire women who can walk in high heels. On top of everything else expected of us.

'Hi, Ben.'

She spoke slowly and sounded amused. Didn't look at us.

'Grace, meet Rebecca and Laura.'

Information is kept to a minimum when Ben makes an introduction. Girlfriends especially. He'd say it was less formal, cooler, but I'd say he likes to keep his options open.

'Grace, I meant to tell you; I'm out of town for a couple of days but Rebecca and Laura are staying here while I'm gone.'

She turned to us with sky-wide eyes.

'Alone? And the fence still not fixed? Are you crazy, man?'

His voice is calm. 'A couple of days.'

She drew shocked breath and let out an equine snort. Whistled.

'What about that carjacking? Another white man was just killed in the city.'

'That's in the city.'

'It's worse out here, man! They come round here at night. They know everyone round here has money.' She pulled her arms tightly round her waist, excited. 'You gotta be careful. You shouldn't leave two girls on their own.'

Ben looked bemused. 'What about you? You live on your own.'

'I've got my gun.'

She patted the white tasselled leather bag that hung from her shoulder.

Ben stared at the sea. Panic pricked in my stomach. Rebecca, studiously interested, wrinkled her forehead.

'Oh, really, you have a gun, what is it?'

Grace unzipped the bag readily and whipped out a pistol that lay snugly in the palm of her hand. 'It's a Glock twenty-six.'

'Oh, a Baby Glock!' said Rebecca, as if spotting a label on a pair of jeans. 'Mm, they're really popular with women.'

Grace shrugged. 'It's cute. Nine millimetres but really reliable. I told Reiney to get me one since he leaves me here on my own. He gave me one of his but it was a huge fucking thing, when I hold it I thought my wrist broke! I said, *no way*, you get me one that fits in my purse.'

She toyed with the gun's sleek contours, touching it incidentally, like a mother stroking the head of her child. I was mesmerized.

She laughed exuberantly. Then took the weapon between her fingers, pointed it at Ben, quiet for a moment.

'Bang bang, Ben.' Grace broke into a wide grin.

'Can't you get Reinhard to fix the fence as well, since you're so cunning?' Ben's smile was a little over-ready.

Grace sucked her cheeks in and squeezed roughly past Rebecca to where he sat. Crouching, her feet bulged through the leather boots, the weapon hung limp to one side, the nose scratched the ground; with her other hand she gripped Ben's square face. Long nails dug into his sweating skin. He looked very pale next to her. 'Ben, man, I'm only his girlfriend, I can't get greedy.'

Sunday morning Ben left. He said the village was a few hours' drive inland, nothing more precise. Rebecca Colt wasn't going to ask.

I don't think she'd expected him to leave so soon after her arrival. His hands rested loosely round her bare waist, fingers stroking the skin of her lower back, darker already so the tiny hairs gleamed gold. She stood rigid, trying to shrug off his touch with a frown.

Even Ben noticed something was up but his ham-fisted concern infuriated her all the more.

'If you go down to the harbour, take your rings and watch off and leave the digital camera behind.'

'Ben, I managed to survive without you for the first twenty-two years and three months of my life. I think I'll cope for another three days.'

'Grace is right, you really should be careful.'

He kissed her airily and when she threw him a twisted smile he decided, as only Ben can, that everything was fine.

Later when I pass her room, she is rolling barely-there beige across her lips, staring in the mirror. Artlessly concentrated in the moment. Lovingly she scrubs the segments of her pink bikini, cheese-triangle dimensions, in detergent powder from a lozenge tin and strings them over the wicker chair to dry.

Over dinner we trashed Grace – so vulgar, so twentieth-century, living off a lover. We could put our differences – and uncomfortable similarities – aside while we picked over the failings of somebody else. Cloudless, with a slight breeze, it was turning into a perfect night until emboldened by our newfound friendship I questioned her more personally.

'How did you meet Ben?'

'He's a friend of my father's.'

Her *father's*. So now I'm Marianne Faithfull. Soon men will want to know me for my fighting talk, a female life-stage I might have dreaded were it not followed by the one where all the men die off, leaving just other decrepit women and no teeth.

'How old are you?'

Young enough that it wasn't rude to ask.

'Twenty-two.'

No wonder Ben looks so smug. No wonder she's so certain. I hadn't realized that girls almost twenty years younger than me are allowed on planes alone. Born in nineteen eighty-three and she's walking and talking and mixing her own gin.

Fear of growing old, like all menace, is somehow enticing. I don't want to be forty but I have to think about it. To muse that thirty now sounds young. Sometimes I wish I could act without thinking. Without being held up by the miasma of remembered warnings

– wise words of parents, peers, government health advice and the green-cross-code man. Just live.

The Lariam must be wearing off because when I wake in the night I think it is a dream.

But no, Rebecca really is sobbing by my bed. Her eyes are reeling. She's whispering in exclamation marks.

'They've got Joseph! He's lying in the garden! They hit him with a brick.'

'Who?'

'He's bleeding! They're in the corridor! Can we escape through that window? Where does it go?'

My bedroom door pushes open. Three ragged figures steal into the room. Their faces are uncovered but I can't make them out in the dark. They grab Rebecca, wielding a rope, bind her hands and legs and tie her to the bed. She starts to scream. They don't realize I'm there at first and so I try to sneak out behind. But one spots me, his eyes widen and he blocks my path, holding a broken brick to my face. It is wet and smells of the sea.

Now Rebecca and I are trussed up together on the floor and the men leave the room. They knock round the house, shouting in Swahili. Her skin feels hot. Silhouetted tears are running down her face.

'I just want to say that if they rape us and I get pregnant, I'm going to keep the baby.'

This is how I cope. Rebecca stares at me.

'You have a very strange sense of humour.'

'When you're forty, you'll take your chances too.'

'I don't want children.'

'You're twenty-two.'

Rebecca looks scared. This strengthens me. I feel older, magnanimous.

'Don't worry,' I say kindly, 'if they were going to kill us they'd have done it already.'

She baulks. 'Who said they were going to kill us? I hadn't even *thought* of that.'

There is a gunshot. And another. And another. Rebecca grabs my arm and pulls at me sharply, her fingers slipping as she shakes. I can't see or hear anything. My senses are obscured by recalled terror. Rubble and dust, glass falls through the air, people scream. Snapshots I've thumbed so often they are out of order. For now I'm walking to the office, buying coffee, taking it out of the shop, hearing the explosion, dropping coffee on my bare leg. I remember the pain of the hot liquid, feeling sticky fingers and the empty paper cup still in my hand, that more vivid than anything. I remember the aftermath when people keep asking 'What did you see?' and I remember that I can't remember.

The door bangs open.

Grace's face is shining. Swathed in a white silk nightshirt, she is out of breath, ebullient. 'I heard you screaming and I picked my gun up and ran over. I saw the men and I just pulled the trigger! Woo-hoo! I just pulled it and they looked at me, like wondering if I was serious or something, and I pulled it again, just over their heads. And they looked at each other and ran for it. Whoa! They were running and I pulled it again and one of the guys was holding his ass!' She laughed. As she grins, her teeth look surreally bright in the dark. She seems huge, high on power. I know it's crazy but at that moment I want it. Whatever she tells herself that shuts out all other voices, the warnings that stall me, it works. She seems so free.

She unties us as if it is as remarkable as unwrapping a bag of fruit then turns to leave.

'Where are you going?' Rebecca's voice is feeble.

Grace looks astonished. 'Joseph.'

He is standing in the garden, facing the house and clutching a hand to his blood-caked head. Says nothing as Grace bundles him into her Mercedes. Looks very small in the front seat, the belt wide and smooth across his wrinkled, bloody T-shirt.

Three a.m. A man lay on the bench outside the police station, a thin white jacket draped over hunched shoulders. At first I think he's in a queue, but no, that is where he sleeps. The building is squat. Paint peels. Inside is hot and smells of sweat. A strip light on the ceiling emits a feeble glow, shadowed from the inside by a mass insect grave. Mosquitoes hum on the outside.

The policeman spoke in English very slowly.

'He must fill in this form to prove that he is the victim not the aggressor otherwise he must pay at the hospital.'

Joseph can't read. Grace, it turns out, isn't local at all. Her first language is French, Arabic her second and while she can shout abuse at night-time intruders, she isn't at all confident in written Swahili. The policeman shrugged. Yawned.

45

'He has to fill in the form,' he said, more insistently, striking the paper with his ballpoint pen.

Joseph still holds his head. He looks straight ahead. Moisture trickled down his neck but he didn't wipe it away. Was he afraid? From the toilet in the corner behind a bowed door, I heard a slow drip, drip, drip onto linoleum.

'I'm going to call Ben,' said Rebecca.

'Why?' I snapped. 'What do you think he can do?'

Grace fished in the bag with the gun. 'Here, take my phone.'

The moment is just a pinpoint. Before and afterwards, expectation, aftershock, analysis, trawling through the wreckage, acceptance, blame and reassessment of the self in the wake of what has happened or what might happen, *that* takes time. Even after this feeble fracas, I am not the same person. We have escaped again, unless escape is just a reprieve.

Rebecca and I sat in the garden, drinking coffee from the silver pot.

'It's just lucky they didn't have a firearm too.' Her voice is restored to full acerbic strength. 'Next time they will, they'll learn, that's the trouble.'

'Quite right.' I was mimicking her self-righteousness. 'Grace should have stayed in bed. She's ruined my best hope of being a mother.'

For the first time since I've met her, Rebecca laughs. Then she chewed her lip and looked up.

'Laura, when Ben answered my call, before I'd opened my mouth he said: "Darling, it's three o'clock

in the morning." He must have assumed I was Grace –
why the hell did he say "darling"?'

I looked out at the sea. Blue water, white sky, how
beautiful it is.

Claire Calman used to have a proper, grown-up job but gave it up when she realized that, if she wanted to be badly paid and have a tough boss, she could become self-employed and at least be allowed to work in her pyjamas. Her novels, *Love is a Four-Letter Word*, *Lessons for a Sunday Father* and *I Like it Like That* are all published by Black Swan. As well as writing novels and short stories, Calman sometimes dabbles in poetry: she was formerly commissioned to write poems for Breast Cancer Awareness Month and she occasionally performs her verse live or on radio. She lives in London with her husband and the world's tallest-known stack of unfiled papers.

The Family

We just had a couple here who were all the way from Kent over in England. The wife had found us from the brochure. I took out an advertisement last year, though Dewy said it was sure to turn out to be a waste of good money and what did I want to go and do a fool thing like that for? But the last couple of years, payin' guests seem to be rarer 'n the way Dewy eats his steak; like he says, 'Jest wipe its ass, Suze, and herd it onto my plate.'

Anyways, they were real taken with our home and family. The wife, she looks up at our grizzly bearskin on the wall, and she says, 'Oh! How amaay-zing!' in her funny voice, like how people must talk in the theatre or somethin', and then Dewy says, 'Careful, now, he sure is mean. Them teeth'd take a bite out o' you soon as look at you.' She seems as she was about to pet its nose and she takes her hand back real quick then, and looks at Dewy as if she can't tell whether he's kiddin' with her. I tells her not to mind him, he's just a big kidder.

See, here's our advertisement. Looks good, don't it? It cost extra to have the colour photograph, but it was worth it for sure. The place looks real nice, don't it?

And I wrote the whole thing myself. Dewy ain't much of a one for foolin' with words. 'Enjoy a warm welcome on our working cattle ranch and beautiful log cabin home. Mountain views. Home-made pancakes and country breakfast. No pets or children. Peace and quiet guaranteed.'

I thought they would stay two, maybe three nights, least that's what they said on the phone when they called up in the first place, but it was just the one in the end. That's the trouble with folks on vacation. If they'd only plan it all out properly and make like a whole itinerary, they wouldn't get in such a muddle. They ate their dinner here though, after they drove down from the city. The wife and I – well, she was a nice kind of lady I thought, though it seemed she'd let herself go some; if I'd knowed her another day, I'd have give her a hint, point her in the direction of Honey's salon in town, get herself a colour rinse, no need to quit tryin' no matter what age you are, am I right? She can't have been no more'n forty. Still, she and I got along just fine the way girls do. We chattered away while they was eatin', and I got out my photographs to show her and told her everything they ought to see while they was here. The husband, every now and then, he looks up from his plate and says to Dewy, 'So, how many head of cattle do you have?' or 'Are you beef or dairy?' Sometimes seems like men ain't quite got the hang of talkin' and such, you know?

Anyhow, all through dinner I see her lookin' around at the walls and on the shelves and the couch and she says, 'Those are really very impressive. Do you make any of them yourself?'

'All of them, for sure,' I tells her and how I like to do different ones each year. This year, I'm kinda into cats. Last year it was all Victorian style, I swear I went just about crazy with those, all the smocking and such. Year before that was bears.

'My!' says the wife. 'How on earth do you have the time?'

'Well, you know what they say – ask a busy person . . . I always have time for my family.'

I wondered if she was kinda slow, not quite 100 cents to the buck, you know, 'cause she starts peering around the room again like she's lookin' for somethin' in particular. 'Oh,' she says, 'do you have a big family?'

Her husband looks up at this point, liftin' his head from the trough, as if he's frettin' he might starve. Well, he weren't like Dewy, but he weren't about to waste away to nothin', that's for sure.

'Here, let me get you some more potatoes there,' I tells him. I like to spoil my guests. Treat 'em better than they are at home, most times. You gotta keep your man full to keep him happy, am I right?

Anyways, right after dinner, the husband, who's ate enough to keep any regular person goin' for a week, heaves himself up and says how they must be goin' for their 'evening stroll'. They never miss and sure they weren't ones for fussing over a little spot of rain, he says. He takes his wife's hand and damn near pulls her out the house and down the track like she was a mule that wouldn't budge or somethin'. Well, it sure is just beautiful here, with the mountains all around, so I don't s'pose I can blame him. City folks can't wait to get out and enjoy our fresh country air, rain or shine.

When they come back in, they look kinda guilty, like they been kissin' in the bushes. 'Cept they're way too old for that and I guess their courtin' days are long gone so I don't know what they been up to. Anyhow. I'm setting there watchin' a video, with some of my family and my kitties Bayberry and Sasketoon.

'Make yourselves right at home,' I says. 'The boys'll shove on up, won't you? C'mon, boys!' I shifted Harry-Lee and Brandon to the bean bags. 'We all set now?'

'Oh!' says the lady. I swear her husband must just about go nutty over her, with her Oh-this and her Oh-that. 'Oh!' she says. '*Snow White*. I used to love this when I was little. I haven't seen it for years and years.'

'Yeah. It's the best, ain't it? But you look through that stack there and pick yourselves one out. The boys and I seen this one thousands of times anyways. Go on – go right ahead, pick one out.'

So she starts pickin' through the pile, oh-ing and aah-ing.

'*The Jungle Book*. Maar-rvellous,' she says, 'and *The Wizard of Oz* too. You certainly have quite a few classics here. Oh, *The Little Mermaid* – that's rather more recent, isn't it?'

The husband's checkin' through 'em faster than shufflin' a deck of cards. Well, you know how men are, always rushing onto the next thing 'fore they hardly done finished the one they're on. So I shoves some of Dewy's tapes towards him.

'These are more your action movies, your guy movies. Lots of killin's and stuff. Dewy likes these the best.'

He holds out a tape of *The Texas Chainsaw Massacre* to his wife and give her a look. She laughs real sudden, then seems like she's only coughing like she got a tickle in her throat. She smiles at her husband then, lookin' up at him in a funny way, you know, like as if they had a special secret or somethin'. Like they was lovers. Kinda spooky way of carrying on when you're married an' all. I don't know why they was smilin'. That movie is real nasty. I sat through about a quarter of it one time till Dewy fell asleep and I could turn it off. Anyhow, then the wife give him kind of a whack with the videotape and says maybe they'll just have an early night, hmm, she reckons that stroll just about finished her off. And he looks at his wristwatch and says how he's awfully bushed too and anyway it's well after nine and they're on holiday, so why not? It's always the way with city folks. They burn rubber tearin' out to be in the countryside then can't hardly stay awake once they gets here.

The next mornin', they're settin' at the table and the husband's eatin' my blueberry pancakes almost faster 'n I can make 'em. The wife's lookin' at the map and planning their route, saying how they'd best be getting on, goodness, their trip has just flown by, and what a pity they could only stop for the one night after all. I'm flippin' the eggs and tellin' them about my sister's place if they're headin' on down further south and how I can call on ahead and make a reservation, I've got the number right here in my head, it's no bother, no bother at all.

'She cooks real good too,' I says. 'And plenty of it. A real nice home. Dried flowers and homey quilts in the rooms, though I hope I ain't boastin' if I say they ain't like mine, of course. They've got two children, though, but maybe you won't mind that. And they keep horses so they can fix you up with rides for sure if you like.'

The wife sits there, quiet for a moment. 'No,' she says. 'We wouldn't mind at all.'

'Well, surely not,' I says. 'Most folks who come on vacation just love to ride, don't they?'

After breakfast, when the husband gets out his billfold to pay, the wife bends down and picks up Harry-Lee. I see her feel his hair between her fingers, strokin' it.

'He's one of the first I ever did,' I says, taking him out of her hands. 'So I guess that kinda makes him head of the family, don't it?'

She smiles and tilts her head on one side, looking at him like she's judging a prize breeding bull at a show.

'You're obviously very accomplished, they're really really good,' she says. Funny word, ain't it, accomplished? 'I'm hopeless at sewing. I can barely sew on as much as a button.'

"Course Harry-Lee ain't for sale anyways. A lady last month bought most of what I had,' I tells her. 'Just about cleaned me right out.'

Thought I should drop a hint, so's she'd know they were for sale 'n' all. I put the price tickets inside the collar, but folks don't think to look, do they?

'Really?' she says, with a little nod, looking round the room at my family. 'Still, you seem to have quite a collection.'

'Yes,' says the husband, grabbing Raggedy Anne from the couch and holding her by one arm as if she were just any old thing. 'I don't expect you're about to run out.' And he give a great big laugh.

I laughed too, seein' as how he's a guest and to be polite an' all, but it weren't much of a joke, am I right? Didn' have a point or nothin', far as I could see. Still, half the time I don't get Dewy's jokes neither, so maybe it was just a guy kinda thing.

Right after that, the husband starts heftin' their bags into the car and saying they must be off. Dewy was down in the bottom field, but I gave them our card and told them how he said to say goodbye and to be sure to visit again and to send all their friends to us and we'd give 'em a real nice welcome. I brought out Harry-Lee and Raggedy Anne and the three of us stood on the front deck waving goodbye until their car reached the bottom of the track. There was a cloud of dust as they turned sharp off the track towards the highway, but we stayed to watch awhile, looking out to where the car had been till long after they were gone.

Mavis Cheek was born and grew up in Wimbledon. Her mother was a single parent and life was not easy. There were few frills such as books and her education at state schools was very basic. She failed her eleven plus (twice!) and was put in the B stream of a secondary modern school, where she tried, completely unsuccessfully, to learn to become a good and dutiful secretary. She left school at sixteen and worked as a receptionist for the contemporary art publishers, Editions Alecto, where she began to learn about modern art. When they opened a gallery in Albemarle Street, she went there and worked with such artists as David Hockney, Allen Jones, Patrick Caulfield and Gillian Ayres, which she enjoyed tremendously.

After twelve happy years at Editions Alecto, she left to go to Hillcroft College for Women from where she graduated in Arts with distinction. She then had her daughter, Bella, and began her writing career in earnest. Journalism and travel writing at first, then short stories, and eventually, in 1988, her novel *Pause Between Acts* was published by Bodley Head and won the *She/John Menzies* First Novel Prize. She lives and works in West London.

Another Woman's Roses

Maggy and Martin lived with their two small children in a large old house in a not-quite-arrived bit of town. Maggy always thought of the house as one of those British Rail sandwiches of folklore – not quite fresh and curling a bit at the edges. She was no interior designer and Martin was a landscape gardener. Landscape gardeners of his quality and style, it appeared, did not deal in plots of less than half an acre. Their own measured thirty-five feet . . . So both inside and outside the house had a vague air of neglect. This was particularly so in summer, when the evenings were light and Martin worked long hours. It was summer, not spring, that always made Maggy restless. The sunshine, which poured into the house during those months, had a way of showing up all the failings – house, garden, face, self . . .

It was in summer that Maggy felt her strongest affinity with a British Rail sandwich. She participated in the school run each morning – intending, always intending, to look bright-eyed and bushy-tailed, or at least to have managed to put on make-up. But she never did. It was a plus if she had even achieved the shower. Other mothers seemed to manage. They either appeared in their lipstick and rouge, or with suntans, or they had pink, healthy-looking cheeks and naturally bright eyes. Maggy's complexion without the slap on was, she assured herself, like yesterday's porridge, and when she watched advertisements for ways to stop tired women feeling tired she thought the actors looked enviably spry.

Going out had become more and more of an effort. She minded, Martin did not. It came to the same thing. On the rare occasions they did dine out in a restaurant (an occurrence – she vaguely remembered – that used to be such a commonplace in the days when she worked that she had once said to Martin, 'Wouldn't it be *lovely* just to stay in occasionally?), her indecisiveness became acute. 'I can't decide between the calf's liver, good for tired blood, or the turbot, good for tired brain,' she famously declared at her birthday treat. Her procrastination took so long that in the end Martin ordered both for her. Which should have made her laugh but which did not. Meaning that, added to everything else, age had apparently diluted her once rich sense of humour. One was not supposed to be like this in the August of one's days, she thought, one was supposed to be serene, still a bit youthful-looking, and contented.

She was thinking along those lines all over again this morning and being very far from serene, youthful-looking or content. Instead she was restless, whey-faced (with a few Oh So Attractive freckles, it being high summer) and seriously disgruntled. The only warmly familiar thing about her today was that, as usual, she was picking up a trail of toys that led from the sitting room to the kitchen and from the kitchen up the stairs. This is me, she sighed as she pushed open the door to Billy's room and deposited his clutter on the jumbled bed. The room smelled of eight-year-old boy. No matter how much you washed them, they had this smell. She took a deep breath and looked about her. This was what she had swapped it all for. She buried her nose in her son's pillow and wondered, idly, when smelling your son, and liking it, became an Oedipal perversion? She smoothed the bed tidy, stepped back, trod on a sticklebrick and swore very loudly. At which exact point the doorbell rang.

She looked up to the ceiling. 'Oh please, *no*,' she said to its slightly flaky surface. 'Not *yet* . . .' She hadn't even begun on Tanya's room. Tanya, at six, did not subscribe to the Girls Are Tidier theory. Last week, for example, Maggy had hoovered up an entire (and quite old) jam sandwich in there and resolved that in future she would do her children's rooms once a week At Least or have the health and safety people down on her. Well – collapse of stout party.

The bell rang again, she swore once more for good measure, pulled up her daughter's duvet, removed a damp swimming suit from its creases and left the room, resolutely closing the door behind her. If there was another jam sandwich in there it could either turn the doorknob and walk out – or wait to be liberated until the next time. She looked at her watch. Oh really! It was only half past ten. Chrissie wasn't due for ages yet. Life, really, was just not fair. As if to remind herself of this, she began limping dramatically as she descended the stairs.

At the bottom of the stairs she paused to smooth her hands across her damp face as if she was ironing out the wrinkles. This friend of hers, this friend who was even now early and waiting to pounce from the other side of her front door, was from a different era in Maggy's life. Once she and Chrissie had *both* been glamorous and living a little dangerously. Now, it seemed, she must take her excitements vicariously. Chrissie, who offered more excitements to the pound than it was fair for a woman in her late thirties to offer, referred to Maggy nowadays as 'a grown-up', which made her feel about three hundred years old rather than maturely wise. She did not like this feeling of sage old age. It was all right if you were a citizen in China, obviously, but this was England. To be old and wise here was practically an insult. Hip and cool was the only way. Today – on Chrissie's birthday – she intended to show how hip and cool she still was. Or she had planned to. Now she would be caught in leggings and her T-shirt bearing the faded legend, 'Be sincere whether you mean it or not . . .' Apart from the outfit being just a little *too* hip in the – physical – sense, the sentiment was wincingly inappropriate.

Chrissie was having an affair. Whereas Maggy found that the summer made her even more weary with its prospect of school holidays and Finding Things To Do, Chrissie – apparently – found it sexy. This was where Maggy came in. Though the deceit made her spine tingle, she went along with it. To refuse would, indeed, be dull of her. Besides, Chrissie was different. She had achieved the wealthy marriage, the pretty child, the large house and two acres in Hertfordshire and the small but perfect television production company. And now she had the lover. To go with the lover she also had a strangely unlined face, perfectly rounded breasts that apparently stayed still when she moved (fascinating, Maggy found this – indeed she had been known to make Chrissie jump deliberately so she could see it in action – frighteningly childish but fascinating all the same) and fingernails that had never seen the inside of a washing-machine overflow pipe.

It was a case of Good triumphing over Evil for Maggy. Part of her wanted to say to Chrissie that playing around could be dangerous. That marriage and parenthood were responsibilities as well as trophies, and that you risked them at your peril. She never did though, because she knew it would sound pious and pompous and she might never see her friend again, and anyway the fact was she quite enjoyed hearing about open-topped cars in Cannes and having sex on Concorde. The problem with friendship and loyalty was that it did not leave a whole lot of space for truth. If she wagged a finger at Chrissie, Chrissie was quite likely to offer her two of her own, and beautifully manicured ones, back. Friendships were precious as you got older and loyalty was gold dust. Fifteen years ago Chrissie resigned from the same company when Maggy was eased out by a new broom. You did not forget support and kindness like that.

And the other thing – apart from her queasiness over

the deceit – was that, well, she had not told Martin about the affair. So that it almost – silly as it sounded – felt as if she were having it herself. It was, she thought, like a wicked bit of sparkling spandex in her otherwise grey-flannel life.

'I don't know how you manage to resist the temptation,' Chrissie said when it first began, and she was only half joking. Her eyes were sparkling with the illicit newness of it all so that instead of upending her café latte over her, Maggy merely smiled knowingly. She did not say that the possibility of temptation in this neck of the woods was, like the existence of the Yeti, highly unlikely. Instead she smiled and rolled her eyes as if to imply that they were simply queuing up round the block . . . Truth was that staying *awake* long enough to recognize temptation if it came up and bludgeoned her with a pick-axe would have been a thrill, never mind doing what Chrissie was doing and actually getting into bed with it. Occasionally when she and Martin stayed up later than half past eleven at night Maggy went to bed feeling she'd achieved something wild.

Bed. With her lover. That was where Chrissie was supposed to be now. Not ringing Maggy's sticky doorbell but lying in tangled hotel sheets, sipping champagne and pretending that she was somewhere else. The somewhere else being Maggy and Martin's house. To be specific, in their spare room. Just in case of the wildest of remotest of possibilities that the Norland nanny, or her husband, Fabrizi, might suddenly try to get in touch with her she had given Maggy the telephone number of the hotel and their illicit pseudonym as well as both mobile numbers, for use in just such an emergency. God help them if anything were to happen and Martin, who knew nothing, reached the telephone first.

'Chrissie? No, mate. Sorry. Haven't seen her for months . . . Hang on, I'll just ask Maggy. Hey, Maggy – have you any idea where Chrissie might be?'

It did not bear contemplating.

Chrissie accepted that this might happen. 'Everything is a gamble,' she said. 'And I'm really grateful to you for covering.'

Maggy took it as a compliment to her friendship and loyalty. Besides, what harm could it do? There was so little of a gambling nature in her life nowadays that she might as well relish somebody else's. So Chrissie should have been arriving at one o'clock today to take Maggy out to lunch, not appearing here and now. And after the lunch she would catch a cab and then a train home for what she called an intimate little dinner with her husband, ten other close acquaintances and the caterers. Chrissie said it gave her an added thrill sometimes going back to her husband after an illicit night somewhere else. Maggy found the idea at once repulsive and absolutely fascinating. Mostly, just like those unmoving breasts, absolutely fascinating.

She rubbed her foot again. So much for glamour. The skin of her heel was calloused and the nails were unpainted. No strappy sandals then. She had fully intended to deal with these fairly simple items of grooming last week but where did time go? There were also one or two feathery, lavender-coloured veins around the ankle which she knew, if she showed them to Chrissie, would be the subject of a lecture on laser treatment. The fact that one course of such laser treatment at Chrissie's clinic would be the equivalent of a month's groceries was best left unsaid. Anyway, Martin – when she pointed them out to him mournfully in the bath – said they were quite pretty. Not that she'd be able to tell Chrissie *that* either.

Martin – who had always got on well with Chrissie – now found the combination of her and her husband a little too much to take seriously. He referred to Fabrizi as The Godfather and said that when both of them appeared together they seemed to be made out of plastic. Something with which Maggy, though she hotly denied it, privately agreed. They tended not to meet up in a foursome any more. Martin never knew what to say to the American's Sincere Desire To Know – and the American was quite clearly all at sea over Martin's complete lack of ambition . . .

'So – where do you see yourself in five years' time, Martin?'

'Bognor.'

'Excuse me?'

After that the two women agreed it was better to meet alone.

Well, Fate, she said to herself, here I am. She put a bright smile on her face to hide the irritation, and flung the door wide. But it was not Chrissie. Nor the postman. Nor the gas man, nor anyone she might have expected. It was a man in a grey peaked cap holding a huge bouquet of exquisite, creamy roses. Their rich, beguiling scent encircled her. She breathed deep, irritation forgotten.

'For me?' she said hesitantly.

He looked at her, surprised, then at the card. 'If you are Christine Demarco,' he said.

And she laughed, taking the flowers. 'No – I'm not. But I'll pass them on to her. She is expected.'

'Sweet,' said Chrissie when she arrived – bare-armed, tanned, in an elegant white linen number. Maggy handed her the bouquet with both hands, as if it were a tribute. 'How very, very sweet,' she repeated, and handed them back. 'I *wondered* why he asked for your address . . .' She looked all sparkly and flushed and bright around the eyes again.

'Are you still in love?' Maggy could not stop the question slipping out.

Chrissie laughed. 'No,' she said, amused. 'And neither is he, thank God. We're just play-acting.'

'Dangerous,' said Maggy, unable to stop herself.

'That's what makes it so enjoyable.'

'Hmm,' said Maggy, as disapprovingly as she dared. And she thought, there, I have said something. At least I have tried. Thus exonerated she yielded herself up to the rest of it all with guilty pleasure.

Chrissie looked at the flowers again. 'Nice thought,' she said, reading the card. And then she linked her arm through Maggy's and said, 'When I get a space in my diary I'm going to take you to my health farm. That's what you need. A bit of attention.'

Embarrassingly, Maggy felt herself nearly in tears.

Once she had been every bit as chic and vivacious as Chrissie. They were known for it – two very desirable young women. If anything Maggy was considered the more attractive of the two . . . It was the sudden realization that she was as far removed from being a woman of mystery as Chrissie was from allowing thread veins to damage her life. It felt as if she had not had any attention from anybody for years – well, apart from the near-toothless lecher in Waitrose carpark, and he didn't discriminate between about twenty-five and ninety-five – yet she always seemed to be handing care and attention out. In that respect Chrissie *was* good for her – because she did, when she had one of those absurd things called A Window In Her Diary, make time to pamper her a little. Of course, she had the money to do it. But so did a lot of people and they never bothered. Friendship was friendship. Loyalty was loyalty. It was a little bit of lying that wouldn't hurt anybody. Martin would never know. And that was that.

When they were leaving for the restaurant, Maggy said, 'Don't forget to take your beautiful flowers.' And Chrissie smiled, went over to their temporary vase, lifted up the little card which said, 'For a very special sexy lady', read it once more, smiled, then crumpled it and put it in the rubbish bin.

'Can't take them home,' she said. 'You have them.'

Maggy, wishing she had remembered to empty the bin, which was overflowing as usual, said, 'Of course you can take them. Fabrizi won't know. You can tell him I gave them to you.' She smiled conspiratorially.

Chrissie said, 'Don't be silly. He'd never believe that.'

Maggy thought, Martin would. Martin would only have difficulty if I tried to pretend a man had bought them. She sighed. Some mystery woman she was.

Chrissie mistook the sigh. 'No – you have them. Why not? Besides, I don't want to carry them with me to the restaurant now. Oh, go on. Where's the harm?'

The smell of them had already filled the kitchen and their stiff, expensive petals were like silk to her touch. She was tempted.

Chrissie snapped her bag shut and tugged at her friend's arm. 'Come on,' she said. 'Cab's waiting.' Chrissie left the kitchen without a backward glance.

That evening, cooking a chicken for Martin and the children, feeling very full herself from the irresistible three courses at lunchtime, she crossed over to the roses and picked up the vase to move it to the sitting room. Just as she buried her nose into their delicate mass and closed her eyes and took a deep, deep breath, Martin put his head round the door.

'Hi,' he said.

She nearly dropped them. She felt herself blushing.

'You're early,' she said as airily as she could manage, standing there trying not to look incongruous with the blooms between them.

'What are these?' he asked, coming right up to them and touching one of the heavy heads with his fingertip.

'Roses,' she said shortly. She felt cornered, trapped.

'Whose?'

'Mine.'

'Oh,' he said.

He did not ask where she got them. He did not have to. The question was hanging in every part of the room.

'Chrissie gave them to me,' she said, a little defiantly. After all, it was true.

Later he noticed that she was not eating. 'Watching your weight?' he said, finding the idea irritatingly amusing.

'It's only because we had such an enormous lunch,' she said, not looking at him and rearranging Tanya's cup quite unnecessarily on the tablecloth.

'Ah,' he said. 'Where did you go?'

'A little Italian place she knows.'

'Ah,' he said again. 'Trust Chrissie to know somewhere little and Italian. Dark and illicit, I'll bet – and only tables for two? That takes me back . . .'

It took her back, too. Where *was* that woman? 'It wasn't exactly the Dark Ages,' she snapped.

'Joke,' he said. But he sounded puzzled.

Thankfully she took the children off to bath them, leaving him to deal with the dishes. She played with them for an exceptionally long time, so much so that they actually began to complain and Tanya demanded to be helped out. Billy sat on the floor wrapped in his towel as she dribbled the last of the soap from her daughter's shoulders and held up the towel for her. She looked at these little beings and thought that, after all, despite the fine hotels and the champagne and the roses, she would not have her life any other way. Couldn't, anyway.

'Nice,' said Billy, rubbing his finger over the patch of little veins on her foot. 'Pretty.' He was copying Martin.

They could always seduce you, she smiled, these little men. 'Yes,' she said, smelling his hair again – even newly washed it was essence of boy. 'You caused those, you little rogue,' she said. He looked at her, wide-eyed.

'Help, Mummy,' wailed Tanya.

She lifted her out and kissed her cheek – cool and fresh and sweet again. These, she supposed, were her roses, and she sniffed them both, suddenly pleased. For all the money that high living could buy, they were still the best scent in the world. At least, when they were clean.

Back down in the kitchen the smell of the flowers had permeated, stronger than the smell of roast chicken and the scent of the children's sickly bubble bath. She went over and opened the back door and breathed in the cool evening air. Perhaps the summertime was not so bad after all if you kept your eyes above the height of the straggly hedge and did not dwell on the tufted lawn or the overgrown borders.

Martin began emptying the overflowing rubbish bin into a black sack.

'Pow, pow, Dad,' said Billy, running to him and throwing his arms around his waist.

But for once Martin scarcely responded.

'Milk or water?' said Maggy, going to the fridge.

The children made their usual mild squabblings.

Behind her, her husband smoothed out a crumpled card, looked at it, and then looked at her as she busied herself around the fridge. He was about to say something but changed his mind. After looking at the card once more – then once more at Maggy – he placed it, very carefully, into the black sack and tied up the ends. Then he went over to his wife and put his arms around her.

'I love you,' he said, surprising himself.

She turned round to face him. The children went on squabbling, oblivious. Behind them the black sack toppled to one side.

'And I love you,' she said with an equal tone of surprise.

He relaxed. If there was one thing he knew about Maggy – one certain thing that he knew after all these years – it was that she could never, ever lie.

'Funny old Chrissie giving my wife roses,' he said. 'As if you needed reminding you were sexy.' He picked up the rubbish sack and went whistling down the path to the bin.

Candida Clark is the author of four novels: *The Last Look*, *The Constant Eye*, *The Mariner's Star*, and *Ghost Music*, published in Auguest 2003 by Review. She has also written film scripts and published poetry, short stories and criticism.

Ronnie's Watch

I

The girl was elbow-deep in suds, cursing the cook out of the side of her mouth. 'Get a move on with those peas.' She shook her head when Julia caught her eye, wiped her wet hands on her apron. 'Do it my bloody self. One scoop or two?'

It was late afternoon, the low season, and Julia was the only person in the café. It was called Gatsby's. She went there for the name, and sat with her back to the wall so that she could watch the kitchen and the harbour at the same time. It had seemed rude to turn away from the performance over her mushy peas. The girl's stiff blond hair was coloured candyfloss-pink at the ends. Her fingernails, exposed after washing-up, were diamanté-tipped. Cheap foundation obscured her face with the suggestion of fresh concrete. Julia estimated her age around her own: late twenties. The name-chain around her neck read 'Baby'.

'Here you go. Cod chips double peas.' The girl looked down at the plate and frowned. 'Hang on, you'll want more chips than that. That's pathetic. Ronnie!'

'No, really.' Julia tried to take the plate back just as the man who answered to Ronnie – cheeks flushed dark as bruised apples, eyes bulging with angina – appeared on the other side of the counter, putting on his coat. 'Fryer's off now.'

The girl breathed in sharply. 'Now listen . . .' and pushed Ronnie through a white swing door at the back of the kitchen. After the shouting, and the lone, guttural screech, Ronnie ran through the café into the starting evening, 'bugger this' thrown away under his breath as he slammed the door.

Julia ate her cod and chips. The only light in the café was from the blue neon sign advertising Teas Cakes Best Fish 'n' Chips. She stood up, counting out the right change, meaning to put it on the yellow Formica table before leaving. The greasy food had made her stomach bloat. The beef dripping it was cooked in made her think of vegetarianism. She wished she had eaten in the open air out of newspaper at the end of the pier, heedless of the dusk and drizzle that had now obscured the view of the harbour. Her teeth were furred with the UHT milk she'd put in her tea. She ran her tongue along them, pushing her plate aside, and stood for a moment in the silent café, feeling for her car keys in her bag.

There was no sound from the kitchen. Perhaps the girl had simply left by a back door? She checked her watch and tugged her sleeve back down over the gold-rimmed face, annoyed at its gleam of expense. She drew in her breath, and played the new game with herself: until she exhaled, she pretended that she had not really come here, had not thrown over her whole life, her work 'begging for bucks' as her mother put it, eyes widening with girlish sulks as though cash were a thing she couldn't comprehend. Perhaps this was true. Her mother had never earned her own living. She, on the other hand, fled 'the family name' by raising money for movies, and in America, too, which only added to her mother's resentment. Still, Julia knew that for all her expression of placid wonder, her mother was secretly totting up figures, same as any market trader: how many thousands frittered away on the Benenden education, those grantless years at Oxford, and that 'starter flat' in Pimlico – all this, for her daughter to flaunt her pursuit of money so openly, and still not married?

Julia did not mind. She had smoothed her mother with a gift and quit the business. She told her about it over tea at Fortnum's, just before she left London for the North. 'Too many schmucks anyhow.' She fell into tandem with the older woman, who gurgled like a baby with delight, her eyes swerving to see if anyone had overheard. She patted Julia's hand, commented approvingly on her decision to wear great-granny Cleo's sapphire. 'Brings out your colouring.' This was more her territory.

'Feels kind of heavy though.' Julia made her hand go limp as though the ring were burdensome. All these years her mother had been telling her what a disappointment she was. Action movies. For goodness' sake! And what would Professor Antrobus have made of all that shooting and foul language? And what if Miss Forsyth, her Latin mistress – but how would such a thing even be possible? – should one day notice her daughter's name in the credits of 'some hideous flick in Blockbusters'? Julia rolled her eyes. But she was honestly surprised at her mother's insight. The idea had often crossed her mind. How could she square *amo amas amat* with power breakfasts on Sunset, where millions changed hands with the Florida orange juice and muffins?

She cleared her throat. 'It's not my business to say what goes into the pictures. I just dish out the dough.' She said this last thing with exaggeration, making her mother clap a hand across her mouth, her eyes glittering with excitement. 'God, darling, don't!'

But now she had quit. Shame had nothing to do with it. She had simply discovered that she was far lazier than she had once imagined. Like many people of her generation – or so she read with gratitude in a copy of *Harper's Bazaar* as she left LAX last month – she wanted more and better 'quality time', to go 'lo-fi' for a while, to 'down-grade', or was it 'down-size'? The first sounded worryingly like reneging on business class. She lifted the collar of her coat. A noise from the kitchen made her look round.

In the blue light the girl stood hunched in a secret drama of dejection. The light gave her theatricality. Julia wondered how long the girl had been watching her. Outside in the dusk, with a high tide, the bridge was raised and boats passed gleaming by to the inner harbour. Julia noticed this, was about to remark on the prettiness of it to the girl before she paid her bill and left, when with heavy feeling the girl half shouted, 'Bloody bridge!' before kicking out at the wall and turning to Julia with a look of pent confession, her shoulders quivering as she chewed her lip, her eyes glassy with emotion.

'You OK?' Julia noticed a deep red welt on her forearm. The girl swore and blew her nose. 'Bloody Ronnie. I'd leave this place like a shot. You'd not see me for dust.' She fisted her hands at her sides.

A woman with a pram leant in through the café door. 'You still serving?'

'Sod off!' The girl rushed at her as though she might charge the glass, slamming the bolt across. 'He'll probably come back.' She peered out into the dusk. 'Usually does after a few jars. *Ronnie*.' She seemed to wring the word out in her mouth.

Julia could feel the Formica press against the backs of her legs as she waited for something else to happen. She felt slightly dizzy, and suspected it was more than a cholesterol rush. Even standing a few yards away, the girl's antics seemed so near, as though she were being forced to eyeball a scene in slow-motion close-up. But it wasn't that, she corrected herself. The shock was that this was all so *real* – that was the word she used to describe it to herself. The café's cheap colour-scheme, with its ornamentation of ketchup and HP sauce, was starting to make her nerves brighten and recoil. If she hadn't quit, she reminded herself, what a storyline she might find here. She couldn't remember the last

81

time she experienced anything like this. She had been thinking of her mother and of Fortnum's, and now she placed her mother in this place and a laugh suddenly coughed out of her like a bad pill spat out.

The girl stared at her, her eyes venomous with resentment. 'It's true.' She half turned away. 'If I had the chance I'd leave this minute.' She plucked a cigarette from a packet of Royals. 'There's nothing to keep me here. I want to start my whole life over.'

Now that the boats had stopped coming back to harbour, the bridge came down, the cars flowed again between the old and new sides of town, and Julia remembered that those were the words she used to describe her decision to quit to her mother. 'I wish you'd stop these silly Americanisms, darling. I really can't make out your meaning half the time.' Her mother had pursed her lips and tried to appear disapproving, but she couldn't conceal her delight in her daughter's homecoming, and the celebratory *fino* sherry had worked its way into all her reprimands. She flashed her daughter a smile. 'I wish you wouldn't. Because you sound like a real *schmuck*.' She giggled as she waved through the lowered window of the Holland Park-bound taxi.

But that had been her expression then: 'I want to start my whole life over.' She had headed north with this vague idea in mind – a woolly notion of shedding skins and temporary impoverishment. The Cartier tank seemed to burn on her wrist as she thought of that duplicity. Nevertheless, she felt a warm impulse towards this girl with her parallel desires. She put out a hand to touch her reassuringly on the arm, and withdrew it quickly. The girl looked at her with mistrust.

'If you want to talk,' Julia volunteered, 'feel free.'

The girl snorted in derision at this last word. 'S' all right for you.' She started to snuffle. Before she properly cried, she darted for the kitchen. 'I'll make some tea.' When she came back, her eyes were dry and she told Julia everything.

Finishing her story, she appeared lighter, less definite, and bored by herself and by the sound of everything she had said – as though she had run through her life a thousand times that day. Once out, she looked at the sum of it with distaste. Was that all there was? It seemed to disgust her. It hadn't taken long to tell. She had a knack for the succinct plot-line and the killer twist. Julia was impressed. She had not considered herself naive until now.

When the girl mentioned, 'to cap it all', how deeply in debt she was, the figure yoking her in an appearance of sudden defeat, Julia smiled. At least she could do something for her. She unfastened her watch. The girl looked at it in dismay. 'You think it's just about good timing?' She rolled up her sleeve to show Julia her plastic Sekonda.

'Trust me, this will help.' Julia felt serene with an intimation of power. She also felt useful, an unusual sensation. She wished a camera could be there to record the moment on the girl's face when she discovered that watch's value. She imagined the shot lingering on her expression before panning out over the empty street outside the dingy jeweller's, or better, pawnbroker's shop. They would probably assume the girl had stolen it. Perhaps she should give her some kind of receipt?

'What about you then?' The girl leant forward hungrily, snapping a piece of rigid blond hair between her fingers. Confession had given her an appetite.

Julia told her about herself. She was careful to knock noughts off all her descriptions. No point in seeming to brag. But afterwards she felt only embarrassment and annoyance at herself for giving so much away. The girl's eyes stretched wide. 'You've got it made.'

When they separated by the water's edge, Julia felt relieved that at least she'd never see the girl again.

That night, she thought of the watch and felt ridiculous. It was a gesture from the movies, not real life. The girl would probably lose it, and gain nothing. She turned over heavily beneath the goose-feather eiderdown. She remembered when she bought that watch. At Cartier on Madison. A weekend spree. She bought one in gold with a lizard strap. One in silver with crocodile. One in platinum with pigskin. She had had to get the pigskin because otherwise, if she was honest, she couldn't tell the difference between silver and platinum. Could anyone, really, she pondered, or were they all lying when they said they could? If she had been wearing the platinum tank, she wouldn't have parted with it. The girl would have had to go away empty-handed.

Julia thought of this as she fell asleep, but she slept badly. The gulls were loud on the rooftops of the rented cottage, and the sea nagged her. By morning she was exhausted. She reached for her watch and it was not there.

II

'Ronnie! Darling!' Julia rubbed her eyes. She must have fallen asleep on the sofa. The heat had tired her. Her limbs felt heavy with lunchtime Chablis. Her shellfish ban had slipped – she suffered terrible allergies if she was reckless – and now she had a lobster headache. She swore. There was a commotion at the front door. More house guests. Her friends had told her this would be a quiet weekend. She stretched and frowned. Now who the hell was Ronnie?

A warm breeze stirred the limp tulle curtains. The French windows were open onto the garden. She slipped outside before anyone came into the room.

The sun had fallen behind the pines that stood at the far side of the garden, beyond the tennis court. It was the end of August. The house shone golden in the last light of day. Gin would soon be mentioned. Champagne, if the new guests were important. She heard a muffled pop from the direction of the library.

On the air Julia could smell the sweetness of cut hay. She crossed the lawn towards the walled herb garden so that she could sit beneath the trellis where bougain-villea and jasmine clung and fell in scented, artful swags. Concealed by the curtain of flowers, Julia had a clear view of the house. She settled back against the cushions on the garden seat and watched as a couple emerged slightly ahead of her friends. She heard the crystal chime as the quartet touched glasses. There was laughter, and the girl who had just arrived gestured towards her. She had been spotted. Someone waved, and Julia cursed, wondering if it would be thought too rude of her not to get up. Perhaps she could pretend to be sleeping. She shut her eyes.

'Jules, stop faking.' Lottie shook her by the shoulder, handing her a champagne flute. 'Come and meet Ronnie and Todd. And don't sulk. You'll love Ronnie. You're very alike.' Julia hated being told that she resembled anyone. It seemed to steal something from her that she was reluctant to give up. She looked towards the house. The others had arranged themselves beneath parasols on the terrace. Their faces were in shade. 'Ronnie's engaged though,' Lottie added *sotto voce*, with a smirk of malice as they walked across the lawn.

'But that's the Bel Air all over.' The girl called Ronnie sniffed and touched her sunglasses. The two men laughed, as though Ronnie had cracked a joke. Lottie's husband Marcus suddenly pointed at Ronnie, blinking colourless lashes as though she gave off too much light. A fat forelock of blond hair hung damp across his tall forehead. His cheeks were rosy with delight as he jabbed his finger at Ronnie. 'My guess is it's Shakespearean.'

Todd was still snickering. 'She's a sphinx, she'll never tell.' He gulped his drink.

'Short for Rosalind, or Rosamund, or Rose-most-fair.' Marcus blew out his cheeks in pleasure, fondling his old school tie. Such excuses to display his education always reassured him.

Ronnie looked bored, as though she had heard men say such things too many times to mention. 'Shakespeare!' She sipped her champagne ironically and smiled, half turning towards the garden as though about to yawn.

'Quite,' Todd agreed.

Julia imagined the girl's parents, and secretly denounced them for the bohemian impulse that must've seized them in naming their daughter. The middle classes were littered with Portias and Hermiones and Rosalinds. She had gone to school with a few score of them.

A noise from inside the house made them all look up. 'Oh God.' Lottie set her glass down unsteadily on the rim of a planter. 'The cats are at the canapés!' She ran inside. 'Help me with the big table, boys!'

'Is it really time for the big table?' Marcus stood up complaining. Ronnie checked her watch as though to find the answer. The men noticed this and laughed as though she had said something hilarious. They went inside. Todd blew Ronnie a kiss as he stepped through the French windows. The fiancée. Ronnie fluttered her fingers at him as he went inside.

The watch glinted where the last of the sunlight fell upon it. Ronnie took off her sunglasses the moment the men were out of earshot. 'One scoop or two?' She lowered her voice and grinned. 'Don't spill the beans. I'm having too much fun.'

Julia's throat contracted. She drew back. The accent

had gone. The stiff hair was now silkily coiffed, and a decorous shade of English mouse, cleverly highlighted. Julia thought that everything about her spoke of good taste, breeding, even. Certainly it spoke of money. 'Ronnie?'

'Oh, the name. *His*. Remember? The oaf with the good right hook. Nicked his credit cards and scarpered.'

Julia drew in her breath.

'Cleaned him out. Signed his name so often that it sort of stuck. But it was you who clinched it.'

Julia could feel her face drain of blood. 'Clinched it?' She felt a line of sweat gather beneath her hair.

'I wanted to start my whole life over, just like you.' Ronnie licked her lips. 'You said a name counted for everything, and I'm not even going to tell you what mine was before. It was a millstone at any rate – just like my parents, God rest their – so I got rid of it. "Ronnie" made me feel better right away.'

Julia's mind raced. If she said that line about names, she had probably been talking about Cartier. She coloured with embarrassment. Her eyes swivelled to the watch. Ronnie shook her wrist in triumph. 'Put it in hock in a joint off Bond Street when I knew what it was worth. Never did thank you properly for it.' There was the sound of banging from the kitchen. Ronnie looked up. 'It's come in handy, I can tell you.' She leant towards Julia as though sharing a confidence. 'You've no idea how snobbish people are. Well, maybe you do. One look at this and they think I'm loaded.' The two men came back outside. 'But Todd thinks Cartier's terrifically nineties, don't you, Todd?'

Todd smiled as he struggled with the table. His thin arms and hollow chest bore the hallmarks of early middle-age brought on by nervous years hunched over the antics of the stockmarket. A heart condition seemed to be pencilled on the silveriness of his skin. Julia could see that Ronnie knew what she was doing.

'Going to get you a Patek Philippe, aren't I, darling?' He dropped the table on Marcus's toe. 'Wedding present,' Todd explained to Julia. 'Cayman Islands next spring. Flying everyone out.' Ronnie seemed to shiver with satisfaction at these words.

'Everyone who's *anyone*,' Marcus chimed in, forgetting his bruised toe in a flash of what he plainly thought was wit. 'That's right, isn't it, Toddy?' He fell almost double with laughter. 'Not flying *everyone* out.' He nudged at Todd for approval. Ronnie looked out across the lawn. Julia had received no invitation.

'You must come, darling.' Ronnie seemed to recover herself, as though remembering a forgotten Christmas gift for servants. She touched Julia lightly on the arm.

Julia drew back and held out her glass abruptly. 'Any chance of a top-up?'

Marcus looked at her in surprise. He had never suspected Julia of bad manners. He filled her glass with a show of gallantry, and saw her in a new light. He made a note to mention this demanding side of her character to Lottie. She had freeloaded here often enough, and anyway wasn't nearly so much fun now she'd given up producing movies and gone to work as a – what was it? – fundraiser, for God's sake, for that dreary NGO. Jules simply wasn't good value any more.

He looked at her indignantly. Ronnie was much more fun.

'Darling, you're too sweet.' Ronnie smiled up at Marcus as he filled her glass. 'And such a spoiler with all this Bollie.' She raised an eyebrow at the label.

But how could she hope to pull this off? Julia tried not to stare at her. The girl's courage was certainly impressive. But what would she do when she was found out? It was just a question of time. She saw her again arm-deep in suds in that café, and remembered her odd response when Julia gave her the watch. 'You think it's just about good timing?' Then, she had been sarcastic. It was an empty phrase. Now, her new life depended on it. If her fiancé had overheard their conversastion of moments earlier, it'd be no-go the Cayman Islands. Julia was aware that she had been holding her breath. She felt slightly faint with nerves, as though the secret was hers. But she had only listened, and given the girl a watch in a rash impulse of charity. The girl was a stranger to her otherwise.

She listened to Ronnie describing something to Marcus. 'One time, on Sunset . . .' A story of million-dollar deals and 'movie-world schmucks' – the reason, according to Ronnie, why she 'jacked it all in'. Marcus gulped at the expression and looked nervously at Todd, who was beaming like a small boy. 'Isn't she wonderful?'

'Now I'm just taking things as they come.' Ronnie settled herself deeper inside her cashmere wrap. 'Felt that it was about time I slowed down, went lo-fi for a while.'

'Good idea.' Marcus grinned. He didn't understand

what she meant. He had a hi-fi in the drawing room, if that had anything to do with it. He wondered if he could throw the expression into conversation, but perhaps it had something to do with a woman's high-fibre diet and he'd be thought effete. He bit his lip and jumped when Lottie came back outside, handing him the plate of canapés. He lowered his voice to a gruff basso and popped a quail's egg into his mouth. Lottie slapped his hand away. 'Wicked child. Guests first.' He wimpered softly, and fell back in his chair.

'Anyway, you won't want to bother about work when we're married, will you, darling?' Todd drew the cashmere closer around his bride-to-be, looking at her fondly as though she were a fragile doll in a box.

'No such luck for Julia.' Marcus turned to her with a hard laugh. Everyone fell silent. Julia could hear a tractor purring in the distance, and the crickets had started in the long grass of the meadow beyond the garden wall.

Lottie's plump hand froze over a plate of devilled eggs.

Ronnie cleared her throat. Her knuckles showed pale around the stem of her glass. Todd put his hand on her knee. She moved away from his touch with a swift recrossing of her legs.

The tractor passed by on the road. The light was almost finished and when Todd lit a cigarette the flame exposed the mosquitoes dancing in the dusk. No-one spoke. Ronnie did not take her eyes from Julia's face. Her smile was tight and urgent. Julia drained her glass.

'Ah, la Favorita!' Lottie slipped off her chair in an appearance of ecstasy. 'Dearest Alice.' One of the Persian cats whispered by Marcus's ankles. He pushed it away roughly with his foot. 'Don't kick poor kitty,' Lottie scolded. 'If anything, it's bad manners, especially as her pedigree is finer than yours, isn't it, darling?' She bent down, addressing the cat.

'Alice as in Wonderland?' Todd pressed his hands together in relief, looking at the cat assessingly.

'As in Keppel, silly.' She flourished on other people's mistakes. 'King Teddie VII's mistress?

'Refuses to purr,' she explained to Ronnie, 'however much we lace her dinner with Sevruga. Isn't that so, darling?'

Lottie straightened up when no-one reacted. She had hoped someone might chastise her for her extravagance. She enjoyed reprimands, and excuses to flaunt her husband's wealth. But he was so rich he never kept tabs on such things as housekeeping. They had someone to do that for them, and besides, they had too many houses. He glanced at her. Her silliness about caviar for cats only bored him. It reminded him of his mother. She had behaved similarly with dogs, feeding them songbirds. Or was that something he had from Shakespeare too? Or something to do with lark's tongues and Henry VIII? He noticed the empty bottles of Bollinger and sighed. He wasn't thinking straight. He knew that someone was owed an apology. He tugged his wife towards him and kissed her.

'Aren't sturgeon on the endangered-species list these days?' Ronnie's voice was gentle and sounded misplaced, as though she had uttered something personal that it was impolite, openly, to acknowledge.

Lottie made a clucking noise as the cat disappeared svelte into the evening. She hated the way cats did that. She wished they'd come to heel like a good setter. 'More nibbles?' When no-one answered, Lottie squared her shoulders in protest and charged inside. The two men turned to Ronnie expectantly, as though she might suddenly take off her clothes. She drew her wrap tighter about her shoulders.

'Fuck!' Lottie's voice sounded frantic in the quiet house. There was the melody of shattering glass on marble and the two men sprang to their feet.

'That girl is so clumsy when she's had a few sherbets.' Marcus laughed, blushing at the commotion. Were they really so impoverished that they had to serve their own champagne? He staggered against the doorframe as he stumbled through the French windows, an arm around Todd's waist for support.

'I might take a turn around the garden.' Ronnie rose to her feet, plucking a packet of Royals from her handbag. 'Sneaky fag. Toddy's dead against it.' She looked down at Julia and smiled. 'Cover for me if I'm missed? Be years before anything happens round here anyway.'

The large house seemed fragile with noise and light as the smashed crystal was inexpertly dispensed with. The garden smelled of damp lavender and rosemary. A cat moved silent through the thorned rose bushes. Petals fell where it passed by.

Rachel Cusk was born in 1967 and is the author of four novels: *Saving Agnes*, which won the Whitbread First Novel Award, *The Temporary*, *The Country Life*, which won a Somerset Maugham Award, and *The Lucky Ones*. *A Life's Work* was her acclaimed and controversial account of becoming a mother.

Sweet Ladies

When the wind blew straight at Doniford the sea stood up in white spikes, like a head of hair in terror or shock. People went into their houses, leaving the streets silently to absorb the cold. Most days the sea was the colour of a pair of eyes, slate grey marbled with blue or brown. It loitered there, rolling, at the foot of the cliffs and charged in and out of the small bay, flinging mud at the sea wall. It was a rough-looking sea, with patches like the patches on a mongrel's coat where its currents ran contrary to itself. There wasn't much in it, either. On Tuesdays the butcher had a stall of local fish. One recent display had consisted of four or five grey mullet, strange, massive, tow-headed things the colour of concrete. Each one was about three feet long and as thick as a small tree trunk. The butcher and his wife had tried to divide them into steaks but they wouldn't go. All day they lay there in their ugliness. When it was windy the butcher's sign went back and forth like a child's swing and up the hill little bells rang outside the row of brightly coloured terraced cottages where lived the determined few who kept boats down in the harbour for pleasure. Their houses, painted china blue or primrose yellow or cream, decorated with flags and bits of rigging and lobster traps, were as though lost on their way to some sunny southern resort; as though orphaned or offered up, through misfortune or mischance, to this grey, inward-looking town that could not offer them the consolation of its affection.

Sylvia Furnish sometimes thought that she might like to live in one of those brightly coloured houses, but considering everything she was well off where she was, in a cul-de-sac off the coast road, where she rented a modern flat on the upper storey of a two-storey house. The flat had a balcony where Sylvia kept geraniums and other flowers in pots. Before she left in the mornings she usually went out there, in winter to sweep and tidy up and take off any heads and in summer to enjoy the flowers. Whatever the season, from her balcony she could see the girls going up the road at that hour. They went all in a row, blowing about in the wind like washing on a line. Most of them were pushing prams or strollers, as well as having one in front and one behind. Three children, sometimes four, and Sylvia didn't think any of the girls was much more than twenty. The wind would lift their long hair and hold it or hurl it about, or prise open their coats. Sometimes one of the little ones would plant himself on the pavement behind, bawling. The bigger children would run ahead to kick old Coke cans and litter at one another. All the while the girls would move through sun and wind and rain in their stately procession, never turning to left or right but with their faces lifted slightly to the sky, as though in consultation with their own mysterious gods.

By the time they came back down the road again Sylvia was in her shop. Having left the older ones at school it was as though they had awoken from a trance or spell. Sylvia would hear them coming in a rabble along the pavement and the whir of buggy wheels was like the beating of wings around her head. There in her shop her heart would shrink within her chest: she forgot to pity or despise them and instead she was afraid, of their taut skin and their pouting mouths sucking cigarettes, of their youthful rudeness and their bodies only just broken open by children. Sylvia sold sweets and tobacco and a few odds and ends of stationery. In the mornings when she unlocked the door the chalky smell of the sweets would assail her from the shadows. It came up like a wall against what she felt was her own bitterness. When she was in the shop her flavour would never amalgamate – it separated and stood on the surface like oil. She felt exposed and set apart by it. It was never her idea, to run a sweet shop. She'd have liked to sell lavender bags and candle holders and glass ornaments that the light came through. Rob bought the shop in 1985 and they ran it together for the next five years. It was just sweets then. Sylvia brought in the tobacco and the stationery after Rob went, because she needed the revenue to pay off his debts. Rob would never sell cigarettes. He was one of the only people in Doniford in those days who didn't smoke. Sylvia gave up because of him, because his life seemed to possess a kind of entirety that she coveted, but in fact she found an existence unbroken by addiction tiring, as if she was never allowed to stop for breath. She kept it up, though. She didn't know what might be waiting for her, back in the old ways.

The girls loomed at the glass. There were three of them today. Sylvia turned away as the bell shrilled and they opened the door. They clattered in with their prams and buggies. One of the buggies was two seats wide, for twins, and they had to turn it sideways and lift it through like a sofa while the babies looked out blankly.

'All right?' said the one called Terry or Kerry, she could never quite hear, catching Sylvia's eye. She was a big girl but her face was a child's face, and like a child she went along with the rest of them but reverted to innocence when you got her on her own.

'Not too bad,' said Sylvia.

The twins were Terry's. Their hair was like flax even though their mother was dark. They sat there side by side pulling at their dummies, which hung around their necks on strings. Sylvia suddenly didn't know how Terry coped with them: they looked so united and strange. Her own two had been separated by two and a half years and that gap had been all Sylvia's leverage, because the difference in age had led inevitably to disagreements which it fell to Sylvia to sort out. When it came down to it her authority had consisted of not much more than that, although she made it look as though it did.

'I'll have ten Lambert and Butler please,' said Terry.

Behind Terry stood a tall, queenly girl who seldom spoke. Sylvia remembered, a few years before, seeing this girl burgeon into young womanhood and believing, sincerely but for no definite reason, that she would not remain much longer in Doniford. It was the faraway look in her eyes and the way she held herself with such dignity, as though she were waiting politely for the moment to come when she could leave and take up her appointed place elsewhere. But then like all of them her stomach had started to grow and now there were two children and a third on the way; and her bearing was just one of those oddities, like Terry's baby face, that lay scattered over Doniford like pickings on the beach.

'That wind could take the skin off your face,' said Sylvia, conversationally, because they all seemed tongue-tied. These girls were small children during her own trouble. They probably didn't know anything about it, or didn't care: it was Sylvia that gave birth and life to it again and again, who freshened up her shame each spring. The people who *did* remember were older now, like her, and more kind if she were honest than they had been before, as if her bad experiences had been broken down and diffused amongst them all by some organic process. One of the girls tittered at Sylvia's remark. It was one she'd not often seen and never spoken to. She was standing with her little boy in the tent of shadow the shelves made in the corner. She wasn't much to look at, but Sylvia looked. She had a white little face with a little turned-up nose and small eyes the colour of puddles. A wedge of mousy hair sat on her head. Her boy was different, he was dark like a gypsy. He was three or so years old. His velvet eyes met

Sylvia's out of the shadows and when he smiled his eye teeth glinted. Without taking his eyes away he reached out his hand and took a bar of something, Sylvia couldn't see what, from the shelf. His hand was so small and naughty as it reached out. It reminded her of her sons' hands as they had once been, grubby and soft and unformed. The other night she had watched a programme on television, about children in Brazil, who lived in the streets and walked about with guns tucked down their shorts and robbed and killed like adults. It was a terrible thing to watch children struggling out of their innocence. The boy had taken a Tracker bar.

'Whatsa matter now?' mumbled Terry softly, bending over so that her hair fell in ropes around her face. The twins were writhing silently in their pushchair. Their dummies stoppered their mouths so that no sound came out. They turned their fair heads from side to side and grimaced, like sleepers having bad dreams.

'What you got, Troy,' said the other girl. She uttered the words not as a question but as the notes of a descending scale; as a retreat or reverse from the battleground of suspicion. Troy smiled charmingly. His crooked teeth flashed like diamonds.

'Nuffin,' he said.

'What you got,' his mother repeated. Sylvia, who knew something about music, heard the notes again. It was a chord pattern, of thirds.

'Nuffin.'

The girl rolled her eyes and her thin lips lifted at the corners. She shook her head and the wedge of hair moved with it. That was to be the extent, it seemed, of her interrogation. She wanted to make contact with the other girls but they were not attending. Avoiding the searchlight of Sylvia's gaze, she had to bring her pantomime of accusation and exoneration to a close without their help. She rolled her eyes again and cuffed the boy lightly about the head. Sylvia had seen him put the Tracker up the elasticated sleeve of his jacket. He had seen her see.

'I'll have these an all,' said Terry, sliding a packet of chocolate buttons on to the counter beside her Lamberts. 'It used to shut them up,' she said to the queenly girl who stood beside her, gazing out of the shop window with the light on her face. 'But it don't any more.'

'You'll have to find somefin else,' said the queenly girl with a faint smile.

Sylvia took the coins Terry pushed at her over the counter. She noticed that Terry was missing a front tooth. When her own children were small it had all seemed to matter so much, how they turned out. She had been hard on them, and for what? There had been no recognition, and although once they had dominated her existence, now they lived lives she had to screw her eyes up to pick out. Steven stacked shelves at some distant supermarket. Paul lived with a woman Sylvia had never met, in a caravan on the south coast. Their father had left when they were twelve and fourteen, old enough to look after themselves, or so he'd probably thought. He left them with the clothes they stood up in. They lost the house, the car, the television, everything but the shop, which was in her name.

'If he wants it, he'll have to pay for it,' she said bitterly to Troy's mother, as the girls were turning to leave. At Sylvia's words Troy's mother put up her head with a little jerk. Her face was like a scrap of white paper. Sylvia thought she might defend him, but she didn't. She said nothing. She just looked at Sylvia with the little white void of her face.

'She ain't got no money,' said Troy.

'That's not my concern,' said Sylvia.

She had forgotten he was just a child. Her heart was thumping in her chest. A sort of white light seemed to send its glare into her eyes, making them water. Terry and the other two were staring at her with their mouths open. They were like cows standing staring in a field. The little boy was looking at her too, but with an expression that struck Sylvia dimly for a moment as almost being one of compassion. He drew his dark brows together in a crooked crease. His round eyes were sorrowful. Slowly he put his fingers up his sleeve and withdrew the Tracker.

'Sorry, lady,' he said.

He replaced the bar on the shelf and gave his mother his hand. Quietly he led her to the door. Sylvia turned away and went through to the back of the shop so that she wouldn't have to witness the removal of the twins' pushchair. After a while the bell above the door sounded its note. Even though she had been expecting it the noise startled her. She must have been miles away. She went out to the front, just in case anyone else had come in. Through the window she saw the girls blowing across the road with their pushchairs, separating and re-forming like the shapes birds made as they flew in their flocks at dusk over the rough darkening sea. The little boy had let go of his mother's hand and run ahead up the pavement. The wind lifted his jacket and whipped it behind him. She had had a rule against her own boys having sweets from the shop when they were small, but she felt that if Troy came back again tomorrow she might be able to find a little something for him. He lifted his head up as he ran into the wind and held his arms high by his sides like a boxer, as though to make himself go faster.

Stella Duffy has written three novels published by Sceptre: *Singling Out the Couples*, *Eating Cake* and *Immaculate Conceit* and four crime novels: *Calendar Girl*, *Wavewalker*, *Beneath the Blonde* and *Fresh Flesh*, all published by Serpent's Tail. Her latest novel, *State of Happiness*, will be published by Virago in 2004. She has published over twenty short stories. With Lauren Henderson, she is co-editor of the anthology *Tart Noir*. In addition to her writing work, Stella is an actor, comedian and improviser. She is currently working on her new one-woman show *Breaststrokes*, and is also a member of Improbable Theatre's acclaimed *Lifegame* company, which has toured throughout Britain, Australia and the US. Stella was diagnosed with breast cancer in 2000. Her current interests include attaining enlightenment and staying alive.

Forty-year-old Women Dancing
Barefoot in Sydney

The city arches wide arms across the sky, harbour smudges right up against the bright yellow day just like the one before and the one to come, Blue Mountains have reverted to gold and green in national homage. Katie in this middle-country for five days only and four old friends flying in; girlie weekend (Perth), kids and husbands (Auckland, Taupo), partners and dogs (Hong Kong) all left behind. Twenty-five years or more packed into each suitcase.

'Daniel', Elton John:
Katie encouraging the others to put on another play, for the school this time, a better audience than their parents, more appreciative, the acknowledgement of their peers. Janet throwing down a library book, furious but not saying it. Joining in outside, inside held back.

Janet adjusts the buckle on her lap, still uncertain despite booking the ticket months ahead. She does not do disease, is all positive thought and visualized

109

harmony. Has had no deaths, parents still hanging on, well into their eighties and well, well, well. Three births, each one easy, each one a perfect child, and then the fourth – child perfect of course, lucky Janet who doesn't know she is lucky – but the body surrender itself, she doesn't talk about that, the long time labouring, the cutting skin, the giving in to the white coats and their fear. She has the scar to prove it, but would rather not look below the belly line now, her failure label. Swallows Rescue Remedy and little white arnica pills as the plane begins its descent.

Katie brushing her hair. Almost shoulder length now, a year's new growth, not back to what it was, but then neither is she. She has moved on, is different, changed. So is her hair. She wants to wear the wig, loved that wig, the swing of the cut, the shine, the shampoo-advertisement gleam. It was her best-ever mask, made her a proper grown-up lady, someone with nothing better to do than go to lunch and maybe attend a charity committee meeting; she looked like one of those women in her wig, it gave her long slim manicured hands. And the possibility of couture dresses. Shakes her mirrored head at the thought even as she considers it. Katie cannot wear the wig; she knows they will think it is a sign. Which it is. But not of that.

Anna collects her luggage from the carousel. She is occasionally crying, one or two tears falling every five minutes from the red wells of her eyes, as they have for most of the ten-hour flight. The big fight with Paul before she left, his accusations of her selfishness, her ready agreement but packing the bags anyway, being here anyway. She needs this more than he needs her. She needs a break from Paul, a break from the baby, a break from her life. And she needs to feel the pulse of Katie's skin.

Nicki and John are laughing. Two just-released teens left at home; this is their time now. John smuggled along on a girlie weekend; Friday night with his old mates, Saturday shopping for the kids, Sunday he'll come along to lunch with the girls. But he'll be waiting in the hotel room when Nicki comes in, warming the bed, minibar bill already marked up, flicking channels with the familiarity of forever. Nicki and John love hotel rooms. Always have. John is looking forward to Sunday lunch.

John is the one illicit kiss Katie never had. Though God knows she hoped, through long university nights of analysis and contempt. He would have kissed her too, but that for all his revolutionary poise they both knew he would immediately go back to the messy room and tell Nicki every last lick of exchanged saliva. So they did the right thing – and wonder even now. Katie is looking forward to Sunday lunch.

Deb waits in the airport foyer, sunglasses on, hire-car keys jangling against the change in her pocket. Janet is already late, always already late. Deb didn't want to share a room anyway, hates the crush of other suitcases, has relished her space even more since she left Mike. Worse still for Deb to share a room with another woman, the silent competition for space men have always yielded to her, too much make-up in the bath-room, the girlie eagerness to try on each other's clothes.

But that neither she nor Janet could afford not to. (And the unmentioned but entirely true added incentive that even with all those kids and her limited budget, Deb would not be in the least bit surprised to find that Janet still has the best wardrobe of them all.)

'Sunday Girl', Blondie:
   'No really, keep it.'
   'Don't be silly.'
   'Deb, you look perfect. It doesn't work on me, I just look even skinnier than usual.'
   'My mum will kill me.'
   'Janet's right, Deb, you do look brilliant.'
   'Do I? Really?'
   Wait. Look. Turn. Hands cupping fleshed-out breasts, stomach held in, four nodding heads, Katie leaves a half-munched nail to confirm.
   'Absa-fucking-lutely. You can keep it at mine, get changed on Friday when you come to stay. Your mum won't even know.'
   'Take it.'
   Deb smiling in the mirror, the others on to something new, not interested now, already persuaded from the moment Janet sighed and then sized her up, Deb's hips and breasts filling out the perfect dress in the way hers never could.
   'OK. Thanks, Jan. But I will have to leave it at Katie's house.'

Only Nicki and John have ever been to Katie's house. Nicki visiting for a conference, something to do with her work, the job that none of the rest of them has ever really bothered to understand, something governmental, some consultation involved, something worth the nanny when the kids were younger and the beach house now and the extra car always. On that visit John claimed he had been reduced to porter and husband-of-the-more-famous. Late-night wine confirmed the truth, his redundancy depression and fear of letting Nicki out of his sight. All passed now of course, John back on track and working too hard again, just wanting a break this time. And a look at Katie. New look Katie. New hair Katie. Still here Katie.

They have booked a restaurant. A place Deb suggested, knowing Nicki would go for something expensive by everyone else's standards and then want to pay the whole drinks bill herself. Deb and Janet drive there straight from the airport, Janet getting changed in the car, cigarette handed to Deb, still-flat tits provoked into shape by a favourite bra, the variations on which she has been buying for fifteen years ever since she discovered the strength of a well-placed wire. A make-up check in the mirror, last quick drag of the fag, then – when Deb has already started her fast stride along the waterfront, Janet has second thoughts and plunges a hand down her front, quickly rearranges herself to a place less obvious, just in case it's too much. Too blatant. She catches up to Deb and they walk on. Scared and not saying it.

Anna is already there when they enter, pupils working hard to counter bright light to dark interior. She has a glass of wine before her and is on her mobile, firing out a slew of questions: 'What did she eat for breakfast? Did she sleep through the night? The green dungarees? Yes, but she doesn't like them, something about the material, her fingers go all bunched up when she touches it. Aren't the pink ones clean? Try them, she likes them better. In the airing cupboard, under her yellow jumper . . .'

Deb kisses Anna's head, sits down, orders two bottles of the house white, as well as bread, olive oil, warm toasted almonds. Janet gulps a mouthful of Anna's wine in greeting, shouts out hello to Paul, and makes a mental note to tell Anna to give it a rest. It took her two children to work out that Sharon probably could dress and feed their progeny all by herself, three to realize she herself wasn't indispensable, four and a slow-healing scar to finally learn to share. She doubted Paul, who'd waited for this baby just as long as Anna, would be as patient as Sharon had been.

By the time Nicki arrives the photos are out and Janet is wondering if she really shouldn't try again, if five would be all that excessive, mightn't it just round things off? Deb is promising herself she'll sit through just one more baby conversation this weekend before she snaps and reminds them all as forcefully as she'd really like to of her own whipped-out uterus and Katie's chemo-shrivelled ovaries. Though perhaps they will be more gentle with Katie. Her childlessness is new to the three mothers. Deb's accident was the trauma of their twenties; she has morphed from childless to childfree in the past years. This is the decade of a new disease. Nicki's progress, though, is way beyond baby photos and she is more than happy to assure both Janet and Anna that by the time their kids make it to mid-teens they will be way too pleased to be away from them for a weekend to mar their free time with photos and calling home to check on what's being eaten. Anna can't believe she's right, but puts away the album anyway, and nods, offering a whispered 'Sorry' to Deb who shrugs it off as she has been doing for fifteen years.

'Alice is still new, you've been trying for so long. Of course you're excited. It's fine. I don't mind, honest. I'm used to it.' And Deb doesn't mind, honest, but she will never be used to it.

Katie is in a taxi three hundred yards from the restaurant. She wants to tell the driver to take her back to the hotel. She wants to run away. She wants to be already drunk. She wants lunch to be over and all the rawness passed and the news caught up on and photos viewed and for the five of them just to be lounging on someone's hotel bed and eating overpriced minibar chocolates that taste really bad with the room service wine, laughing about some stupid thing that someone else once did in 1978. But first there is the kissing and the greeting and those looks, veering from shock to relief to pity and back again. First she must be witnessed. Before she can be just Katie, she must be seen to be still there. Still here.

And it's fair enough. Katie knows she is silently asking the impossible. That her journey be both acknowledged and ignored. That she is seen to have changed entirely and stayed exactly the same. And she has glimpsed them often enough in the past eighteen months to know that the faces, those first-look faces, cannot but remind her of before and after. Or worse – of during. The first-look faces are her bedroom mirror every morning and evening, they are all the shop changing rooms, each return hospital appointment. The constant reminders that on the one hand it really did happen. And on the other, she is still here, these faces are pleased she is still here, and this has been hard work for them too, they were scared too. Good and bad, two hands clapping.

The taxi stops, driver repeats the fare twice, Katie leaves a tip and balls up her receipt. She walks into the restaurant.

Anna thinks thank God.

Deb thinks oh God.

Nicki is pleased, this is what she had expected.

Janet realizes she didn't know what to expect.

Katie smiles wide and is surprised not to cry.

'Sharon sends her love.'

'Josie is so sorry she couldn't make it.'

'John's really looking forward to Sunday.'

'Paul says hi.'

'My mum sent you a big hug. And this scarf. Hand-made.'

'Emma?'

'Oh, I never really see Emma any more.'

'Me neither. Not properly, not really. You know, we're all so busy. She's got her job and the kids. And I don't think Marcus is much help.'

'This Woman's Work', Kate Bush:
  'But why, Emm?'

116

'You know why. Janet can't come here. I don't want the children to know about her and . . . that woman.'

'Sharon.'

'Yes. Her. Janet's changed.'

'Ah – no she hasn't. Janet's always been like this.'

'What about that bloke she went out with when she was at college?'

'It was a phase.'

'My kids know about it, Emma. Sharon's brilliant with them. They all play together. It doesn't make any difference.'

'It does to me.'

'Right.'

'Well then.'

'Fine.'

Late lunch flows into early dinner becomes jetlag heads and time for bed. The conversation is easy. There are the kids to catch up on and work and Katie's visit and everyone's parents, surviving and dead, and the husbands and partners, detox and diet, new shoes. Always new shoes. Not much is said about it, Katie's difference. No-one is sure what words she wants to use. They are waiting for her to make the first move. And Katie isn't ready yet either. There is a whole weekend to come. For now she will just do what they always do. Talk, reminisce, get drunk. They always get drunk. Twelve on her mother's home-made brandy. Fifteen under the stage at school. Seventeen and the boys were there too. Nineteen for Emma's back-garden twentieth. Twenty-three in London, twenty-five in

Barcelona, before-and-after-forty in Sydney. Not everyone makes it to every gathering; unlike Deb and Anna, Katie was never much of a traveller, but whenever four or more of them are together in the same room, there will be wine. Katie hated the not drinking when she was ill. She felt even more left out, left behind, gone before. And even though every sip is now loaded with what-if and maybe, too many alternative books read, too many scare stories surrendered to, she drinks wine glass/water glass/wine glass/water glass with the others as the Southern Cross falls into place.

Saturday morning there is coffee. Decaff and real. Biscuits, cake, low-fat muffins. And then the shops. First the kids' presents which Anna dreads and Janet loves and Deb bears, always just about bears. Then on to the easy bit. A long stretch of clothes only Nicki can afford easily, or Katie maybe, with her European money tripling in value in the south, but still they look and touch and feel until, in a fit of credit-card excess, Katie and Deb and Anna make their way to the changing rooms.

The stretch top doesn't suit Katie. She knew it wouldn't. Cannot get used to the change in shape. Sees the difference clearest of all when looking in the mirror. Anna will buy the skirt, but only to wear in another three months, when the baby weight has gone, when she is herself again. Deb has a pile on the counter she will get regardless; she has always been their credit-card queen. Fuck Mike and fuck his new girl and fuck her youth and fuck the ring she no longer wears. Anna pulls back the curtain to show the skirt. It is a good fit now, will be better still in a month or so she says. Nicki and Janet disagree, say nothing, care little for later. Everyone thinks the top is perfect. Katie will not buy it, cannot buy it. Nicki asks why not and Anna kicks her. And then Katie asks, do they want to see?

Anna does. Deb doesn't. Nicki is dying to. Janet doesn't think she cares either way. Katie wants to show. Wants to be seen.

In Nicki's hotel room, John out with his local mates, a rumple of new clothes on the unmade bed, gift toys and airport books on the floor, there is a viewing. The scars are longer than Anna expected. Deeper and less tidy than Janet had imagined; she had not pictured a gouge right down to the ribs, or the long, misshapen rip under Katie's arm. It is not as gross as Deb would have thought. The heavy red lines on thin skin make Nicki cry. She wants to kiss Katie's scars. When Katie is dressed again, Deb unveils hers, how the fifteen-year healing has made a pale life-line of her own near-death experience. Katie wonders about waiting fifteen years for the reveal, thinks how she should have paid more attention to Deb's loss back then. They were young back then, Deb came through it, she remembers Anna being attentive to Deb's pain, Katie herself didn't yet know enough to acknowledge the loss, Deb's future-fears. She does now. Janet and Nicki offer up caesareans; Nicki's easy and quick and unimportant now, Janet's identical in appearance, entirely the opposite inside. Janet moans when she shows off her cracked body. Anna's milk begins leaking again. Deb is surprised that even now, after all this time, she still wants aching, leaking breasts.

Katie wants to keep going. Nicki wants John. Janet wants more and knows she is never going to be satisfied. Anna doesn't know what she wants, questions now if she ever did. Nicki opens champagne and the words begin.

Katie talks about radiotherapy, dark room, door closed. About chemo and the burning pain in her veins, that weird perineum feeling, repetition of weeks, sucking cherry drops to get rid of the taste. Cherry drops she can't even smell now without retching. Katie talks about the difference, the fear. But she kept working throughout and was strong and Katie always keeps going – Anna cannot imagine no Katie, never has been able to, hates Katie for saying it out loud, for getting that close. All five lying together across the two double beds, glasses emptying and trying to understand. Janet thinks about Sharon, what she would say if she were here, how her view of these women is a holiday imprint, cool drink in each pair of hands, cares missing. No-one understands.

Nicki opens more fizz, real champagne now, stupidly overpriced all the way from France and yet apparently worth it, they drink to each other. Each one entirely separate from the others, wondering how she got here, thinking how is it that they all understand each other and yet no-one really knows me, not even these women who have known me for ever.

Katie and Janet have a nap on Nicki and John's bed, they hold hands. Katie has a room in this hotel too, but hers is smaller, less impressive; it's nicer to sleep here with the balcony and the view and the wide water behind the door. The others go downstairs to the long-lap pool and jacuzzi in this painstakingly cool hotel. They are quieter. Afternoon champagne and Nicki's tears. Then Deb and Janet and Anna do a hotel room run, leave the taxi meter turning outside as they speed upstairs to get clothes, return to Nicki's hotel for the dressing up. There are power showers and shared clothes and trying on new make-up and, because Katie wants it, because she has demanded it – even though it is the last thing she feels like doing now the time has actually come – they go out. They go out dancing. Anna's cousin who lives here has recommended a place. Dinner would be better, late meal, quietly taken, more wine, more talk, proper talk. Or just cocktails, silly ones with wide glasses and extra cherries because Janet has always loved them. But they go dancing.

Most of them are wearing each other's clothes and make-up – not Nicki, she likes her own things too much to go for anyone else's, though she is always willing to share. Janet is in Katie's wig. It suits her. It does not mean anything else on her. Katie might give it away at the end of the night. Anna leads the way and they walk into the basement bar. She orders tequila. Nicki shrugs, downs it. Will have just one or two. The others whoop and begin again. First floor the music is way too loud, way too young. Everywhere the other punters are young: ten, fifteen, twenty years younger than them, but on the first floor they all know it too well. Second floor is a darker room. There are beautiful gay boys in every corner and Nicki comes alive in ultra-violet light. Anna orders more tequila, Katie pays for doubles. Downed again. Behind the ultra-violet is another exit, downstairs now to a different ground-floor bar, slower here, softer lighting, flagstone floor. The music is a techno-salsa, easier to move to, in the brighter light these women are clearly not twenty and the room is packed with bright young things. Now Deb buys the tequila and they begin to dance. Anna is the first to take off her shoes. Nicki's shoes, not quite the right fit. Then Katie, then Deb, Janet next, Nicki finally, pushed into it, given into it, glad of yesterday morning's pedicure. Tequila-drunk and still breathing and keeping going. Anna's left breast is leaking again and now there is nothing funnier. Nicki remembers warning her husband not to stay out too late and then ignores herself, ignores John in the bed in her head. Janet orders drinks, the DJ smiles at them, they are louder now. The music switches to a more insistent beat, feet happy to be on the flagstones. A too-young man moves in on Anna, she turns him to face Deb, who sends him away with only the slightest regret. Katie feels the new hair grow dirty and smoky, Janet's scalp itches under the beautiful wig. Arms entwined, singing along to words they do not know, back to this place where they are all the same again. An hour later it is too late. Ugly stepsister feet cram into discarded shoes, mascara and lipstick have no solutions to offer, the air outside is warm and dry on damp skin, taxis take a while and the hotel returns are quiet, tired, gentle.

Eight hours later Anna is hungover. Horribly, painfully, hungover. At brunch-into-lunch they discuss cures. Suddenly they are sixteen and reddened knuckles, sore back of the throat doesn't seem such a bad solution. Anna slowly shakes her head, then wishes she hadn't tried to move. She cannot do it. Has never been able to make herself throw up. Will not go back to bed, does not want to waste this last time with the others, her baby-free, Paul-free weekend. Endures instead. On the tip of her tongue to confide and explain, reveal the baby is not the longed-for dream she had expected, cannot face either their knowing or their surprise. Says nothing, sips water, holds it in. Deb resolves to take Anna to the airport too. They can leave a little earlier, have a serious talk once Janet is on her plane. Anna in hangover can be forced to reveal, always has. At sixteen and twenty-three and now at thirty-nine. Deb is sure she'll get the juice. Orders a Bloody Mary meanwhile. John arrives with gifts for the girls, eyes wide for his late-night wife, special soft kiss for Katie.

In one car driving home, two different planes crossing too many time zones, a silent single bedroom and the last hotel bed, five women feel an itch in their feet. They will do this again, have done it in various combinations for over twenty-five years, it is what they do. For good occasions and bad. They will do this when they go from five to four to less. Their children and partners will think them excessive and fading-lovely. They will be right. This is just another group of giggling girls. Entirely ordinary. Hugely different, exactly the same.

Helen Dunmore is a novelist, poet and short-story writer. Her latest novel is *The Siege*, published by Penguin in 2001, and her most recent collection of short stories is *Ice Cream*, published in 2000.

Esther to Fanny

I am an orphan. I say these words aloud to myself and hear them move around the room and then disappear into the carpet. They sound like a lie, even though they are true. An orphan is small, scared and hopeful, battling bravely in an institution or bowling along a country road in a dog cart towards a new home where she won't be wanted at first. Orphans have red hair, wide vocabularies and a carpet bag containing their earthly possessions. An orphan is a child with a destiny.

I know the literature. 'Orphans of the Storm: the journey to self-actualization in literature for children.' We don't yet teach a module with that title, but we may well do so one day. It has exactly the right ring to it. Our students like modules which demand opinions rather than extensive reading. My studies in English Literature have brought me here, to this room where words sink into the cord carpet, to this university staff flat in a concrete block full of students.

They are arriving now. Parents are unloading cars, lugging TVs up echoey staircases, checking the wiring on the communal microwave, opening and then quickly closing the bathroom doors. Soon they'll be gone and the kids will be on their own. Big, bonny temporary orphans with credit cards.

My mother died during the summer. I practise the words and they too disappear. When last term ended I was a woman with a mother whom I visited each weekend. Some colleagues knew why, others didn't. I had learned a new vocabulary. I would say 'Macmillan nurse' and on one or two faces there would shine complete understanding. On others, not a flicker.

Esther to Fanny, this is Esther to Fanny, come in. I listen. I'm not daft enough to think there's going to be any answer. My name is Esther. My mother's name was not Fanny.

Last term I read out to my students a letter from a woman with breast cancer. This letter was addressed to a woman called Esther. The writer's name was Fanny, Fanny Burney, and in her letter she described a mastectomy performed on her without anaesthetic, in 1811.

It isn't my period. It didn't fit into the module at all, and some of my students were annoyed at the waste of their time. But I thought it was worth reading to them, all the same.

I came across Fanny Burney's letter by chance, while I was searching yet another website for information about mastectomy. And there was Fanny Burney's portrait. Her face was composed but she looked as if something had amused her very much a few minutes earlier. I began to read her letter to Esther.

The eighteenth century is not my period, but it has

always appealed to me. There is something about those small, fierce, brave people who dressed elaborately, smelled awful, gushed about feeling and worshipped Reason. Fanny Burney, for all she lived forty years into the nineteenth century, is one of them to the bone. I am glad it's not my period. I wouldn't want to add to it, deconstruct it, contextualize it, demystify it, or explain it in any way.

I didn't ask my students to analyse Fanny's letter. I read it out to them, that's all. They are too big and bouncing, healthy and beautiful. They frowned and shifted in their seats and flinched and probably felt glad that things like that only happen to really old people. Fanny Burney was fifty-nine! No wonder she got ill, what else could she expect? Besides, at fifty-nine, should you really care so much about your life any more? It is the deaths of children and young people that rate as tragedies, just as it is children who make real orphans. Fanny Burney's mastectomy, performed without anaesthesia, gave her another twenty-nine years of life. I watched my students doing the calculation, and reckoning that it was hardly worth it. Who wants to suffer in order to be old for even more years?

No, I am not doing them justice. They flinched, as I did. Unconsciously, some of the girls brought up their hands to cover their breasts, as I'd done. Fanny got through to them. 'I don't see why she agreed to have the operation. I mean, I'd rather die than go through that!' one girl said after I had finished reading. 'I mean, she wasn't young, was she,' she added, glancing at me.

Esther to Fanny. No, you weren't young. My mother

wasn't young, either. She was even older than you. She was seventy-three. If she didn't receive the very best of modern medical treatment, she certainly had the nearly best. She had a mastectomy, radiotherapy, chemotherapy. Two years later she developed a secondary in her left lung. She had more radiotherapy, oxygen, a nebulizer, massage, physiotherapy to keep her lungs as clear as possible. They gave her baths in a jacuzzi at the hospice. She liked the jacuzzi, or at least I think she liked it. She was so polite that it was hard to tell.

My mother had everything. GP appointments, clinic appointments, a second opinion, referral for rehab, referral to pain clinic, a place in a trial, a re-referral, another X-ray, a series of blood tests, a change of consultant, a lavender massage, a Macmillan nurse, a commode, a bell by her bed and a tube up her nose, a bed in the hospice. She was so lucky to get it, that bed in the hospice.

Esther to Fanny. You had none of that. Each doctor in your story had a name. They trembled, or grew pale, or stood aside hanging their head at the thought of the pain they were about to give you. They colluded with you in sending your husband out for the day. They knew, as you did, that he would not be able to endure witnessing your operation. They told you the truth: 'Je ne veux pas vous tromper – Vous Souffrirez – vous souffrirez beaucoup.'

Yes, they were clear about it. They were men of the eighteenth century, even though the century had turned. They told you that you would suffer a great deal. They told you that you must cry out and scream.

They stammered, and could not go on, because their sensibility was as powerful as their sense of reason. When the moment came for the operation to begin, you wanted to run out of the room. But Reason took command in your fierce, bright eighteenth-century mind, and you climbed onto the bedstead where your breast was to be amputated. There were seven men around your bed. I wonder how they smelled, and how often they washed? They were the greatest doctors of their age, but probably they didn't even wash their hands before they cut off your breast. They put a cambric handkerchief over your face, and through it you saw the glint of polished steel.

But they also cured you. They cut off your living breast and scraped you down to the bone to search out the last cancerous atoms. You screamed all the time, except when you fainted. You recovered, even though everyone concerned in your operation was left pale as ashes, in their black clothes. You saw the blood on them as you were carried back to your bed. You were about to live for another twenty-nine years.

It's a strange story to our ears, Fanny. How exquisitely you act out the hard logic of the eighteenth century, and keep your eyes open under the cambric handkerchief. It is only semi-transparent anyway, so you see most of what goes on as the men prepare to operate upon you. They could have found a thick black piece of cloth and tied it around your eyes as a blindfold, but they didn't. I have the feeling that they respected you too much.

And the emotion around that bed! Imagine if one of

the doctors treating my mother had turned ashen, and wept. If he had told her the truth. 'Vous Souffrirez – vous souffrirez beaucoup.' Nobody said it. But you suffered, Mum. You suffered a great deal. There was a smell in the hospice which we never mentioned, although I know you smelled it as well as I did. It was the smell of death, literally: it was the smell of the cancer in the old man who shared your two-bed room. He was curtained, out of sight, but we could smell him. I had never known that such a thing would be. Sometimes I would gag, and turn it into a cough. 'It's not very nice, is it?' you whispered once, sadly, pitifully. But in a very soft whisper, so no-one else would hear.

Esther to Fanny. I am glad that you screamed throughout the twenty minutes of your operation, except when you fainted. To restrain yourself might have seriously bad consequences, your doctors told you beforehand. What miracles of sense and feeling those men must have been! Knowing that you would scream, you must scream, and anticipating it by actually charging you to scream and informing you that to do otherwise might be dangerous for your health. Knowing that you would have enough to contend with, under that semi-transparent cambric handkerchief, without any false shame.

My mother hated to make a fuss. She was very grateful to all the doctors and nurses. If they didn't do their jobs well, she had an answer for it. They were understaffed, run off their feet. 'That nurse over there, Esther, she's got an eight-month-old baby, she's been up half the night with him cutting his molars. I don't know how she does it.'

132

I wanted to shake that nurse until her teeth rattled. She was late with the drugs round. My mother was waiting, waiting. There was sweat on her yellow face but she wouldn't let me ring the bell. 'For God's sake, Mum, it's what they're here for. They're supposed to be taking care of you, that means bringing your tablets when you need them.' But my mother turned her head aside wearily. 'It doesn't do to get across them. You don't know, Esther.'

Esther to Fanny. You were utterly in those doctors' power, just as Mum was. You saw the flash of steel through your cambric handkerchief. You felt and heard that blade scraping your breastbone. You were a heroine and the doctors treated you as one.

We have moved on. We have chemo and radio and prostheses, and scans to show the travels of those 'peccant attoms' of cancer which your doctors feared so much that they scraped you down to the bone. What can I say? I can't re-read your account without flinching. You couldn't re-read it at all.

Mum is dead and I'm an orphan. Two things that don't sound as if they can possibly be true. Mum didn't want to cause any trouble, and she didn't cause any trouble. The doctors barely noticed her really.

My students are pounding up and down the stairs with their posters, IKEA lamps, armfuls of CDs and clothes. They are flushed, healthy, on the whole averse to study but only too pleased to be back at uni with all their friends. Some of them will choose my module on Elizabeth Bishop. These days it is perfectly possible to get to the end of a degree in English

Literature without venturing into the eighteenth century at all.

Esther to Fanny. At the end of your long letter you apologized to your sister. 'God bless my dearest Esther – I fear this is all written – confusedly, but I cannot read it – and I can write no more —'

I put my hand out to touch that semi-transparent cambric handkerchief which time has laid across you. Your letter cuts like polished steel, although I am not, dear Fanny, your Esther at all.

Esther Freud was born in London in 1963. She trained as an actress before writing her first novel, *Hideous Kinky*, published in 1992. *Hideous Kinky* was shortlisted for the John Llewellyn Rhys Prize and was made into a feature film starring Kate Winslet. Her other novels include *Peerless Flats*, *Gaglow*, *The Wild* and to be published in July 2003, *The Sea House*. She lives in London with her family.

Just One More

Heathrow had never looked so enticing. The silent queues of people, the shops and magazines. Nell turned her eyes away from the occasional sprawling family, the double-buggy and scattering of crisps. She stood up straighter, breathed more deeply, strode through departures with nothing but her bag. 'Shall we get a babysitter and come to the airport every week?' she said to her husband, and dizzy with their freedom they sat at a chrome table, light and empty, and ate cinnamon pastries and drank tea. Later they meandered through duty-free, and then on into the mall of shops. Electrical equipment, watches, pens, leather shoes and belts. They were wandering, nonchalant, past the Disney store, relishing the novelty of not having to go in, when they heard their names over the tannoy. 'Urgent call for Mr and Mrs Leonard . . .'

'Oh my God!' Nell clutched Patrick's arm. 'Something's happened!'

'No, it's not that.' He looked round wildly for a clock. 'We forgot to board. They're about to close our flight.'

Stunned, they ran along corridors, over carpet-covered

intersections, onto the escalated floor where people stood immobile as they waited to be moved along. 'Excuse me, excuse me.' They pushed past, arriving finally, breathless, at their gate.

'We've called you three times,' an air stewardess told them sourly. 'We were about to remove your bags.' And she hurried them along a rubber corridor and straight onto the plane. One hundred and seventy people looked up as the door slammed shut, and within minutes of strapping into their seats, the plane was rolling off along the runway.

Nell and Patrick grinned at each other. It was four and a half years since they'd set off anywhere like this alone. Alone. Nell reached into her bag. She'd been warned she might need photos to calm her on the plane, and before anxiety had time to grip her, she slipped out a brightly coloured packet and started flipping through. Blue skies. Pebbled beaches. The children, both with ice-cream beards. Here they were, playing in an inlet: Maeve, pot-bellied in pink shorts, Sam, his hair as straight as straw. 'Nell?' Patrick was talking to her, and she had to tear herself away from gazing at them, noses scrunched with laughter, eyes all glittery with sun. 'Do you want a drink?'

'Look,' she said, holding up a picture, the two of them last summer, naked except for arm bands and a selection of jungle-book tattoos. Patrick raised one eyebrow, and in his sceptical expression she saw the true reflection of their family life. Only that morning Sam had kicked her as she bent over for her shoe, and it made her shiver to think of the violence with which she'd turned on him, every fibre of her body hungering for revenge. 'Naughty boy,' she'd said instead. 'Naughty boy to kick.' And then Maeve had fallen down the stairs. She was wearing plastic dressing-up shoes which had tripped her on a fold of carpet, and by some miracle Patrick had turned from the open door where he'd been waiting for their cab and caught her just before she hit the floor. 'Is it too early for a Bloody Mary?' she asked the air stewardess.

'It depends what time zone you're in.'

Nell glanced at her watch and saw that it was still only five to ten.

'Are you tired?' Patrick asked.

Tired? Nell looked around her. Their hotel room was calm and white. There was a high, wide bed, and an armchair under the window. A huge black television was fastened to the wall. 'No.' She could hardly remember such a restful day. 'I'm not tired.' She walked out onto the terrace. Their hotel was in the middle of Manhattan and above them, sparkling, was the Chrysler building, its silver-petalled spire glinting in the sun. Ten storeys below a man was watering a potted plant on an oblong strip of roof garden, and lower still, a woman was arranging furniture on a bright green astroturf lawn. 'Do you want to phone?' Patrick was behind her. 'And then we can go out.' It was afternoon here, a balmy autumn day, but in London it would already be night.

Nell's mother sounded tired. Yes, the children were asleep. But Sam had come down three times to see if she was back yet with his present, and then Maeve woke screaming, her juice beaker having turned inexplicably upside down in her cot.

'Oh,' Nell gasped. 'She shouldn't be having—' but just in time she bit her lip. 'Mum, thank you so much, I'll phone tomorrow, and if there's anything, just call.'

'Don't worry,' she said, 'they'll be absolutely fine.'

Nell and Patrick walked into the Village. They looked into windows, traipsed in and out of sleek and silent shops and stopped at the Manhattan diner where the sandwiches were all named after Hollywood stars. Patrick ordered a 'Whoopi Goldberg', with black forest ham, while she opted for a hot roast beef 'Tom Cruise'.

'How's yours?' Nell asked him and then she stopped. 'Oh my God.' She put her hand out. 'You've shaved off your moustache!'

'Two weeks.' Patrick wasn't smiling. 'It's taken you two weeks.'

Nell stared down at her plate. 'I'm sorry,' and then she looked up quickly to see if there was anything else she'd missed.

'Accept it,' he said. 'I had to bring you halfway round the world before I could get you to notice that I'd shaved.'

'I did think there was something . . .' She was sure she remembered thinking how odd he looked at some point recently, but then she must have got distracted. Wasn't it two weeks ago that Sam's tongue swelled up with the human form of foot and mouth?

'I'm only joking,' he said, then, 'I shaved it off this morning.'

'Bastard, how could you?'

'Even so,' he said, 'even so it took you all day.'

'One day!' And she tried to swipe at him with her Tom Cruise.

It was warm bright autumn in New York, whereas London, when they'd left it, had been a sodden mass of leaves. Even the air smelt different here, lighter, dryer, the scent of pretzels mixed in with the sea. They went into a bookshop and began to leaf through postcards, city guides and magazines. There were thick stacks of books heaped on tables: recipes, photography, gardening, art. Nell picked up a book of photographs and it fell open on a picture of two naked men. Instinctively she went to close it, and then, realizing she was alone, she opened it again and looked. The men were muscled, oiled, their chests shaved, but what struck Nell most was that each one was motionless, waiting, as if they had all the time in the world. She looked across at Patrick, innocently engrossed in a search for something under fiction, D to G. She put the book down and picked up another. Here were photographs of women, their bodies draped with shrouds of gauze, their breasts, some real, some swollen with silicone, their nipples all hardened by an invisible breeze. One girl lay side on to her, her arm raised above her head, her armpit white and milky, her pubic hair trimmed into a heart. Nell swallowed. She was quite weak, suddenly, with desire. Was this how Patrick felt when she shrugged him off at night, unable to imagine what more blissful indulgence there could be than sleep?

'Pat?' She wandered over to him. 'Actually, I am feeling a little tired.'

'Oh.' He looked disappointed. 'I thought maybe we could see a film, go out somewhere to eat.'

'Yes, of course, you're right.' She felt herself blushing, heat fighting through her like a knife. 'But maybe just a little lie-down first?'

Patrick turned away and put the novel he had chosen back into its slot. 'If you have to,' he sighed, and she realized the language she was talking had become so foreign to him that he had no idea what it was she meant. They walked back to the hotel in silence. Patrick with his hands in his pockets, Nell fighting to keep alive the images that had sparked her. The bodies so powerful and languorous, men and women with nothing on their minds but sex.

Patrick kicked his shoes off and flicked on the TV.

'Mmm.' Nell had climbed into the bed. 'It's gorgeous in here.' She let her legs stretch out against the ironed sheet, felt the quilt fold in around her. She nudged Patrick with her toes. 'Pat,' she said, but her eyes were drooping, her body sinking, and before she could help it she had fallen asleep.

'Nell.' Patrick was shaking her. 'Come on, wake up.'

'What?' For a moment she couldn't think where she was. 'Oh yes.' Patrick had drawn the blinds and switched on a lamp. 'Did you sleep?' she asked, sitting up beside him, and he said no, he'd found three episodes of *Frasier* that he'd never seen.

'So,' he said, 'if you get up now, we could still just catch a film.'

'Or we could stay here.' She had her arms around him now. 'We could stay in bed all weekend.'

'Really?' Patrick was looking hard at her. 'Are you sure?' And with one more quick look to check that it was really her, he began tugging off his clothes.

Later, in a haze of contentment, they lay stretched out on the bed. Patrick threw a heavy arm across her and let out a long sigh. 'That was a safe time, wasn't it?'

'Safe?' Nell kept him suffering for a moment. 'Yes,' she said, 'of course.'

'Just think.' He was staring up at the ceiling. 'The little horrors. They'll be waking up in two hours' time.'

Nell woke at ten and ordered breakfast in bed. She eased the blinds a little and light fell in bars of gold across the floor. This is heaven, she thought, pure heaven, and she pulled on a thick white dressing gown. Croissants, orange juice, a plate of melon, pineapple and kiwi. Even the tea looked like nectar in the thin china cups. They ate and drank amid the snow peaks of the quilt, and then they made love again. 'Should we call?' she asked, once they'd showered and were ready to go out, and then she remembered it would be the children's crankiest hour just before they had their tea. Patrick didn't answer and they stood there for a moment looking at the door.

'We could wait an hour?' he suggested, and like truants they rushed towards the lift.

Armed with their city guide they took the subway to Chelsea and wandered along cobbled streets, a land of car lots and warehouses, where behind each derelict facade a secret world of art galleries was opening up. At first they held themselves aloof at the door of each experimental show, but the more they walked and looked, the more they saw, the more open-minded they became until they were standing happily in front of a giant screen of multicoloured letters, their arms outstretched and reflected back at them, while the letters settled on their shoulders and formed words. Eventually they found themselves in a room full of projected images – a man standing at a window – a girl swimming, accompanied by such soothing music that she and Patrick felt compelled to sit down on the floor.

'Let's do this every year.' She squeezed his hand.

'Yes,' he said. 'November 2000. I'll remember it. Christ, when you got pregnant I didn't think I'd have to wait until the next century to get you back.'

It was so warm they took a cab up to the entrance of the park, and the first thing they saw when they got out was the tower of FAO Schwartz.

'Presents?'

Patrick shrugged. 'We might as well.'

'Do you want a Toy Present or an Edible Present?' Nell had asked the children. 'Edible!' they'd shouted. 'And Toy,' Sam said, and grinned. But just then the cab had arrived. Maeve's arms clamped tight around her neck, and Sam flung his head back, hitting it against the banister with a roar of pain. 'Shhh now, shhh.' She'd tried to calm them. 'Mummy has to go and buy your present.'

'No. No present.' Maeve sobbed. Nell had looked out through the open slice of door. She could feel her spirits sliding, her heart fill with despair. Why was she doing this? Who was it for? She didn't even want to bloody go to New York! 'Mum,' she had called, frantic, to her own mother who was clearing away the breakfast things. 'The taxi's waiting!' And she began to prise her children's fingers from around her neck. 'I know what,' Nell tried. 'Who wants a sweetie?' She had a net of gold and silver coins in the pocket of her coat. She'd bought them at a garage, the genius that she was, and now she tore at the string, sending them spinning off over the tiled floor. She could hear the taxi revving and a car behind it hoot. Both children leapt down from her lap.

'Come on.' Patrick was at the door. 'Goodbye, kids, be good,' and as the children ripped off the first rounds of foil and pressed the chocolate discs into their mouths, she kissed them, hugged them, and then turned and ran. 'It's all right,' she heard her mother say as the first choked cry rang out, 'who's going to dress up as a wizard?' and clanging the gate behind her, Nell leapt into the car.

'So, what would they like, do you think?' There were shelves of games, tiers of stuffed animals, whole rooms of trucks and bikes. The choice was so overwhelming that they had to remind each other their children were barely two and four, and would be quite happy with a revolving lollipop and a pot of bubbles that promised not to burst. They took their purchases and walked into the park, past the ponies and traps, past the break-dancers, and on towards a meadow of long grass. They lay side by side, pressed against each other, and let the sun soak into their skin. To think we used to do this every weekend. Lie in a park with the Sunday papers. But hard as Nell tried, she couldn't find a time when it had been as special as it was now.

The next day, like a miracle, it snowed. Soft white flakes settled in the corners of their window. Their room was white inside and out now, and they spent all morning there, bathing, smooching, ordering up snacks. Eventually they wrapped up against the cold and went out into the street. The noises of the city were hushed, the dirt of the pavements purified, and they walked arm in arm, admiring the trees, their thin branches laden with snow instead of blossom. They walked on and on until they were on the Upper East Side, where they gazed into the crystal splendour of the shop windows and nodded smiling at the passers-by.

On the plane on their way home Nell was rummaging for a pen when she found the packet of photos. There was Sam, buried up to his neck in sand, and Maeve in a frilled white bonnet looking so beautiful it brought tears to her eyes. 'Look.' She held them out to Patrick. 'Aren't they the most beautiful children in the world?'

He laughed at her. 'Of course not.'

Nell leant against him. 'Shall we?' she whispered. 'Shall we try for just one more?'

Patrick started as if he'd just been stung. 'I don't know what you mean.'

'One more . . .' Of course he knew what she meant. 'Baby.'

'Are you completely mad?' He turned towards her. 'Think about it. More screaming. More fighting. More sleepless nights.' And then he seemed to relent. 'OK, have one more, and watch me, I'll just go and kill myself.'

He smiled serenely, picked up his paper, and leant back in his seat. Nell looked down at her lap. She could feel the happiness knocked out of her. Could almost see it running down a gutter to a drain. But why did she want one anyway? Why did she want another child? And she thought of their afternoon in Central Park, the feel of the warm green grass against her back, and she knew that without the restrictions of their daily lives, that moment could never have been as precious as it was.

'Oh, for God's sake,' Patrick said, after she'd sat like a statue for an hour. 'Just one more. If you promise.'

'What?' she said. 'To bury you at sea?'

'No.' He whispered into her ear, 'That we'll go a little more often to New York.'

Free Spirit

You'll never tie me down. I'm a free spirit; I go wherever the wind takes me.

Last night it was Paris, by the banks of the Seine. She'd been sleeping under a bridge; she was sixteen; dog-tired; beautiful. Tinfoil and spent needles littered the floor around her bed. I knew at once that she was the one. Her long river-coloured hair trailed across the greasy bricks; her eyes were closed. She made small introspective sounds as I touched her; her skin mottled; her eyelids flickered. Sometimes she seemed ready to speak, but there was no need for words between us. We were already too close for that. Her fists clenched; she clawed the air; her neck and her pale arms blossomed. She was alight and lovely with fever.

It was quick; that's the only drawback with these short affairs. In less than twenty-four hours it will be over. But the wind keeps on blowing; a scrap of tinfoil from under our bridge escapes in an updraught and is carried up over the Pont-Neuf and over l'Ile de la Cité to descend in a shower of confetti on the steps of a church where a young couple poses, smiling for a photographer.

Choices, choices. Who will it be? The bride? The groom? More interesting to me are the guests: the teenage boy with a scattering of *herpes simplex* around his sullen mouth; the grandmother with her caved-in face and hands knotted beneath her white gloves. They are all beautiful to me; all equally worthy of my attention. I leave the choice to the scrap of tinfoil; there's poetry in that. It spins, whirls. Faces lift to the sky. For a second it brushes the lips of the balding man, a second cousin with a flat, impassive face who stands slightly apart from the others. Him, then. I follow him home.

His flat is on the Marne-la-Vallée line; small and obsessively clean, the flat of a man who has no friends. There are no beer cans discarded beside the sofa, no dirty dishes stacked in the sink. Instead there are books: scientific manuals, medical dictionaries, anatomical charts. This man gargles with Listerine four times a day and his bathroom cabinet is filled with the paraphernalia of the hardcore hypochondriac.

Not that I mind; in a way it appeals to me. This is a man who does not understand the nature or the extent of his own desires; beneath his prissy exterior, his obvious fear, I sense his secret longings. Besides, I enjoy a challenge.

Once again, there is no need for words. He is irrationally afraid of me, and yet he welcomes me with something approaching relief, as if he has been awaiting just this moment. There is a desperation in his resistance which gives spice to our meeting, and when finally the barriers are broken, he responds even more quickly than the girl, who was already weakened by hardship and encroaching pneumonia.

But I can't be tied down. Twenty-four hours is all I can give him, and already I sense that our wildly opposite natures are causing problems. He wants intimacy; to stay in bed all day with the television on and cool drinks by the bedside. I'm a social animal; I need contact to survive. I'm already beginning to miss the nightlife, the clubs, the busy heat of Paris. I escape when he is asleep, the moment the cleaning woman comes to look over the flat.

She is all unsuspecting; she peers over him cautiously (it is past twelve) as if to check him for fever. 'D'you want me to call a doctor?' she queries, then, when he does not answer, she shrugs and gets on with her work. That's all I need. I escape unnoticed, the brush of her hand the only contact between us.

The cleaning woman is old but tough. She lives near Pigalle. It's my favourite part of Paris; bright, ugly and seething with life. She takes me to the Sacré-Coeur, where she prays and I prey, passing from tourist to tourist and running voluptuously over the well-fingered stonework. The air here is hot with incense; from here penitents will wander down the Butte de Montmartre into Pigalle below, where the whores and the rent boys congregate and the strip clubs are just beginning to get busy.

I'd like to stay with the cleaning woman, but life's too short. There are hundreds – thousands – of others out there waiting for me. I pass quickly from one to another; a nun gathering alms at the door of the basilica collects more than she bargained for; the old gentleman who gives her a hundred-franc note receives an unexpected handful of change; later that night, a lad who swears he is fourteen will meet us both in the dark archway of a closed Métro station, and after that the young lad (who is really nineteen and doing good business) will take me to a club, where I shall mingle freely among the revellers, dipping into drinks, sharing cigarettes, touching flesh and enjoying the warm, damp air.

They are all equal to me: young, old, healthy or corrupt, male or female. Twenty-four hours is all I can ever give them; but in that time I give them my all. Who next? And where? Will it be a needle, a kiss, a lost coin picked up from the streets and carried home? Will it be a cube of sugar in a crowded café or the gleeful tramping of a fly in a pâtisserie window or the furtive hands of a pervert on the Métro or windblown dust sticking to a child's lollipop? Whatever it is, I'll be there. You may not see me; I won't speak a word. But all the same, you'll be mine. We'll be closer than lovers, you and I; tighter than DNA. Nothing will mar the perfect physicality of our relationship; no quarrels, no seduction, no lies. You will give me your self, and I will give you mine, entirely. For a while.

And afterwards, I'll take the road again. No regrets. Maybe I'll go to America, in a crowded, air-conditioned plane. Or to England, by the tunnel. Or maybe back to Africa, or Asia, or Japan. I'll see the world ten times over. I'll meet millions of people. That's why I don't stay anywhere long. You can't tie me down. I'm a wanderer. A traveller. A party animal. I'm a free spirit, and I go wherever the wind takes me.

Maggie O'Farrell was born in Northern Ireland in 1972, and grew up in Wales and Scotland. She now lives in London. Her début novel, *After You'd Gone*, was published to international acclaim, as was her second, *My Lover's Lover*.

The House I Live In

is tall and narrow, with many rooms, all stacked on
top of each other. The staircase winds back and back
on itself like a hank of wool held on a pair of hands.
The floorboards lean towards the street; if you dropped
a marble from your pocket, it would roll, slowly at
first, then picking up speed and direction, towards the
windows. The walls refuse to meet together at a perfect
angle. People who move in here try to shove furniture
into the corners, and when they see the ungeometry of
the place, that nothing will ever fit, they curse and
swear.

The windows at the front look out on to the matching
faces of the houses opposite, and at the back, these days,
patches of gardens, with sheds, paths, flowers and large
iron arches with a wooden seat at the end of two chains.
Children come and sit on the seats and swoop up then
swoop back, their cries left behind, imprinted on the air
where they were just a split second ago.

Before, there were slatted-doored privies and an alleyway, running like a feud between the two terraces –
rank-smelling, filled with rotten food and rats with tails

like whips and a creature with the head of a dog and the thick, bristling body of a pig that once snip-snapped at my ankle as I hurried past, a parcel of dripping held in my hands. But that was before.

These streets were built on a marsh, a damp well of land that belonged to a rich man who lived in a large house over the hill and beyond the trees. He built them quickly, draining the soil and covering it in a lattice of branches to buoy up his buildings like ships on the sea. In wet weather, the houses remember. They creak downwards, into the earth: wainscots strain and split, walls fracture, window frames and chimney stacks loosen and rupture. Some people nowadays dig up the foundations and buttress them with concrete. But it won't work, I want to tell them. Houses don't forget.

Neither does the soil. When people lift up the tiled paths that were made then, by the rich man's men, seeds that have lain dormant in the soil for a hundred years spring upwards into the light, triumphant and gleeful. Everyone wonders why marsh plants are suddenly filling their dry-soil gardens.

The rich man put in as many rooms as he could, then filled every room with a family, then asked for rent. All day, people were running up and down the stairs in their wooden-soled shoes, babies cried, men shouted, women cooked and cleaned and tried to feed their children. We all queued up for the privy out the back.

I know all this because my mother told me. Before. Money follows money, she would say, from the poor to the rich. That's the way of things. And she would look at me across our room and shrug.

All houses were the same design. Streets and streets of them, all identical. My mother said when we first came here she used to lose her way, especially in the dark, in this maze of blueprinted streets. Except for this one. My one. It was always slightly different. It stands at the junction where two streets meet, at the end of a row, like the final book on a shelf, and is slightly askew, slightly foreshortened, as if a piece of it has been bitten off and swallowed.

My mother had hair so black it was almost blue. Her hands were marbled with frozen rivers that stood up underneath the skin. Her face is indistinct to me now, but I know it was pale and angular. I see it as if through steam – a white oval with wide brown eyes.

There was no father. Or none that I remember. My mother told me I was born in East London, a place where the air was crammed with different languages, the smells of strange foods, dyes and the throat-catching stench of tanneries.

She said she walked all the way here, me strapped to her back with some old sacking, through Shoreditch, then Islington. She lost her way around King's Cross, she said, the great, panting, fire-breathing engines frightened and distracted her, she said. But she walked on, further north, through markets and shops and factories and then on again into rows of houses being built. It took her all day. She needed rests and I was heavy. When she got to the house, the sun was setting.

Our room was the smallest, right at the top, right at the back, at the end of a long, long row. Looking down to the ground was so vertiginous it sometimes felt as if we were in mid-air, like the crow's nest of a galleon, above the street that wound its way towards the heath.

The people in all the rooms of all four floors of the house came and went: babies arrived, husbands left. At one time my mother and I, lying side by side in the narrow bed, fitting into each other like pieces of a jigsaw, counted thirty-eight of us, including the new twins on the first floor – scrawny, bawling creatures with identical rodenty faces.

Knowing your numbers, she said, was very important, would distinguish me from all the rest. So when she returned from work late at night she would push her feet up close to the fire until they steamed and, taking a piece of chalk, would write on the floorboards: 1 2 3 4 5 6 7 8 9. These I remember. Her in the act of writing my name, I can picture: I see her bending forwards over the floor, the grey-white chalk gripped in her fingers, damp hair scribbled on her neck; I can see her arm moving up and down, forming the loops, lines and curves of my name. But the name itself, the mark in chalk, is gone.

My mother worked for a glove-maker in Camden, her needle puncturing and pursing together the finest leather, flayed from the backs of young goats, to make new, close-fitting skins for the hands of the rich. From the window, she could see barges with coal, lime, iron ore and lead gliding through the brown, brackish water of the canal.

Sometimes she would bring back tiny triangular scraps of leather. Off-cuts, she called them. I would rub them over my face when she left me alone during the day. They were the softest things imaginable.

She told me not to leave the room while she was out. She warned me. But I did. Of course I did.

I liked the staircase, the way it wound round and round, how you could stare at the wall until your eyes blurred and then you could make yourself forget which floor you were on. I liked the solid smoothness of the banister handle. I liked sliding down it. I liked the struts, white and evenly spaced as ribs. I liked to wander past the rooms, listening in to other people's lives. Those rooms seemed much fuller than ours, more exciting, more interesting. From behind the bevelled doorplates came the sound of shrieking, laughing, shouting, gasping. I hated being alone.

There was a stove on every landing, a coughing, belching, crouched black monster, and in cold weather I could curl myself around it.

Somehow, though, she always knew.

'You went out of the room, didn't you?' She would hold me at arm's length, searching my face.

I would always shake my head.

'You did. I know you did. We'll get thrown out. We will. And then where will we be?'

One day I was down by the door which led out on to the street, where the light came in red, blue, green and yellow through the writhing patterns of coloured glass. If you pressed your face to it, the street beyond was a fabulous, one-colour world, like the lantern show my mother had taken me to see one year on the heath. One of the twins, walking about now in a grime-smeared vest, appeared next to me. Together, we stared out at a blue street, where people were moving through aqua-marine air, where a blue horse toiled up the street, dragging a cart of blue coal. Next to me the twin was gripping a thick slice of bread, clotted with red jam. He wasn't eating it, not at all, just letting bits of it ooze through the slits in his fingers. And I was so hungry. So very hungry.

It was easy to take it from him. I was twice his size, and his hand was small and pliable. I pushed it between my teeth in one go. He stared at me, astonished, for a few seconds, then he opened his mouth in a wide, wet square of misery and yelled. And yelled and yelled.

When my mother came back later that day, she sat right in the middle of the sag in the bed and cried, her face clamped into her hands.

That night she told me something she'd never told me before. That in the middle of the city was a big, grey building, built on four sides around a big, grey court-yard. It was a foundation, she said, which looked after the babies of unmarried women.

She'd gone there, she told me, just before I came. She filled in forms, signed her name at the bottom of documents and, from the huge, cross-barred windows, saw lines and lines of children in grey uniforms crossing the courtyard like ants.

After I was born, she wrapped me up and carried me there through the city. She said it was a cold, cold day.

The Thames, someone told her, was frozen in parts, great blocks of ice riding the filthy tides. I picture her, breath steaming from her mouth, walking up the big, grey steps.

There were twelve steps, she said, count to twelve. I did. She only got to number nine before she turned round and went back. Count to nine and back again. I did.

The next day, she stood over me with a long piece of dark red material. A scarf or a shawl I'd never seen before. She snagged one end of it around the end of the cast-iron bed and tied it firm. I realized too late what was happening. I made a dash for the door, only half-dressed, but she was too quick for me. She grabbed my arm and lifted me, kicking and squealing, over the boards where letters and numbers had got rubbed to unreadable runes.

We tussled and fought each other for the first time in our lives together, my mother and I, me twisting and turning in her grip, her with her lip bitten between her teeth, silent tears coursing down her cheeks. Some of them fell on to me in dark circles, I remember.

'I have to do this,' she cried as I thrashed around. 'I don't want to but I have to. I'm not supposed to have you here. They,' she pointed down to the floors below, 'know that. I'm sorry,' she whispered, kissing my hair, my face, my hands. 'I'm sorry.'

After she'd gone I lay for a while on the floor, exhausted and spent. Then I examined her work: a stretch of material tethered me to the bed, an intricate knot bound my ankles together, heavy and dark as a human heart.

Every day this happened. And every day we fought and wept.

Then one day she never came back.

I waited and waited, my feet held out before me, ready for her to unravel her undecipherable knot, as she always did, even before taking off her coat.

The room got darker and darker until the window was pitchy with gloom and the room sunk into invisibility. I sat awake on the floor and watched a weak grey light waver back into the room.

I knew I shouldn't cry. Boys mustn't. But I wanted to. On the second day, the water in the kettle ran out. I tried again to untie the knot, but it was complex, tangled, dense. I couldn't free myself. And any second now she would appear through the door and she'd be angry if I'd untied myself. The skin on my ankles split and bled as I kicked against my bindings. I licked out the inside of the kettle, and then its lid.

On the third day a strange, high keening sound filled the room like smoke. I cocked my head from side to side to listen to it, curious, awestruck.

There was a sudden drumming from the floor below me, as if horses were galloping over the landing to save me. But it was only Mrs Bunt from the room below, banging on the ceiling with her broom end.

I slept and woke, slept and woke. Light rose and faded in the room. I lay crooked on the floor, watching a crack in the wall spread, widen and fragment as Mrs Bunt drummed and drummed on her ceiling. I dreamt strange, hectic dreams: blue horses dragging blue carts laden with my mother's inert blue body; my mother climbing up and down and up and down a flight of stone stairs; the twin downstairs gripping a tiny mannequin of my mother in his fist and squeezing, squeezing.

Sometimes the knot seemed very far away, as far as the trees shielding the rich man from us, and sometimes it was so big it was all I could see.

Then I had a very long, heavy sleep, as opaque and thick as the night dark. It was dreamless and compressed and close. When I woke, something solid and heavy was crashing at the door. I stared at it, relief washing over me.

She had come back.

I wanted to cry but knew I mustn't. The latch was straining on its screws. I was just moving towards it, to ask her where have you been, why did you leave me like that, when the door burst open and three men stepped inside.

I knew them – they lived downstairs. They didn't look at me at all. I spoke to them. I said, where is my mother, can you tell me, where is she, but none of them were listening.

Their expressions frightened me: odd, stretched, fearful.

One of them leant down and picked up something that looked like a bundle of clothes. He picked it up carefully and gently as if it was a very precious, very rare thing. Don't, I said, that's my mother's. Then I saw that the bundle had feet and a long red swathe of material was falling from it, like a tail, like a wound, and I was speechless.

I was speechless for a long time after that. I think I forgot how to speak.

Some people moved into our room, mine and my mother's – two men. They strung a curtain between their beds. One was very tidy, hung up his clothes, combed his hair every morning; the other scattered things around him like snow. I hated them being there. They ignored me. And I had nowhere to go.

The Bunts moved out. I was on the first-floor landing as they left. The twins saw me as they passed by, I'm sure of it. They gaped and stared, then clung to their father's leg, screaming my name, over and over. That was the last time I ever heard it.

I hung around our room. I drifted up and down the stairs. I waited by the front door. She might come back, she might. At any moment. I slipped out of the door, once, when one of the brothers was off to his job in the morning, ready to find my way to Camden to look for her. But outside the house, I felt my strength and substantiality ebbing away from me, as if there was different air out there, air I couldn't breathe. I slumped on the doorstep, gasping, suffocating, and just managed to crawl back in when someone else, a woman now living in the room next to mine with her squalling crowd of children, opened the door to come in.

The alley out the back was flattened and low walls

put up. Flowers stretched themselves up the brickwork. A man with luxuriant side whiskers moved into the whole of the lower two floors, along with his wife who never seemed to blink. Imagine, all those rooms between just two people.

She carried a handkerchief constantly in her right hand, into which she sneezed, meekly and quietly, like a cat. The man called her Pussy. He spent hours grooming his side whiskers, combing and oiling and waxing them. I stared into the mirror with him, fascinated. The smell of hair oil. The long fingers teasing and primping. The intent, absorbed look on his face. There was no reflection for me.

Pussy had a tiny bird in a cage, as yellow as her hair. All morning, she would bend and peer at it, pushing bits of food through the golden bars, trying to entice a melodious warble from its soft yellow throat. That bird hated me. Whenever I came near to look it would roll its ochre bead of an eye, screech and flap about, crashing its feathers into the bars. This made Pussy weep.

They never saw me. Or at least I don't think so. He would shiver in my presence occasionally, as if he felt a draught threading in from a gap around a window or from under a door. She would stare glassily in my direction at times. But then she looked at him in this way, too, so it didn't really mean anything.

Upstairs, at this time, were a brother and his two sisters. He read aloud to them every night, at great length, from a book with a leather casing and gilt-edged pages, fragile as onion skins. They were as bored as me,

I could tell, although they smiled whenever he looked up, their eyes swimming with suppressed yawns.

This is where I discovered that if I concentrated really hard, shut my eyes, held my breath and thought about the ball of displeasure in my chest, I could move things. I really could. Almost as if I were still a real, flesh boy.

His pen, his pipe, his shoes, his snuffbox. His glasses were my favourite. They were loops of wire, the size of small coins, surrounding glass. He barely needed them, I was convinced, but I think he liked the way they looked, the way they felt, the embracing press of them on either side of his nose.

I would uplift them and put them under papers, inside drawers, behind cushions, down chair arms. I couldn't carry them far, somehow, but it was enough. It made his face puce with rage and he would storm about, whirling papers, antimacassars, books around him like the great north wind. It made me laugh for the first time in years.

But one day I made the mistake of hiding them in the elder sister's sewing basket. He struck her twice, once on the arm and once on the shoulder, two glancing, sharp blows. Crick crack. She fell back against the fireplace and even before she had stood upright again she was apologizing, over and over, I'm sorry I'm sorry I'm sorry. I never touched his glasses again.

He would never have struck the younger sister. I saw the way he looked at her, like a cat looks at a bird, his tongue licking around his teeth.

She saw me once, the younger sister. It was in the big

front room on the second floor, their drawing room they called it, though I never saw them doing any drawing, ever, in their whole time here. I was leaning on the arm of her chair. The brother was reading from his accursed book again. I was feeling that dense hatred in my chest, that hard knot of badness within me, its contours, its dips, the way it has sat there ever since—

And my mind was running over ways I could get to him without him taking it out on his sister, when I saw her, the younger one. She had turned her head to look at me, only six inches from her. I saw it in her eyes, that sentience, that knowingness, that sudden realization.

I was so shocked I was motionless. I watched her face fade to a greenish white, saw the tiny, golden hairs on her wrists raise themselves, her skin shrink into bumps.

She shut her eyes and turned away, back to her brother. Deliberately. Determinedly. She knew I knew she knew I was there. I could see the violet pulse in her temple, the rapid rise and fall of her chest. I touched her sleeve and she shuddered as if feeling the clammy, webbed tread of a goose across her gravestone.

She died soon after, in the back room at the top. My room. Coughing up blood into a basin. I have to admit I was quite pleased. I thought I might finally have some company, that that might be how it worked. I liked the younger sister, you see, there was a restlessness in her face that appealed to me.

I was there the moment she died – we all were. Her sister sat beside the bed, holding her hand; me cross-legged on the bed, holding the other. The brother was over by the window making obscene, spiralling noises.

And I saw it, her spirit, her soul, whatever you want to call it, lift up out of her body, stretch into the air, and then vanish like steam.

Just like that.

I was furious. Why hadn't that happened to me?

They all left – the brother and sister, something wordless solidified between them like ice, and Pussy, her husband, and the yellow bird from downstairs, all muttering about damp air and disease.

The rooms were empty for a while after that. I slid down the banisters, climbed up the stairs, slid down again. I walked through the big rooms, criss-crossed by draughts. I pressed my skin to the cold of the windows to see out. People passed below me and no matter how hard I banged on the glass, they did not look up.

Three dishevelled men arrived with lots of implements: wooden frames with blank cloth stretched over them, fistfuls of hair-tipped brushes and tubes of pungent-smelling colour that made my eyes water. They set up their paintings, leaning their imperfect backs against the walls, and soon the floorboards were smattered with bright shoeprints.

I liked them. Creamy-skinned women would come and shed their clothes, one by one, into a small, neat pile, then lie back on cushions, the pink-brown eyes of their breasts tipped up towards the ceiling. The men stared at them, frowns pleating their faces.

Four more painters arrived: three men and a woman

who dressed like a man, her trousers tied around her waist with a length of haired string. She saw me sometimes. But only after she'd swallowed down a black-smelling liquid from a green bottle. She never believed herself the day after, so I stopped bothering with her after a while.

They had big parties, clearing the sofas and the paintings from the big room on the ground floor, which reached right from the front of the house to the windows at the back, draping the walls with cloth and winding up a small box until music etched itself into the air. The room would heat up then. Sometimes I would stay with them, watching the men holding the women to them as they danced, the flat of their hand pressed into the small, low curve at the base of their backs, their feet moving together as if they shared a secret no-one else had. And sometimes I would go up to the room above, feel the heat rising to my face and gaze down through the lighted fissures to the movement in the room below.

You can miss great gouts of time, like this. You can sit or lie down for a rest, close your eyes, and all of a sudden a decade or more has gone by. The artists were thrown out. One day a man in a coat cut from smooth, soft cloth stepped in through the front door and told them all to leave. I wondered for a moment if he was the rich man whose house it was, come back to reclaim it. I was going to ask him if he knew where my mother was. But then I remembered he had probably been dead for years.

Two couples lived here for a while. On evenings

when their spouses were out somewhere in the mist-veiled, street-lamped city, the man from the lower floors would climb the stairs to see the woman from the upper floors. Together they groaned and struggled and clutched each other beneath the tight clinch of bed-sheets.

I didn't like them. Didn't like the first husband's grease-sheened skin. Or the downturn in the mouth of his wife. I made it my business to walk about at night, moving things around. They didn't stay long.

Next came people with children. They were the first children I'd seen since the Bunts. A boy and a girl. She had wide, watery-blue eyes and hair pulled into two stiff plaits, a white line drawn through her scalp. When the parents weren't looking, the boy would give the plaits a sharp tug.

'Please,' the mother would say when the girl cried out in pain, without looking up from her sewing, 'don't be wearing. At least try and behave.'

They had the whole house. The whole house. For only four of them. The father, Arthur, had many tools, like the artists a long time ago, except he painted the walls with his brushes, and hammered nails and shelves into the asymmetric rooms. He liked doing this, I could tell. It made him happy. If he could have pulled the whole place apart and rebuilt it, he would have done it.

Caroline was given the high room at the back. My room. I took this as a sign.

One night I crept in, slowly, slowly. Her bed was in the same position as my mother's, pushed up against

172

the outer edge of the house. I curled my fingers around the brass bed end and stared at her. She looked as if she'd been dropped from a height, her arms flung wide, her yellow hair fanned out behind her. She breathed heavily, as if with difficulty, through her mouth.

I looked at the floor, at the seam of light coming in from around the curtain edges, at the door where there were still holes made by the latch being ripped off by the men from downstairs.

'What's your name?'

I turned. Caroline was looking straight at me, her face softened, blurred by sleep. One of her knuckles was burrowing into her cheek. She yawned, her eyes rolling back in her skull, then focused on me again.

I don't know, I tried to say.

'Mmm,' she said. Then she turned over and went back to sleep, dipping below the surface of consciousness and sinking away from me.

She introduced me to all her dolls, one by one: 'This is Rosie this is Isabel this is Imogen this is Claire and this is Jenny. She lost an arm. Richard pulled it off and threw it into the pond. That was in our old house, before we came here. Daddy said he'd get it back, but he couldn't. He spent hours and hours and hours with a net, but all that came up was weeds and plants and things like that.'

The dolls were odd creatures. Rigid, unyielding limbs and glassy eyes that rattled inside their head. But I listened to all their names, determined to remember them.

She showed me her books, dense packages of pages with columns of letters marching across them, and pictures of children playing.

Downstairs, her father was taking a chisel and a mallet to the fireplaces, wrenching them away from the walls, then covering the scars with boards and plaster. Richard was hurling stones at birds in the garden.

'This is where I keep my dresses.' She pulled at the closet door that had always stuck in damp weather. 'This is the one for best.' She pointed at something white and blue and thin. 'This is one my cousin gave me. My cousin Cecile. She's horrible. When she comes round she —'

Suddenly her mother was in the room, the door slamming behind her. 'Who are you talking to, Caroline?'

Caroline bit her lip, uncertain. She glanced at me, cross-legged on the floor beside the bed. 'I wasn't talking,' she muttered.

'I heard you, Caroline, coming up the stairs. There's no-one here.' The mother spun round, her eyes circling the room. 'There's no-one there,' she repeated. She marched to the window, her hand flying up to the lock. 'It's freezing in here. Have you opened this window?' She seized her daughter by the hand. 'Come downstairs with me.'

I tiptoed up behind the mother one day when they were all out. Amy, she was called. She was sitting in the big room downstairs, where the artists used to have their parties, a cardigan on her shoulders, her legs crossed.

She was leafing through a book stuffed with scribbled bits of paper and newspaper cuttings.

I came up behind her chair, softly, softly. I breathed on the tiny, short hairs at the nape of her neck, I rubbed my fingers over the wool of her cardigan, I sniffed at the soap smell of her hair, I inhaled as much air as I could into my lungs, and then I yelled,

BOO!

Amy leapt several inches in the air, letting out a small shrieking squawk as if she'd been burnt. The book flew up into the air like a bird, pages, notes, cuttings falling from it and fluttering to the ground. She sprang from the chair, her shoesoles slipping and skidding on the loose pages all over the floor, putting up her hands to cover the back of her neck.

'Who's there?' she screamed at the room.

I laughed and laughed and laughed, rolling around on the carpet her husband had laid, tiny nails held painstakingly in his mouth as he tacked it down at the edges.

'Who's there?' She scurried out into the hallway. The light through the front door made her skin a kaleidoscope of wild colour. She bolted through it and out into the street.

Who's there? Who's there? It's me, of course.

Two days later, she let a priest in at the door. He was being choked by a white band around his neck and the bones of his face pushed up through the flesh. His eyes were pale and darting.

They stood in the hallway for a while, him saying words like exorcism, soul, damned, over and over again.

'We're going to cleanse this restless spirit away,' he said to her, his hand on her sleeve, 'don't you worry.'

I thought of soap bubbles, whirling around and around before being swallowed down into the black gullet of a drain. I didn't like the sound of this. Not one bit.

The priest sparked a match against the sandpaper rasp of a matchbox and lit a tall, thick candle. He walked up and down the stairs, along each landing and into every room, intoning long, melodious words which merged into each other: *in nomine patris et filii et spiritus sancti amen.*

From his left hand he scattered drops of liquid which sat as raised silver beads on the hem of his cassock, as if the nap of the cloth refused them entry.

In the third-floor front room, where the brother had struck his sister twice, crick crack, the priest stopped. The fireplace she fell against was still there – Arthur hadn't managed to prise it away from the wall, but he'd covered it with a thin screen of wood and plastered over it. You'd never have known it was there at all. Out of sight, out of mind. Or something like that.

'I sense . . .' The priest trailed off.

Amy leant forward, her ringed hands clasped together. 'Yes?'

'I sense,' he began again, '. . . an . . . old presence.'

The end of his sentence rose, as if he wasn't quite sure, as if he was waiting for her to speak. Which she didn't. I circled their ankles like a cat.

'Possibly . . . female?' He scanned her face.

She frowned. 'My daughter did say it was a child,' she said. 'A boy.'

'A boy a boy a boy a boy,' he gabbled. 'That's what I meant. A male presence. An old spirit, is what I mean. I sense an old spirit.' He passed the back of his hand over his brow and stared down at the black book in his hand as if he might find the answers there. Clearing his throat, he began again: *in nomine patris et—*

AMEN! I bawled. AMEN!

Amy flinched as if slapped across the face. 'There!' she hissed at the priest. 'There! Did you hear that? Did you?'

The priest gazed at the ceiling. Was he hoping I'd be swinging from the frilled lampshade?

She was moving round the room in tight, nervous circuits, dodging the furniture. 'And it gets so cold.' She stretched her cardigan around her. 'Do you feel it? It's freezing in here all of a sudden. Freezing. Do you feel it?'

The priest held out his hand as if checking for rain. 'Um. Yes. I think . . .' he began, clearing his throat again, 'I think what we have is a very unhappy child spirit. It's interesting, don't you think, that it chose your daughter as the person with whom it would communicate, because maybe it's trying to tell us something, to get through somehow. Often, in cases like this, the spirit wants to speak and once it has spoken, it will be at rest.'

She nodded, desperation distorting her face.

'Maybe,' the priest struggled on, 'we should ask it what it wants.'

'Do you think so?' Amy was doubtful.

The priest squared his feet a few inches apart on the rug and, still clutching the lit candle, addressed a point midway up the wall. 'What do you want?' he said in a clear, slow voice. 'Why have you come?'

He waited. The words hung like gas on the air. He closed his eyes, straining for sound. Amy glanced down at his shoes and pursed her lips, then back at his face. I clamped my hands over my mouth to silence my laughter.

'Can you tell us?' He was using the same slow, silly voice. 'What is it you want from these people?'

I had to stuff my sleeve into my mouth. But a kind of suppressed snort escaped. I couldn't help it. He looked so ridiculous there in the middle of the rug in his black dress with his eyes closed and his candle held up like a weapon. Amy glared suspiciously in my direction.

He sighed. 'Let us pray,' he said to Amy. She arranged her features into a pious sneer and placed her palms together. 'Dear Lord,' and he launched himself into a long, monotone slew of words.

My laughter ebbed away. I waited for them to finish, to see what would happen next. But he talked on and on. Amy fidgeted slightly, tweaking at the material of her skirt, opening one of her eyes a crack, then closing it again.

I crept forward. I trod on the polished, reflective toes of his shoes, tugged the hem of his cassock, tickled

178

Amy's ankle bones, blew up her skirt. And there was a great furore of stampeding feet, shrieks from Amy, muttered exclamations to God from him and they ran right down the stairs. I was laughing too much to follow them. I hadn't had so much fun in years.

I was hoping the priest would come back. But he didn't. There were others, though. Exorcists, spiritualists, diviners – the lot. A man with a curling blond beard and wide, flat hands told Amy to put mirrors opposite every doorway 'to drive back bad spirits'. A woman with trailing, reddish hair claimed that I was hungry and that they should put out plates of food for me. She was right. I was hungry. But how could I eat their food?

The mirrors gathered thin films of dust on their surfaces and opaque holes appeared in their silver. The plates of food became fringed with green mould. Arthur threw them out eventually, going round the house with a rubbish bag, muttering about mumbo-jumbo.

Caroline knew not to talk to me again. She avoided meeting my gaze, wouldn't answer me when I spoke to her. Sometimes I still used to watch beside her bed at night. She asked to move to another room. They kept that room, my room, stuffed full of boxes, old furniture, toys they had outgrown – and locked. After a while, I really believe she stopped seeing me altogether.

One day I caught her reflection looking in one of the mirrors they still had around the house, and I realized she was no longer a child at all. She had grown up without me.

Richard left, then Caroline. Amy left one morning,

too, on a stretcher. She'd been ill for a while, spluttering and complaining into a handkerchief. She never came back. Arthur sawed wood for shelves, replastered the stairs, built a greenhouse, filled in the cracks that filigreed the walls in wet weather, laid lino on top of other lino and laid carpets on top of that. He fed crumbs and slivers of suet to the birds, on a bird table he'd made himself. He walked around the perimeters of the garden wall, his back bent. When winter came around, he would sit at the window, looking out at the sky. I sat with him.

He stopped going into the top floors of the house. They became cold; the wallpaper he'd put up curled at the edges and eventually flopped forward to the floor. He slept in a bed on the ground floor and every day a woman would arrive at the door with a meal for him on a plastic tray.

He ate it alone, standing up in the kitchen.

I was upstairs when he fell – somewhere, hovering about, drifting. I heard a series of regular thuds, like a stick held against railings. I came down.

Arthur was lying at the bottom of the stairs, beside the front door, right where the Bunt twin and I had been standing before I took his crust of bread. His body looked splayed, uncomfortable. His face was pressed up close to the cold tiles as if he loved them, as if he worshipped them.

Arthur, I said, Arthur.

He'd already gone. I hadn't been quick enough to see the rise and disappearance of his soul, or to try and catch it. I sat down on the bottom step.

Days and nights turned into each other, then back. I zoomed up and down the stairs, rattling the window-panes at passers-by. Nobody came. Arthur's skin turned a silvery blue. When the sun shone, he was dappled with the colour of jewels from the front-door glass. I'd always been afraid he'd take his chisel to it one day. But he hadn't.

The phone rang a couple of times, then cut dead. The plants drooped and yellowed. The milkman came up the path once a day and I tried to speak to him through the letterbox but he just turned away.

One evening I was sitting on the bottom step again with Arthur when the thundering thuds of the people going up and down the stairs in the adjoining house gave me an idea. I walked up and down, pressing my ear to the wall like a doctor in search of a heartbeat. It was thinnest on the second-floor landing. I'd never tried this before. I breathed in and just as the cold grain of the bricks bit into my skin, I breathed out, dissolving myself, mingling myself with the mortar of the house, and pushed and pushed and pushed.

When I breathed in again, I was standing on a landing. It looked just like my landing. I blinked. It was like the reflection of my landing in a mirror: there was the looping staircase with the exact same fluted banisters, the door to the room that had been Pussy's sitting room, the four steps down to the lower landing, the window to the garden. But all the wrong way round.

Then I saw something that nearly made me faint. A big, mottled, white-pink animal, on the landing above, looking straight at me, lips drawn back to reveal a row of long, serrated teeth. It stretched out its neck and shouted,

WOOF,

then that rumbling, strangled noise from its throat.

I knew it, of course. It was the creature that had chased me down the alleyway a long time ago. I'd always wondered where it lived. I took a deep breath and pushed my way back through the bricks, quick as I could, terrified I might leave a limb, an ankle, a wrist behind which it could clamp its fangs around.

Caroline appeared, just when I had given up, when I had taken to sleeping in the doorway near Arthur, to keep him company. She fitted a key into the teeth of a lock and let the door swing open. She stood over her father's body for a few seconds then moved towards the phone. And when I looked into her face, I saw that she was old, older than my mother had been.

She had Arthur's body taken away. A few days later, a large, red van emblazoned with letters I couldn't read pulled up outside and men in overalls started taking everything from the house and loading it into the waiting mouth of the van, until everywhere was empty, empty, empty.

This was the hardest time. I slept a great deal. And when I wasn't sleeping I would drift from empty room to empty room, wailing. They looked the same, all of a sudden. I could no longer tell them apart. Sometimes I forgot where I was in the house and that would make me cry more. I hated being alone. The floorboards creaked up and down, depending on the rain; the cracks Arthur had filled in widened and spread. The wind whistled down chimneys to fireplaces no longer there.

Occasionally, people would come and walk round the house, peering up at the ceilings, tutting at the fallen wallpaper, rapping their knuckles against Arthur's plastering. A man in a suit the colour of wet earth and a smile that came and went too fast always came with them. An 'agent' he called himself. I didn't like them. I didn't like any of them. I didn't want them to live here. So I cried louder and louder until the backs of their necks prickled and they left as quickly as they could.

It was raining the day the young couple came, water rushing down the guttering to form rivers in the street. I was feeling the house shifting, remembering, the timbers creaking. He came in first, shaking the rain from his coat. When I saw her, something slipped and coiled inside me. Her hair was so black it was almost blue and she had big, dark eyes that skittered around the hallway, taking in the glass, the tiles on the floor, the staircase leading up to the rest of the house.

They held on to each other by the hand, as if they were afraid the other might vanish if they let go. The agent with the smile was with them but they ignored him, mostly. They didn't like him either, I could tell. On the landing, behind the agent's back, the man kissed the white of her neck, rubbed his palm over her cropped hair.

In the third-floor front room she looked at the wall

where Arthur had hammered a board and said: 'I bet there's a fireplace behind that.'

The man turned to the smiling agent. 'So how come it's been on the market for so long?'

The agent stopped smiling. Then he recovered himself and bared his teeth. 'You know . . .' he circled his hand in the air, '. . . market forces.' He turned up the collar of his coat as if he was suddenly cold.

'They've dropped the price a lot, haven't they?' the man persisted.

'A little,' the agent conceded. 'They're eager for a quick sale, I believe.'

'But why hasn't it sold? I mean, round here houses go overnight. What is it about this one that . . .'

The girl slipped out of the room and up the stairs. I followed her, tiptoeing so that she wouldn't hear me, so that she wouldn't know I was there. In the back, top room she stopped. She sat on the windowsill, just as my mother used to when she brushed her hair, letting the tangle from her brush fall from her fingers to be lifted away by the breeze. The man stuck his head round the door.

'What do you think?' he whispered. 'Do you want it?'

She just smiled.

He went downstairs, to measure something, he said. She stood and wandered to the edge of the room. I stayed close to her. I wanted to look into her face for a long time; I had this feeling it would have all the answers to everything I had ever wanted to know.

She nudged the edge of the lino with her toe, then

184

bent down and tugged at it. It peeled back easily, like damp paper. There were two more layers (Arthur had liked lino). She knelt on the bare boards.

'Hey!' she shouted to the man, 'there are great floor-boards under all this stinky lino.'

I saw her look down. She reached out her hand. Across the boards where she was kneeling were scratches. Deep, frantic scratches in the wood where I had kicked and kicked against my bindings, the nails in the soles of my boots scoring the wood. An incomprehensible intersection of lines, like Chinese characters.

She touched them once, twice, rubbing her fingertips along their grooves. Then she looked up. Straight at me.

I waited, holding my breath, for her to scream, run away, shut her eyes. But she didn't. Her hand on the floorboards stilled. The black centres of her eyes swelled and stretched. In the street below, someone shouted.

She stood up slowly and went downstairs, wending her way through the house. I flitted behind her, trying to stop myself from grabbing hold of the loose material of her trousers or touching her hand with my icy fingers or pressing my cheek to the warmth of her neck.

In the garden, the man was pacing up and down the width of the house, counting his steps, muttering about how it was going to need underpinning. I stood in the doorway. She squinted up at the house. She was standing where Mrs Bunt used to hang her carpets and beat them with a wicker bat, near where the privy used to be. She sniffed the air. I knew she was smelling the ghost of that foul alley. I knew she'd be back.

185

When they moved in, they filled the house's foundations with concrete, pulled down all of Arthur and Amy's curtains and ripped up all the lino so that the windows were bare and sunlight spilled in over the wooden floorboards. The man scuffed with his toe at the coloured-paint shoeprints left by the artists, shrugged to himself and left them there.

The girl grew her hair. The man liked it, I could tell. He liked to push his fingers into it and draw them out again slowly and when she leant over him at night, he pushed his face into it, so that it covered him on all sides like a tent.

They were always touching each other. When one of them left the house, the other would wait, eyes straying to the door.

But I was sick of women. They pretend, they forget, they leave and they don't come back. I wanted the man to see me, just once, just so I knew a man could. I tried everything – loud noises, stamping, crying, shrieking, wafting, hovering, shouting, touching, tugging, moving things around. My complete repertoire. Nothing. He looked through me as if I wasn't there.

It made her jump, though.

At first, I thought the girl was ill. She started dozing on the sofa during the day, her face soft and confused in sleep. I could stand just above her then, my face warmed by her breath. She would no longer run up the stairs, but plod, yanking herself up each step, gripping the banister.

Her stomach puffed and swelled out and one day while she was dozing, her cheek creased red by the cushion, I pressed my palm to it. There was a quick, sudden twist of movement, like something shedding a skin, and then I understood.

The man painted the top back room a deep red, tutting as the paint pooled and dripped into the crack in the wall made by Mrs Bunt's banging. I watched from a corner, my teeth set into each other. No child would live in this house but me.

I was right there when the first pain came. She and I were climbing the stairs. I was waiting for her to catch up, standing on the landing where the stove used to be, where my mother would get live coals to light our fire. As she neared me, she snapped in two like a tree hit by lightning, buckling over, a long, low sound escaping her lips.

She lowered herself down to the top step, her legs stretched out, breathing in and out like a pair of bellows. She clenched her hands together, then released them. She pushed her hair back from her eyes. She counted to nine and back again. Then she did it again.

The phone rang twice then cut dead. She didn't move, sweat dampening her face and hair, her hands gripping the rounded bones of her knees. I was anxious suddenly. What if something went wrong? What if the man didn't come back? What if—

A scream razored the air. I moved past her to come and crouch in front of her. Her face was pallid, marble grey, her eyes screwed shut. I reached out and put a small, cold hand on the dome of her belly.

Her eyes sprang open. She studied my face. Then I watched as she was clenched again by pain. Her mouth stretched open and she gasped and as she did so I felt the air around me stir and rush, as if I was moving.

I panicked, tried to still myself, tried to grip on to the solid, worn wood of stair-tread. But I was being pulled, dragged by something bigger than me, stronger than me. As she breathed in to the bottom of her lungs I felt myself yanked inside her. And swallowed.

Everything is very hot and close and airless. I am being pressed and I cannot breathe and I cannot make any sound even though my mouth is open and I am screaming. I am screaming for the feel of the familiar wooden boards under my feet, for the touch of coloured glass under my fingers, for my mother. But she never came back.

I am being pushed now, towards something, or through something, and I have not felt anything like this before. Or maybe I have but I can't remember. I don't like it. I want to get out. I batter my fists against this thing that is restraining me, squeezing me, and I am still battering them when I realize I am out in the open and that terrible noise drilling into my head is me.

I open my eyes.

I am back, it seems. Almost as if I never went away. I inhale again, ready for another outraged yell. She is not going to get away with this.

Then I realize they are bending over me. Both of them. Right over me. I stare back, thrown, still furious. They look as if they have something they want to tell me.

She is looking straight at me. He is looking straight at me. They smile.

Sarah Parkinson is a comedy writer, radio producer and occasional actress. She produced the highly acclaimed series *Late* for BBC Radio 4, and a series about Catholics in comedy for BBC Radio 2, for whom she also co-devised and wrote the literary panel game *Speaking Volumes*. Her writing credits include *Kate and Cindy* and *Five Squeezy Pieces* (Radio 4), *Barking* (Channel 4) and *The Suicidal Dog* (BBC), a short film which she co-wrote with her partner Paul Merton. Paul also directed her in *Unf***ed* at the Edinburgh Fringe Festival. Sarah was diagnosed with breast cancer in February last year, caused it is thought by IVF. With Paul's help and love, and that of her family and friends (including the wonderful Stella Duffy), she is recovering well, and has finally learned how to live one day at a time.

Saving Grace

It really was too bad of Grace. Natasha drummed her fingers on the car steering wheel and tried to ignore the persistent cries of 'Mummy' from the back seat of the 4x4. God, she hated the school run. She glanced in the narrow rear-view mirror, and sighed. She could see faint blue shadows under her eyes. Proof that she hadn't had enough sleep. David didn't seem to understand how important it was that she should have time to rest. It was stressful enough being the mother of two small daughters without having to get up each morning to attend to their every need. Surely he could have given them their Frosties today? Well, if Grace couldn't be relied on she'd have to get an au pair again. Not that it had been a success the last time. She blamed David for that. It had been completely unnecessary and hideously expensive to call out the emergency doctor. And the doctor had been very off with Natasha, which was unusual – Natasha prided herself on having most good-looking men eating out of her hand within minutes of meeting her. But he – well, he had looked at her in a very cold way after the au pair had given an account of her average day and he had diagnosed nervous exhaustion. Good God, she was here to learn the language, wasn't she? She wasn't going to be able to do that sitting on her substantial arse in the kitchen eating *Waffeletten*. After all, the girl (what was her name, Inge? Inde?) was only hysterical in the way that all teenagers were hysterical. She remembered a very similar experience in her own youth where Saskia Robbins had been asked to a May Ball instead of her. She too had cried for over an hour, and it had taken her a very long time to get over it. In fact, it hadn't really been till Saskia had been in that awful road accident and had to have reconstructive surgery to the lower part of her face that she had been able to forgive her properly.

And now Grace had let her down as well. When only the other day she had been saying that of course she didn't mind driving the kiddies to school, it was no trouble, it was on her way to work anyway, they were such sweet little girls, and it was nice for her really, not having any little ones of her own to look after. And she had seemed almost speechless with gratitude when Natasha had also allowed her to look after the girls' new puppy, which had just proved too much of a nightmare with Natasha's white carpets.

Grace had no right to let her down, Natasha thought, jabbing at her horn as an elderly man dawdled across the pedestrian crossing. Natasha thought of Grace's lank greying hair, the heavy shapeless body shrouded in an ill-advised emerald-green coat, the sensible lace-up shoes, the – ugh – hairy legs still visible through the American tan tights, the eyebrows that beetled across her forehead in two straggly lines – heavens, had the woman no idea about personal grooming? – she should be pleased to have a neighbour as glamorous as Natasha. Perhaps her mother took up a lot of time – she seemed to recollect Grace saying that she visited her every day, but even so. Natasha would never let herself slip like that. She knew the value of a good night's sleep and a vigorous physical (and occasionally carnal) work-out with Igor, her personal trainer. No chance of that today. She was going straight back to bed when she got home. No point in going to the gym looking like this. Her friends would start talking pointedly about facelifts, and she didn't want Igor going on about her 'beaudy-full laff lines' again. Bloody Grace. Ringing her up at the last minute, all subdued, couldn't come tomorrow, something urgent . . . leaving a pause, as though she wanted to say more but wasn't sure if that would be right. Well, Natasha was blasted if she was going to start getting all touchy-feely with someone who'd just let her down. She'd said a cold, clipped, 'Well, thanks for letting me know,' and then put the phone down in a fury. Bloody Grace.

Was it too late to book herself in with Janice for some colonic irrigation?

'Hi, Grace. It's me, Suzy . . . hi, are you there? I just called work and they said you were off today . . . hi . . . Pick up, pick up! Hope you're OK – sure you are, probably just skiving! Anyway I've sent you a couple of e-mails but you haven't replied and, well, the thing is, listen, sis, I hate to do this to you . . . yeah, I know that's what I always say but the thing is I'm having a fantastic time here and I've just met this guy called Greg – he's a surfer too, and he's so – God, well, fantastic, I mean what a body, like just all muscles and – wow I mean I can't even begin to tell you what the sex is like and I know you're not really into all that but like think amazing and double it. Anyway the thing is I'm running out of money again and I just really don't want to have to come back to cold miserable England yet. I could get a job in a bar I guess but the thing is that Greg and I want to go and travel around a bit – apparently there's an amazing beach about twenty miles to the south where you can just surf and smoke and – well, you know. So I was wondering if – pretty please, sis, you could possibly lend me some more dosh. I mean, I promise I'll pay you back and yes I know I said that the last time, and I haven't yet, but I absolutely promise that this time I'll get a job somewhere and stick at it and not get sacked this time or anything. So the thing is maybe you could wire me some money. I guess if you can manage it about five hundred would be great, that should mean we could stay here another month. Wow . . . amazing sunset. Anyway, can you ring me back and let me know soon where to pick up the cash? . . . Oh, and listen, I'm sorry I haven't rung for a while but it's just like so amazing here it's hard to fit everything into the day. Oh, and love to Mum – tell her I'll send her a postcard soon. Bye . . .'

Roger stretched out his legs and gave a slight wince as his sciatica reminded him that he was getting old. He scrolled down through the report again. The girl had typed it out properly. So what was it that was bothering him? The headings were right, the subsections made sense, but somehow, it just seemed, well, turgid. You never expected a document on drainage options to exactly fly off the page, but he prided himself on the fact that his reports were pretty legendary in the department. 'Want something written with a bit of style, a bit of elan? Then ask Roger!' would go the cry. Some would say that it was his aptitude at report writing that had been behind his meteoric rise within the environmental division, from team leader to field manager to field director to departmental sub-director all within the space of twelve years. Board meetings had seemed to fly by when it was one of Roger's reports they were discussing, the points all seemed clear, even Simpson, his closest rival, was unable to pick holes in them. And his introduction of the 'where to now?' section at the end, a sort of brainstorming summary of the future options for sewage disposal, or rainwater dispersion – well, they were a chance for the department to loosen up, to warm to their themes, to forge the new path.

He looked at the final paragraph. It was flat and uninteresting. He could feel a few droplets of sweat breaking out on his forehead, a forehead that was substantially higher than it had been twelve years ago, a forehead that now almost reached the back of his head. What was different?

It was Grace's fault, he realized. Where was she? She was usually here, at her desk. And he'd got used to popping in and chatting with her about his ideas.

Indeed, in the early days he'd even taken her out to dinner a couple of times, just after his divorce. Nothing romantic, you understand, but he'd seen she had a good brain, and not all women were happy for you to talk about drainage all night, as he'd found out to his cost when shortly before she left him his ex-wife had thrown most of a Royal Worcester dinner service at the wall, narrowly missing his head. But Grace was different. She had gazed at him myopically through her thick spectacles in frank admiration as he had held forth about cesspits versus septic tanks. And not only that, but she had some very pertinent comments about their respective tonnage. He'd been able to incorporate them into his next report.

Of course, he had eventually put a stop to the romantic dinners. She'd turned up one night wearing a blue dress, her hair up and her eyes slightly red-rimmed from a new pair of contact lenses she was trying to get used to. It might have been all right, Roger reasoned, except Simpson somehow got wind of these assignations and Roger, to his embarrassment, had heard him talking in a loud voice about how Grace looked like a be-spectacled horse. Roger liked Grace, yes, but he certainly didn't want to be seen as sad.

He still let her sit with him in the canteen from time to time. He would run his ideas past her, while she toyed with a dubious fishcake. He made notes and she seemed happy enough.

Roger sighed as he read the last paragraph again. Where was she? Personnel had been quite unhelpful. They said she'd phoned in sick. Maybe he could go round, take this report? Even if she'd lost her voice, she could still make notes. He could leave it with her.

That's what he'd do. He lifted his buttock slightly and emitted, with some satisfaction, a silent fart. He felt better already.

Grace sat on the edge of the hospital bed. She knew that if she got into the bed she was admitting that she was ill. Maybe if she just sat down here, by the blankets at the end, someone would come along and tell her it had all been a mistake, that it was very sensible of her not to get into the bed, that now they would be able to give it to a properly ill person. She decided not to drink any water out of the jug they had provided. She would keep drinking from her little bottle she had brought in with her. That way they wouldn't have to wash the glass.

If she waited long enough someone would come and tell her it was all right.

That she was OK.

That she didn't have cancer.

'Ah, Miss um er . . .'

'Sherborne,' the nurse said helpfully.

It was the surgeon.

'You don't mind?' He gestured to a bunch of twelve-year-olds wearing white coats. 'It is a teaching hospital.' He made it sound as though, if she refused, she would be single-handedly denying the next generation any hope of medical skill at all.

'No,' she said faintly. 'Though I think there may have been a mistake—'

'This lady presented,' the consultant continued, 'with swelling around the aureole and palpable lump in the right upper quadrant of the left breast. Upon core biopsy it was identified as an invasive cancer, and a wide local excision and removal of the lymph nodes will take place later this afternoon. As advised in the Macmillan guidelines, she was given a definite diagnosis, within two weeks,' he concluded triumphantly.

'Um, actually, I did come to see you six months ago and you gave me a mammogram and told me there was nothing to worry about.'

'Yes. Well, mammograms can miss up to twenty per cent of lumps, I'm afraid, particularly in younger women with their denser breast tissue.' He looked at her distastefully, as though she had deliberately set out to make his job difficult with her stubbornly dense breast tissue. 'We've found it now. I'll see you in the operating theatre.' And he swept on to the next cowering woman.

Grace felt hot tears at the back of her eyes. She suddenly felt very angry. This wasn't fair. She was a good person, wasn't she? Or maybe she wasn't. She thought about how sometimes she was irritated by her mother's ceaseless demands on her. How her little sister seemed to treat Grace as a very dull bank account. How her neighbour Natasha had not even asked her how she was. How Roger (she swallowed, remembering how once she had thought tall, lanky, balding Roger was the answer to her dreams) had begun to annoy her with his inability to give her even a little bit of praise. Maybe it was her fault. Maybe she was being punished for being so horrible.

Grace suddenly wanted someone to put their arms around her, to tell her it would be all right, to hold her and tuck her up in her cold, unfriendly hospital bed.

But there was no-one. No-one came to look after Grace. She was all by herself.

It was Christmas, and there was a tree in the ward covered with ragged tinsel and faded decorations. It reminded Grace of herself.

Through the next few days, Grace, her left breast now slightly smaller than her right, a hideous paisley bag on her shoulder to hold the bottle that was draining fluid away from her wound, walked slowly around the ward. She talked to the other women who were in for the same operation. They laughed together sometimes, that black humour that people always call Blitz spirit, though there were plenty of nervous breakdowns during the Blitz. And she listened to the women, and heard stories of exhausting children, and demanding spouses, and unrealistic expectations, and she heard herself tell her own story.

She didn't like what she heard.

* * * * *

Dear Natasha,
Just to let you know that I'm going to be away for the next six months, so am letting you have your key back. Used it today just to let Rollo in. I've put some food down for him in the kitchen, but have left the sitting room door open so he can run about. Hope

this is OK. Know you come back early on Tuesday afternoons to work on your 'abs' with the personal trainer chap, so Rollo won't be alone for long. Have left a small gift each for Chloe and Allegra. You are probably getting used to the school run by now, anyway – they are delightful children and I know David would love you to see more of them, and indeed him. He found some of Igor's underpants there a couple of weeks ago, but I was able to convince him they were mine. I think.

Hope my being away will not inconvenience you too much.

You may hear some banging from next door – I've finally decided to have that conservatory built. Apologies for any noise.

Best wishes, Grace

From grace.sherborne@aol.com
To suzysherborne@hotmail.com

Hi there little sis

Hope all is well in sunny Thailand. Thank you for your messages, e-mails etc. Glad you're having a good time.
Unfortunately I'm not going to be able to lend you that money – I've finally decided to have that conservatory done, and it's taking almost everything I've got. You know I always wanted to knock through from the sitting room, but then you needed some-

where to store your stuff and somewhere to stay when you were, well, between holidays, and, well, it just seemed to be too complicated. But then this marvellous leaflet dropped through the letterbox about this storage place where they keep it all under lock and key and so I've put it all into a couple of their little cabins for you. Have paid for the first month for you but you will have to be back by the 15th to sort out what you want to do with it after that.

Of course, this does also mean you won't be able to stay with me. In fact I'm having the whole place redecorated and I've rented a little cottage by the sea while it's happening. Just feel I need to get away for a while. Doctor's orders, I suppose you could say. Without going into it too much I've been told to take it easy for a while.

But I've had a wonderful idea – you can stay with Mum instead. I won't be able to pop in every day now and she would love to have you. She is still quite forgetful, but I have organized Meals on Wheels and social services – it's the company she needs really. And she will enjoy asking about all the lovely places you've been. Every day. And of course she won't charge you any rent, so you'll be able to save up and pay off your debts. I am going to need that £4,000 to pay the decorators. Quite soon.

Anyway, you will still be able to get me on e-mail, though I've decided not to give out my new address just yet. I will write to Mum, and ring in from time to time.

Enjoy the flight home.
Love, your big sister,
Grace

Dear Roger,
I hope you are well.

I am returning your reports, 'I can't stand the Drain', 'The Sewage Crisis' and 'Not only but Silo'. Although I am sure they make fascinating reading, I am at the moment reacquainting myself with George Eliot's work. You might enjoy *The Mill on the Floss* – water features quite heavily in that.

Although your handwriting is very hard to read (it always has been. I'm sure you must realize that's why your reports often included parts where I just guessed what you were trying to say! It was very kind of you never to correct me), I think I deciphered a 'Best wishes for a speedy recovery'. It was either that or 'Do your best with these, I need them by Thursday'. Anyway, it is now the following Monday, so many apologies. I hope that crucial departmental meeting on Friday went well.

I am afraid that as you might already know I am now on indefinite sick leave, so I do hope Angie will be able, in time, to decipher your handwriting and enjoy those delightful fishcake lunches in the canteen. Unfortunately, as she is a keen sportswoman (along with her fiancé Gordon in Acquisitions), I fear it is unlikely. Not every secretary will listen to endless drainage solutions in the hope of the occasional compliment on her layout.

In the meantime, many thanks for a most instructive twelve years.

Best wishes,
Grace Sherborne

* * * * *

The sun was very high in the sky as the slender woman with the chic grey cropped hair opened the latch of the gate. Nasturtiums tumbled onto the pathway, and cornflowers and poppies filled the front garden with their exuberance. The woman smiled. She had planted nasturtiums in her seaside cottage too, that March, not knowing, in the bleak brown-ness of the early spring, if she would be alive to see them bloom. But she was. There, and now here. She let herself in through the newly painted bright green door. There were a few leaflets on the mat – pizzas, mini cabs, as usual – but she stepped over them, amazed instead by the golden floorboards, newly sanded, which seemed to reflect the sun as it streamed in. Light poured into the flat through the vast French doors of the new conservatory, and there was suddenly no division between inside and outside, but instead a brightness which seemed to fill the rooms.

It filled her as well. She watched the motes of dust dancing in the beams of light, and thought, I would never have done this before. Just stopped and watched.

She suddenly felt incredibly, terribly happy.

She thought of her sister who had found Grace's cancer a huge inconvenience. Grace had felt so sad when she'd realized that just because you look after someone else, it doesn't mean they look after you. She thought of her mother, whose favourite had always been Suzy, no matter what Grace did for her. Suzy had managed to bring back a souvenir from Bali, not the surfer Greg, but an intestinal parasite which she had not yet named. Grace hoped the three of them were happy living together.

Grace thought of Natasha, and the 'For Sale' sign outside the house next door. David had finally had enough and taken the children to his mother's. She thought of Natasha with her full life and her empty head, and offered up a quick prayer that the children would take after their father – whoever he was.

Grace thought of Roger, forced into early retirement after an interdepartmental coup organized by Hector Simpson. They had emailed to see if she wanted to contribute to his leaving present. Instead she had enrolled him on a correspondence course, entitled 'So You Think You Could Be A Writer?'

Grace thought of how horrible her treatment had been, and how she had changed, losing hair, weight, responsibilities. She thought of how many amazing people she had met through it. And she felt sad for the old Grace, and then happy for the new.

'Jo,' she called through the front door. 'Jo, come here!'

A tall, red-headed woman with smiling eyes came up the path, carrying several bags of organic carrots.

'It's time for your juice,' she said merrily.
'Kiss me first,' said Grace.
And Jo did. In front of all the neighbours.
It really was too bad of Grace.

Justine Picardie is the author of the best-selling *If The Spirit Moves You*, and her first novel, *Wish I May*, will be published by Picador in January 2004. She is a *Vogue* contributing editor, and also writes for the *Daily Telegraph*. A co-founder of the Lavender Trust (set up after her sister Ruth died of breast cancer), Justine lives in London with her husband and their two sons.

The Fat Lady Sings

It was in the south of France, three weeks before her forty-first birthday, that Annie realized she had become invisible to men. She'd taken her boys to the Riviera for the first few days of June; her husband was working (harder than ever) and the holiday was a half-term treat for them, after her twelve-year-old son had finished his exams and the nine-year-old recovered from the indignity of his newly fitted orthodontic brace. They were booked into one of those white wedding-cake palace hotels on the promenade: kind of tacky, too expensive, but easy, overlooking the beach, and with shops and restaurants nearby.

So it should have been fun, but there was something depressing about their first night, as she stood on the scales in the hotel bathroom. They didn't have scales at home – hadn't for a year or so – but she seemed to have gained a stone since the last time she weighed herself, a couple of months ago in the doctor's surgery. This can't be right, she told herself, hurriedly checking her figures, converting kilos into pounds (and heart sinking, like a stone); but the mirrors told her otherwise, reflecting back the heavy truth. Annie resolved not to weigh herself again – they were on holiday, after all, and she needed a break from worrying – but there were mirrors everywhere in the hotel, full-length mirrors, unlike at home; in the bathroom and behind the wardrobe doors, in the lift and lining the lobby. And though she tried not to look, she barely recognized her reflection, as if she were seeing herself in distorting fairground mirrors, the ones that used to make the boys laugh when they were little, at the steam fair that came to the local park every August.

But now Annie wasn't laughing. She felt like crying, especially when it started raining on their second day here, heavy rain from the low grey sky. For years, she'd thought of herself as thin: five years ago, in fact, she'd been very thin, too thin, actually, when she'd suspected her husband of having an affair. But now, my God, without realizing, she'd got thick around the middle, pot-bellied; and at night, in the darkness of the hotel bedroom, while the boys slept peacefully, she grasped heavy handfuls of flesh, unable to believe it was hers. Middle-aged spread – that was what her mother had always complained about, warned of, even, but Annie hadn't listened, believing herself immune, as daughters often do.

And now it had come to her, and she hated that she cared, but she did, casting covert sideways glances at herself in the mirrors they passed; shocked each time by the hefty woman who looked, startled, back at her; both of them surprised to be caught staring at one another – the thin woman inside Annie's head, the fat lady in the mirror – neither willing to acknowledge the other.

It was like being a teenage girl again: that same disconsolate obsession, after years of being . . . well, if not perfectly content with her body, then at least not thinking about it very much. But as she regressed into adolescent angst, the difference this time round was that men weren't sizing her up. Annie found herself turned into a matron, as if overnight: though not the sort of imposing *grande dame* before whom men snapped to attention; no, just a middle-aged woman who apparently merged into the walls.

On the third evening she'd taken the boys to a restaurant on the seafront where they'd all eaten pizza and ice cream (no point starting a diet on holiday in the south of France). And the waiters hadn't even bothered with fake Latin charm, couldn't even remember to bring the bill, all too busy falling over themselves to serve the single Barbie blonde drinking red wine alone at another table. I bet she's had Botox, thought Annie, giving the girl the once-over; maybe even plastic surgery. And suddenly, she could understand why her friends at home were taking themselves to the gym, not to mention discreet dermatologists. It was too much to suddenly disappear (and how curious, to vanish in the eyes of men, just as one was growing in size).

'They think you're a single mother,' said Marcus, her elder son, observing her being ignored by the waiters. 'Or a widow,' said Jack, her younger one. But Annie guessed the waiters thought no such thing of her; indeed, did not think of her at all. Later, back at the hotel, she rang her husband for reassurance, but he sounded too tired and stressed about work to care about her petty insecurities. 'I love you,' she said, but Bill seemed not to hear, and afterwards, when he put the phone down, Annie wondered if she was mute now, as well as invisible.

The following morning, the Riviera sky was still as grey as the tarmac streets, and it was raining into the Mediterranean. Over breakfast – croissant, pain au chocolat, brioche with strawberry jam, all of which Annie ate, gloomily, steadily – the boys told her their dreams, which was not at all what they usually did in the mornings (like their father, they were more often monosyllabic when they awoke).

'I dreamt that there was a nuclear war, and you died,' said Jack, to Annie.

'What about Dad?' said Marcus.

'He wasn't there,' said Jack.

'I dreamt Mum died as well,' said Marcus, 'or maybe she just disappeared.'

'Well, I wouldn't worry,' said Annie, buttering herself another hunk of French bread. 'I'm the picture of health.'

They wandered around the shops afterwards, in the miserable drizzle, but she didn't even attempt to persuade the boys to let her go clothes shopping for herself. Instead, she spent over a hundred pounds on surfers' t-shirts and shorts for them, her lovely, growing sons, before scuttling into a pharmacy to buy some vitamin C, as if that might cure all her ills. 'Mum, your bum is showing,' hissed Marcus, appalled, as she bent over to reach the vitamins on the lowest shelf. How fortunate, she thought, pulling her jumper down over the offending bottom, not to have had daughters, even though she'd once longed for a third child, a girl. Just as she was finding herself in this apparent dead end, this pre-menopausal vanishing act, a daughter would be flowering, ripening into desirability.

Not that Annie wanted to turn back the clock. The last time she'd been in the south of France was as a student twenty years ago, with another girl, her best friend, during the long university summer holiday, and that had been unsettling in a different, more dangerous way. They'd had very little money, the two of them – just enough to buy bread and cucumber every day, after paying for a fleapit hotel – which meant that they were both thinner than when they'd arrived; but the constant wolf whistles (more like catcalls, really; more jeering than admiring) were disturbing rather than flattering. One morning they'd taken a bus to another town, up in the hills, and at the final stop – where they found themselves to be the last passengers on board – the driver had refused to open the door, mouthing obscenities at them, clutching at his groin, until Annie had started screaming at him. Afterwards, walking away from the bus stop, taking a short-cut through a small wooded park to avoid the noonday sun, another man had appeared from the trees, like in a bad B-movie, gesticulating at them and fumbling with his trousers. Annie had made the mistake of laughing, which seemed to make him angry, and he had grabbed hold of her friend, blonder than she was, and they had both started hitting him, scratching him with their nails, until at last he gave up and ran away.

So much for Latin lovers, then. It was better being invisible, she decided, as the sun came out after lunch and she walked with the boys along the Croisette. They stopped at a kiosk to buy ice-cream cornets, and two sweating, fat, middle-aged Frenchmen pushed her aside, barging their way to the front of the queue; but still, it wasn't the end of the world. And then she realized something else – that other women could still see her, even the glamorous mademoiselle with waist-length hair who nudged her slightly, by accident. '*Pardon, madame*,' said the girl, politely, and Annie smiled, to show she didn't mind. A little further along the promenade, towards the children's playground, an older woman nodded her head at Annie, very slightly, as if in acknowledgement of something, and Annie smiled again, grateful to discover that she was not quite invisible, after all.

The boys were too grown-up for the playground, they said, and the little fairground was closed until the weekend, so they scrambled over the rocks together, towards the marina where rich men's yachts were berthed, sleek and huge and gleaming. Why was it that boats could be big, and still beautiful, wondered Annie; though she wasn't sure if she really liked the yachts, more like white plastic Tupperware containers, all nestled up together in a row; and she wondered, too, if that was how her husband thought of her these days, like Tupperware, everyday and reliable, rather than something more desirable. 'Fragile' – that's what he'd said when he first

touched her, all those years ago. 'You're so fragile.'
She'd been slender, then, and he made her feel fragile,
not at first, when she was sure he'd loved her, but
soon afterwards, and she'd started feeling more anxious,
insecure, as if he might break her. It got worse when
she was pregnant with Marcus – as she grew bigger
every day, she'd felt smaller inside, shrinking under her
husband's distaste. Afterwards, run ragged with a new
baby, and Bill away more often than ever on business
trips, Annie had got skinny again, and stayed that way,
despite a second pregnancy. Not that being thin had
kept him loving her; and slowly, she'd begun to care
less. Careless – was that what she'd now become?
Letting herself go – that's what women said about each
other, didn't they? Annie sat on the rock, turning her
face up to the sun, feeling the warmth spread through
her body. 'It's not over till the fat lady sings,' she said to
herself, quiet enough for the boys not to hear, as they
threw stones into the murky harbour water.

Annie wasn't entirely sure what that meant – nor what
it might mean to her – but still, she started humming, a
French nursery song she'd learnt at school, just the tune
because she couldn't really remember the words. And
then, because the humming sounded rather quiet (like a
small bee, she thought), Annie started singing the bits of
words that she knew, la-la-ing the rest. 'Sur le pont,
d'Avignon, on-y-danse, la-la-la,' she sang, getting louder as
she went along, remembering herself as a little girl,
remembering how she'd imagined other girls, bigger
girls, dancing on the bridge, dancing over the water,
letting themselves go so fast that no-one could stop

them. 'Mum!' said Marcus, looking embarrassed, but she didn't stop singing, because he and Jack were smiling, too; and so was a man fishing nearby, from a little jetty. The man waved at her, and she waved back, because she'd finished her song by now, and then she stood and stretched her arms, as if reaching up to touch the clear blue sky. But she wasn't quite big enough for that. Not yet, anyway.

Polly Samson's collection of short stories, *Lying in Bed*, is published by Virago. Her stories have been read on BBC Radio 4 and BBC Radio Scotland and have appeared in the *Observer*, *You* and the *Sunday Express*, and in the anthologies *Girls' Night In* (HarperCollins) and *Gas and Air* (Bloomsbury). Her novel, *Out of the Picture*, published by Virago in 2000, was shortlisted for the Arts Club First Novel Award and has been translated into German, Greek and Latvian.

Low Tide

This is what Hal remembers from before. His earliest memory. The darkness closing around him like a shell and he's curled inside, staring out. A crack of light, the sheen of white gloss at the edge of a door, a thin slice of shining passageway. It isn't like anywhere else in the world, this passageway, because it has brown glazed tiles.

At the far end, Hal's parents are at the kitchen table, talking beneath the glare from a bare bulb. He can hear them all the time he's in his cot. Their voices hiss, the radio hums. Hal rubs wet fists to and fro, cheek to ear, ear to cheek, but it's no help with the pain.

It takes all Hal's strength to haul himself up, and when he's hanging over the rail he sees what a dizzying way it is to the floor. He tumbles, then lands with a soft thump onto blankets that have been folded there. Maybe he crawls, maybe he stumbles towards the voices and the light; he's only aware of them getting closer and wanting his mum.

As soon as she sees him, Anna sweeps him onto her lap. She's soft and cool and tastes like salted butter.

He cries because of the pain in his mouth and his throbbing, hot ears, and then there's the burning of his dad's finger, rough as a cat's tongue, rubbing whisky onto his raw gums. The whisky is fire at the back of his nose; it makes him feel sick, but it stops the pain for a moment, or at least replaces it.

Hal has no idea whether all small children can recall their babyhoods but it's fun to show off sometimes.

'How on earth do you remember all this?' Anna says. 'I mean, right down to the colour of the tiles at Checkpoint Road.'

Hal can tell that his mum's impressed. And he's not making it up, remembering the shiny brownness of the tiles is proof enough of that.

'I used to lick them because I thought they were chocolate pudding,' he says, and watches Anna's big grey eyes crinkle at the corners. There's nothing better than making her smile; Hal thinks she looks kind and pale, like an angel. And he knew she'd be happy if he remembered something about the way things used to be; and she mustn't be sad, especially not today. Not in front of his dad.

They're on the train, heading south, and he can't wait to be there at the sandy beach that's been on his mind ever since his dad sent the picture. It was a postcard with swirly giant's writing, 'Wish you were here', engraved in the sand. 'The seaside, the sea,' he chants, bouncing so hard on the old-fashioned dusty velvet seats that their tangled innards creak and ping beneath him.

'Bim! Bom! Bum! And the beach!' Hal resorts to

made-up songs, listing everything he sees out of the train window: fields with cows, big stone houses, mud and pigs and tractors and horses, fields where hay and straw are mystery packages coated in plastic, shiny and black as liquorice wheels. 'In my day, it was all square bales,' Anna says.

'Thing I remember about Checkpoint Road,' she says as they pass a deserted racecourse, 'was the day your dad kicked a football, right through someone's window . . .'

'Why did he do that?'

'By mistake, of course!' she snorts. 'We had to run like mad, with you in the pushchair and the shopping, and everything falling about.'

'I was scared as hell,' she says. 'We were only kids. There's no way we could've paid for the window. The pushchair always felt like a toy to me, like I was still a little girl clopping about in my mum's shoes, pretending.' Hal looks up and notices that her eyes are sparkling. They always do when she talks about the happy time.

'One more station and we'll be there,' Anna says. 'Start putting your felt-tips away.' Hal sees her reach into her bag for a small square of mirror, sees her grimace at herself in it. Then, and much to his surprise, she glosses her lips with some pinky stuff from a little pot and, with a little brush twisted from a tube, sweeps her eyelashes into black spikes.

'What're you gawping at?' she says, nudging him as she spritzes her wrist with a short burst of sweet, lemony perfume. The train judders and squeaks as it slows, then stops.

'Are we here, Mum? We are?' Hal wants to whoop but there are other people still on the train so he knows he must behave himself as he tussles with the door.

Hal leaps onto the platform, ready for anything. 'Is it a bird?' he wants to shout out loud. 'Is it a plane? No, it's Superman!'

It's so bright outside, still. It makes you happy just to look at it, the sky as thin and blue as airmail paper, sunshine, and – now Hal can't suppress a squawk – his dad at the barrier. Hal's dad, waiting for them in a dark blue mac that reaches almost to the floor. The fabric spills around him as he crouches to the ground on one knee, his arms held wide, and Hal can't wait to throw himself against him. His dad has long hair! Hal can see it lift from his face as he moves.

Hal has never imagined a train station like this: open-air, not even a tunnel for the tracks to disappear into. He can hear seagulls screeching, though he can't see any yet. A white picket fence runs all the way to his dad, the only other person there. Hal feels Anna's grip tighten around his fingers before she releases him.

'Come on,' he urges, wanting her to run with him so that they will reach his dad together.

But she's not moving and his dad is grinning like the Joker. For a moment Hal forgets her as everything goes blurry and he flies through the air into his dad's arms.

'You're so big!' says his dad and Hal wriggles as Christopher's coat wraps around him. 'You're heavy now!' he says, his chin sandpapering Hal's cheek. This part is always a shock to Hal: the roughness of his dad's

224

skin, especially when he hasn't seen him for a while, and there's the lovely, horrible smell of tobacco in his hair. Hal hangs over Christopher's shoulder, he's almost winded with excitement, shouting, 'Come on, Mum!' to Anna, who's still fussing with a buckle on their bag.

'Wait until you see where I'm living,' says Christopher. 'You'll love it. You'll be able to see the sea from your own bed.'

When she catches up, Hal thinks Anna looks like she's been sneezing. Swimmy eyes and red cheeks give it away. 'Here's Mum,' he says, feeling rather grown-up; as if he's introducing his parents to one another, like it's his party.

'You all right, Anna?' His dad must have noticed her face too.

Anna sounds short of breath. 'Almost two years, isn't it?'

Hal watches her eyes as she scans his father up and down, not settling on anything in particular.

'You look different,' she says, frowning slightly. 'Is everything OK?'

Christopher rubs his chin, as if he's about to tell them a joke. 'No beard, is that it?' he says.

'You didn't have one then, did you?' she says.

Hal notices that so far all his parents have done is ask each other questions.

'Will you last?' says Anna, turning to Hal. 'Do you need the loo?'

Hal can't think about toilets at a time like this.

'No!' he yelps. All he wants to do is run and leap about.

'Can we go to your new flat now, Dad? Can we see the sea?'

'Do you mind walking, Anna?' asks Christopher. 'It's all downhill from here.'

'Whatever,' she says.

'Do you want me to take the bag? And . . .' Hal feels his dad's breath in his hair, nuzzling his scalp. 'And I'm glad you came, Anna, after all. You can't imagine how much I've missed' – he gives Hal a squeeze – 'this.'

'We'll see how it goes then,' says Anna.

Hal wishes she'd hug him too, or hug his dad, or just touch one of them to show she's there with them. But she's looking away from them, back along the track.

'Yeah, suck it and see,' says Christopher, and when he laughs Hal catches Anna biting her lip.

Anna maintains several feet between them the whole way to his dad's and walks with the bag squashed to her chest. Christopher doesn't set Hal on his feet like he expected him to but walks with him hugged to his side. 'Big bear, little bear,' he says. Meg floats briefly into Hal's mind. Because of Meg, the word 'girlfriend' will for evermore make Hal think of someone with a sing-song voice and soft hair.

Meg and his dad usually walked arm in arm. Or they swung Hal between them, though sometimes Meg complained that it made her back hurt. Meg had lots of really mad jumpers, dayglo pink and green stripy ones, and Hal's favourite, which was electric blue with yellow smileys on the front.

Hal clings around his dad's neck so that when Christopher swallows he feels his Adam's apple knock against the skin of his arm like a knuckle. It's funny seeing his dad without Meg.

'Breathe that air,' his dad says, swelling out his own chest so Hal is hugged even tighter.

The hill winds towards the sea, between rows of houses painted in the soft colours of ice creams and biscuits. Gulls, the only white in the sky, call out like nasty babies. 'Better than pigeons any day,' Hal says.

At the foot of the hill, between the road and the sea, there's a wide stretch of sandy ground dotted with caravans.

'Look, there it is, my flat, above the café.' Christopher points up at a couple of windows on the corner, opposite the caravans. 'Any closer and I'd be in the ocean,' he says. 'What do you think?'

They had stopped in front of a big mermaid painted on the front of a café. 'Wicked!' She is all pink-skinned and smiley, leaning against one side of the door, combing her golden hair which falls in a cascade, framing the café's entrance.

'Did you paint her, Dad?' Hal breathes in deep, preparing his chest for pride.

'No, Tamsin did her,' Christopher replies, and Anna says: 'Tamsin?'

'She's one of the waitresses here,' he explains. 'She painted the mermaid at the same time as I painted the inside of the place, but it's only ordinary blue.' Tamsin's uncle owns the café, he says, as well as three guest houses. Nothing touched since the seventies. 'All coffee and cream,' he says. 'Plenty of work painting that lot. That's how I got the flat. Perk of the job.'

'I might have guessed,' says Anna, with a mysterious sort of a snort.

Beyond the mermaid door the café is closed but smells oily. Christopher leads them behind the tall counter and up some creaky stairs of cracked tomato-red linoleum. The cooking smell seems stronger when they reach the top than it had been among the empty tables. The stairs emerge straight into a sitting room with a sloping ceiling. Hal's eye is drawn to the big telly in the corner.

'Doesn't this chip-pan stench get right in your clothes?' asks Anna, sniffing loudly.

'Mmm, doughnuts,' says Hal, appreciatively. 'Smells lovely.'

'Don't know about doughnuts,' says Christopher, 'but we can have our breakfast down there tomorrow if you like. Nice eggs straight from the chickens out the back. Come and see, Hal, you can watch them from the window here.' Christopher scrunches back the brittle-smelling net curtains for Hal to see out. 'You'll probably get woken by that randy old cockerel down there before you get used to it,' he says.

'We're only staying the two nights, don't forget,' says Anna. 'I don't suppose that's long enough to get used to anything much, not even clucking.'

Hal is fighting back some annoying tears, holding his dad's hand and looking out of the sitting-room window at a run of sagging chicken wire and the hens scratching the earth in the garden below. He can smell the ancient dust in the nets and the window tastes bitter, like match ends.

'Funny,' says Anna, joining him there. 'Your dad, not being in town.'

'It's the siren's song,' says Christopher, moving to stand behind her so they almost touch. 'The sea,' he says into her ear, so close that his lips almost brush her neck. He points to it out of the window, his arm over her shoulder, while she stands very still with her hands on the sill. He must think she's blind, Hal thinks, but all the same he's subsumed by a sudden wave of happiness.

In fact, you can't see anything much worth looking at *but* the sea; there's the garden with its tufty chickens and edging of frothy blue and mauve hydrangeas, there's scree, rusty metal rails, sand and caravans as well, but the vast blue glitterbed of sea fills their eyes.

'It's where a Pisces *should* live,' Christopher sighs, his hand still resting on Anna's arm.

Hal says: "You're Pisces as well, aren't you, Mum?' but she doesn't even nod, though he's sure she's heard him. Instead she pulls away, says: 'I suppose it was Meg's idea? Moving out here?'

Why does she have to bring Meg into it? Hal wishes she wouldn't. Normally Anna calls Meg 'Smeg', though Hal doesn't have the faintest idea why. He just knows it would be very rude if she started calling her Smeg right now, here.

'Yeah, Meg wanted to move here.' His dad says it quietly, like it's a confession. Or an apology.

'Right,' says Anna. 'So where—'

'It was the silence. I think it got to her.' Christopher interrupts her before she asks. 'That, and I've stopped drinking.'

'Right.' Anna flushes again, stepping back into the room. 'So, it's goodbye Johnny Walker.'

'Yeah, him as well,' says Christopher, propping his backside against the windowsill, his arms folded, facing where she stands with nowhere to run to in the middle of the room.

'Good,' she says finally, and Hal wonders what he can say to stop everything feeling so awkward.

'Can I see my room now, Dad?'

Sometimes Hal wished he had his own bedroom in London. At home, his bed is in the corner of his mum's room because it's only a one-bedroom flat, and he's supposed to sleep in a dark space between the wall and the bookcase that Anna's pulled across the room to divide his space from hers. Because of bad dreams, he usually sleeps in Anna's bed with her; she never seems to mind too much. He prefers her side of the room because of the window. The good thing about his part is that she lets him draw on the wall, but the bad thing is that he's already used up most of the bits he can reach. Some of his drawings make him cringe they're so babyish. Silly smiling figures with legs growing straight out of potato heads, instead of having bodies which is how he can draw people now. It's good that she lets him draw on the wall though: normal pictures can be taken down and thrown in the bin, even if you use lots of Sellotape and Blu-Tac.

'So, what do you think?' Christopher stands at the door and waves his arm into the small room, like a salesman. 'Do you like your bedroom?' Hal catches sight of Bob the Builder smiling at him from a poster and thinks: How long is it since I've seen you, Dad?

'I like the curtains,' he says. 'Did you get them just for me?'

'Yeah. I thought they were kind of like Action Man's curtains,' says Christopher.

Hal notices that they don't quite reach the bottom of the window, but who cares? They're made of green and grey camouflage material. And the bed!

'Oh, Dad, cool! It's Action Man's duvet.' Hal bounces on his knees because of the sloping ceiling.

Christopher says to Anna: 'I got the stuff from Army Surplus and had Tamsin from the café run it all up for him.'

Anna nods, smiling. 'You've done well, Chris,' she says.

'Do you want your mum to sleep in here with you?' asks his dad. 'I think the bed's just about big enough.'

'Where else?' Anna's smiling, her head on one side, her face shining in the late light from the west. Hal's sure he's never seen her look so beautiful. With her long golden hair and pink lips she'd pass for a mermaid any day.

'Sofa?' suggests Christopher, and Hal glances at his dad and catches him wink.

They're both laughing now, and although he doesn't know what the joke is, Hal joins in when Anna punches Christopher lightly on the arm.

'You don't change, do you? Shouldn't *you* take the sofa? I'm your guest.'

Anna looks so happy that Hal decides to try to make

his parents laugh at every opportunity. He pulls silly dinosaur faces while they eat cheese on toast and sliced red apples.

'Has he gone mental, or what?' says his dad.

Hal takes off most of his clothes and dances in his pants in front of the telly when they curl on the sofa with mugs of tea to watch *Top of the Pops*. Blur are number one and they're much better than Oasis. He's glad that his parents agree with each other about things.

In the bathroom, his mum and dad sit cross-legged on the floor while Hal splashes around, pretending he can swim. The bath is old and it's like sitting on grit and his dad's soap doesn't smell so nice: it's yellow streaked with grey like a piece of old marble. It's a shame they keep talking, though, because Hal can hear the sea when they're quiet. It feels special hearing the sea swell and sloosh against the sand at the same time as you're sliding to and fro, your own waves slip-slapping against your skin.

'Lovely colour you've done,' says Anna, looking around the room, nodding like she's in a shop, like she's about to buy something she can't quite afford.

The bathroom is freshly painted in a pale green, misty like seedless grapes. Hal looks for signs of the grape colour on his dad, but he's clean. Usually Christopher has speckles caught in his hair, sometimes on the backs of his hands, like sugar strands on a cake.

Hal catches Anna gesture at the bath. 'He's very proud of you, you know,' she confides in an audible whisper, then adds at normal volume: 'He told his new teacher all about you when he went for his try-out at proper school, didn't you, Hal?'

Yes, Hal had felt rather boastful at the time. 'My dad's a painter,' he told Miss Sanders.

'Of walls,' Anna said. 'Not pictures.'

'And he did the laundry. It was a really big job.' Hal wanted Miss Sanders to be really impressed. Just as Hal himself had been when he watched his dad paint around the laundry machines in swift, unwavering lines, as if the grey paint simply unwound from his brush like tape.

Christopher and Anna are deep in conversation, so it's hopeless trying to listen to the sea. He interrupts them, asking for more hot water. His dad is telling his mum that he's going back to school. 'It's time I got some exams,' he says. 'And Janine says she'll lend me her computer if I do a course at the Tech.'

'Can I do the hot tap again?'

Anna says: 'What about Hal?' She doesn't look very pleased all of a sudden and Hal wonders if it's just because she hates his Auntie J so much. As his dad mumbles on about computer courses and grants, Hal thinks about Janine, about the last time he was allowed to see her.

He'd been with his dad and Meg and Auntie J at the stock cars and his mum had been horrible to Auntie J when she brought him back in a taxi. She'd snatched him through the half-open door with such

233

sudden strength that his feet flew in behind the rest of him and Auntie J said: 'Not so rough!'

Hal had to catch his breath. It was as though he had been stupid and she was saving him from the wheels of a car. She smelled cross, like raw onions.

'It's late, so—' And so angry, she spat few words as he shrank inside his coat. She grabbed the carrier bag of clothes from his Auntie J, who didn't smile at Anna. Come to think of it, they'd given that up months before. Auntie J's face was all pointed and foxy above her fur collar and he had tried to wave to her, making the movement as tiny and close to his coat as he could.

Back inside, Anna pushed him to the bathroom. He saw her hands shake as she undid the toggles of his coat.

The monstrous pipes chugged, while Hal stood, silencing himself, a soft, naked thing in the steaming, windowless cube of bathroom. Anna was kneeling, holding him so tight that he could feel her heart banging against his ear. She made him get into the bath too hot, he danced from foot to foot, the water stinging prickles up to his knees.

'I can't sit down,' he yelped.

'You'll be able to in a moment,' she told him, grim-faced, as though he'd done something bad, as though he deserved it.

He flinched more later, when he heard her confess how she had felt undressing him. 'Full of hate,' she said into the phone. 'Like I was skinning an animal.' He understood then that the bath had to be hot to wash Meg away. He heard her crying while she spoke to whoever it was she always spoke to. 'I can't help it.' He could hear her blowing her nose. 'I can't stand it if he smells of her.' And he remembered how she shuddered when she chased the suds down the plughole with the rubber spray.

In the grape-coloured bathroom, Hal curls up on the floor with a towel. Christopher says: 'You're too big to be a little egg now you know!'

'I'm not.' Hal tries to burrow, to get snug, but his dad's towel is thin and grey and the carpet smells disgusting, like Brussels sprouts, or something worse.

'You'd have to be a socking great ostrich, not a baby bird,' says his dad. It doesn't matter. Hal wants to get up off the floor anyway.

'He's still my little egg at home,' says Anna, returning from the kettle. 'We have big big towels, don't we, Hal?'

It's true. Hal likes warm, dark spaces. At home he crouches into a ball on the bathroom floor and Anna tucks the towel around him. He curls into a small, delighted eggling, while she pretends to walk in and find him there. 'Who left this little egg on the floor? I wonder what's inside?' She has to crack the little egg all over for ages before he emerges from the secret, dark space. He hatches into the light of the bathroom.

'Why, it's a sweet little bird!'

'What's a goo goo? Can I have one?' Hal is woken, as Christopher predicted, by the sound of the cockerel. 'It's not cock-a-doodle-doo at all,' he says. 'Listen. It's cook a goo goo.'

Anna gives him her tender, pale-lipped, morning smile from the pillow beside him and for an instant he can't work out why she's there, her hair all fuzzy over her usual old pink sleeping shirt. He must have dreamt about snuggling up to her in his dad's bed, after the noise and thinking it was the cockerel and, even though it was pitch-black, managing not to bang into anything on his way through the sitting room, and the sound of the sea, and their breathing getting louder, guiding him to them. Anna's skin was buttery, warm; she wasn't wearing the pink shirt in the dream. She had groaned and rolled towards him and then he fell asleep, enclosed by her bare arms and her lemony scent.

Anna sits up and rubs the sleepy-dust from the corners of her eyes. Hal catches a faint whiff of warm lemons when she lifts her arm. Weirdly, he can still recall the early morning smell of his parents together, at Checkpoint Road it must have been, from when he used to crawl between them before it was light. Lemons like now and warm and sort of eggy, but not unpleasant. He had never got into his dad's bed with Meg. He always just sat on the covers, though Meg said he could get in with them if he wanted, when it was winter, and she and his dad watched cartoons in bed all morning, turned up loud because of the traffic.

Hal stretches and looks around him. Mostly he looks at Anna, as she untangles her hair with her fingers, and he tries to sift memories, to separate dreams. He would ask her if she's been here all night, but he catches sight of three brand-new shrimp nets on bamboo poles leaning against the wall and excitement bubbles up inside him. 'Let's go,' he says. 'Get Dad out of bed and let's go to the beach.'

It wasn't really the best beach for swimming, his dad said, because of all the rocks, and it feels like hours before they catch any shrimps. Hal's neck began to ache from staring down into his net.

'Let's pretend we're shipwrecked,' says Anna. His dad had been talking for ages to a couple of men with motorbikes up the top, where they had bought the Disney buckets and some cans of Coke from a kiosk that also sold ice cream.

'We'll have some later,' said his mum when he asked, and she told him they'd have to earn their lollies by catching enough shrimps for supper. She'd been boasting all morning about how good she used to be at it, not that she'd been near the sea, oh, since who knows when. Her feet were bare, and she had rolled her jeans to above her knees and she was wearing her red bra as a top because she'd only packed Hal's swimming things, not her own.

'We're going down now, Chris,' she said to his dad, who was leaning against the wall, watching one of the men roll a cigarette. She muttered: 'You'd think he'd introduce us.'

Hal shouted over to his dad, asked him if he'd get him an ice cream.

'Yeah, in a minute,' he said, and then he nodded towards Hal and said to the men: 'That's my kid, come for the weekend from London. That's Hal.'

Hal felt he and Anna were very alone, on a desert island probably, in spite of all the other people on the sandy part of the beach. They flinched in their bare feet over sharp black rocks, headed for the wider pools that the tide had left behind. They settled by the shallowest and dipped their nets into lukewarm water full of seaweed and promise, but pulled up nets full of nothing more exciting than sand and bladderwrack that smelled of sewage. Further up the beach two seagulls squabbled noisily over a crust left over from someone's picnic. They pulled it between them like a tug of war, until a girl about Hal's age, in a bright orange swimsuit, ran at them, flinging sand.

Hal is still watching the girl as Christopher catches up with them, flicking the end of a roll-up at the water, just as Anna caught the first shrimp.

'Dad, you forgot the ice cream,' says Hal, but he doesn't have time to be disappointed because of Anna's excitement.

'Look, look,' she says. 'Oh, Hal, it's quite big.'

'Yeah,' says Christopher, peering into her net, 'practically a lobster.'

'I'll get you a lolly in a minute, Hal,' promises Anna. 'Now help me get the prawn into the bucket.'

'Shrimp,' says Hal, studying the minuscule sliver of grey, jumping against the gauzy green net like a cartoon flea.

Christopher prises a limpet off the rocks by bashing it with a stone so that it oozes orange goo. He throws it into their pool. 'There, now you'll get somewhere,' he says, dusting his hands together, casual but expert. There are five or six much bigger shrimps in Anna's net. Christopher wanders off with a heavy stone to hammer more limpets and Anna announces that she can't bear to touch the shrimps after all.

'They feel too acrobatic, too alive,' and Hal has to tweezer hers as well as his own off the nets with his useful little boy's fingers and hop them into the buckets. For a while he and Anna forget all about his dad.

As far as Hal is concerned, there is only him and his mum, foraging for their food on the island; it's a matter of life or death. For a moment he doesn't even notice when Christopher reappears at his side.

'I think there'll be some monster ones in this pool,' he says, throwing in a handful of smashed-up limpets, steering Hal to a deeper pool, much further out, which is shadowed by a large, overhanging rock.

'And, look, there's room for a little bum on this comfy ledge. Come and fish with me,' he says plaintively. Hal looks round. Anna is still picking seaweed from her net.

His dad pats the rock beside him, adding, in a scratchy voice, a bit like a baddy in a film: 'Come with me, Hal. We can talk of many things: of shoes – and ships – and sealing wax . . .'

'What? What do you mean?' Hal doesn't know why his dad has suddenly started talking rubbish.

'Of cabbages – and kings . . .'

'I don't like it when you do that voice.'

'And why the sea is boiling hot . . .' Christopher continues all the same. 'And whether pigs have wings.'

Christopher raises his eyebrows so they almost touch in the middle, while Hal stabs the sand with the end of his net, feeling hot and prickly and stupid. Why was it that he could never understand what grown-ups were talking about?

'It's from *Alice in Wonderland*.' His mum is at his side. She explains. 'Me and your dad had to learn it at school. The walrus and the carpenter get all the little oysters to go for a walk with them and then when they're far from their beds they gobble them up with bread and butter.'

'Dad, I remember when you had oysters once,' says Hal, so suddenly it felt to him as though someone else had spoken through his lips. 'You hit the oyster with your hammer and a bit of shell went right in your eye.'

'Yes, that's right,' says Christopher, looking along the bamboo of his net, down into the pool. 'What an amazing memory you have!'

'Yes, and you went to hospital for an operation.' Hal could remember his dad's eye, the red on it, like a marble rolling around in a horrible wet pouch where he had pulled down the skin for Anna to look.

'You're getting confused,' says Anna, wandering back to the bucket with an empty net.

'No, I didn't go to hospital,' says Christopher.

'Yes, you did,' insists Hal. 'Mum and I came to see you and you were in a bed with a blue fuzzy blanket and the floor was white and I slipped over and then we left you there.'

'I think you might be muddling things up a bit,' says Christopher, turning to watch Anna walking away.

'I'm not,' insists Hal. 'You swore and Mum was crying.'

Christopher turns back to face him. 'Really, Hal, it did hurt like hell, but I just rinsed my eye with Optrex. Honest.' He jumps down from the rock, although Hal had been about to join him there on the ledge. 'Talking of boiling hot sea, I think these poor little things might be fish soup if we don't change their water soon.'

Hal has to help him. They tip all three hauls into one of the nets, the shrimps buck and jump like rain hammering a puddle, while Christopher replaces the water in the bottom of the buckets by scooping them into the sea. Hal is pleased to see his mum coming back from the top. He knew he was right about the hospital. Everyone knew Hal had a brilliant memory and he would never forget his dad there, with his black pirate's eye patch and his hair all messy; how lonely and sad he had looked when they left him.

'Hi, lovely!' Anna treads like a cat over the sharp rocks bearing lollies. 'That's enough talk about hospitals.'

As they all start back up the beach, Hal blows into his wrapper and for a split second the orange lolly smokes and freezes to his lips.

＊   ＊   ＊

When you look close you can make out each in-dividual shrimp, microscopically tiger-striped and curled round. When it is time for them to be cooked, Hal passes each little bucket in turn, so his dad can sort them all into a big sieve before swilling them under the

241

kitchen tap. Hal watches as the water flows through them while Anna stands at the stove, heating oil in a pan. When it is bubbling, Hal cranes his neck to watch as Christopher tips them from the sieve into the frying pan.

The shrimps fall as a rain-coloured mass. There is a furious burst of sizzling and wriggling, like boiling water, but they don't *look* like boiling water for more than a split second.

'Ugh, they remind me of foetuses,' says Anna, throwing down the spoon as masses of little bodies turn livid pink. 'Hundreds of human foetuses' – Hal thinks she must have burned herself – 'eight-week-old foetuses, like that photo in Janine's book. The one she made me look at.' Tears start to spring from her eyes.

Christopher grabs her wrist. 'Don't start,' he hisses. She pulls herself free, her hand a fist. He grabs her again. 'Don't ruin things, Anna,' he says.

She's yelling, pulling free: 'You're the one.' Yelling: 'You're the ruiner.'

Hal doesn't know what to do. It's like being caught in hailstones with nowhere to run.

'Anna!' Christopher shouts her name like it's a swear word and Hal wants to scream 'No!' Perhaps he does but his dad is shouting louder.

'God, Anna! Is there to be no forgiveness?' There is a shrill, 'Fuck you!' as someone sends the frying pan flying onto the floor, in a clatter of metal on stone. Oil and shrimps explode, something splashes up and burns Hal on the leg, a flash of pain, but he doesn't cry.

Hal runs from the room. He buries himself under

the camouflage quilt of the unmade bed. He breathes noisily into the pillow until it is warm against his face. He tries not to kick his leg where it is hurting. He rubs his fist back and forth, ear to cheek, cheek to ear, because of the pain. But it is no use.

'Some things are unforgivable.' She is screaming.

This is when Hal remembers something from before. Even though the shouting is reaching its peak in the kitchen, something is forcing its way through all the noise, worming its way from the dark sludge at the back of his mind.

It's the hospital. But it isn't his dad propped up in bed in a room of blue and white and disinfectant. It's her. His mum. Hal wants her to cuddle him but Anna's hands rest in a knot on a fuzzy blue blanket pulled across her lap. Above the blanket, her face is as white as the shirt she's wearing.

When it's time, she rises from the bed, but one hand stays put, like she's warming her tummy through her skirt, and they leave the hospital through glass revolving doors. It's drizzling, cold. Headlamps glare from puddles all the way down the long street. His dad's coat is hairy, rough. It's the last Hal gets of him before he's pushing him into the minicab after her. That's when Hal sees the stain. He sees something on her long washed-out skirt as it folds around her legs before she sits down. It's just a darkening like spilt ink where her skirt's all creased from sitting on the bed. Anna arranges herself, carefully, and Hal is so distracted by what he's just seen that he fails to register that his dad isn't joining them. The door shuts with a heavy clunk and

Christopher turns heel on the pavement. Hal sits beside her, but his face is pressed to the window, trying not to lose sight of his dad walking away along the wet street. The driver starts the engine and Hal continues to wave to the dismal, grey figure until he can't see him any more. It's only when they turn the corner that his mum tells him where they are going.

Reach

Wednesday, and Kim's mother goes up to the school for parents' evening.

'She's doing badly, then.'

'Well, no, not exactly. She can read and write. Quite well for a seven-year-old, as it happens.'

Her daughter's class teacher pushes Kim's report around on the desk with her fingertips and Alice waits for her to pull the words together.

'She's just not an easy child to reach, Mrs Bell.'

Home is the end house of the terrace above the sea-front. From her bedroom window, Kim can see over the rooftops to the old pier and, beyond it, the last curve of sand before the headland. Seagulls hover on thermals, suspended, and Kim watches them at the window, swaying, waiting. From here she will see her mother when she comes home from the school.

In the door and then chopping, no sitting down between and no hello either. But this is not unusual. Kim's description of her mother in one of her schoolbooks: she always cooks with her coat on.

Kim waits an extra minute or so after her mother has passed along the path beneath her windowsill to the back door and the kitchen. Face still pressed to the wall, and so still hidden from the street below, Kim listens a while to the pot and pan noises, then goes downstairs to find Alice: early evening, getting dark, working by the blue light of the grill-flame, chops spitting underneath. Kim stands in the doorway a minute or so, but Alice does not turn. An evening like any other: potato peelings on the counter, mother's back at the sink. Kim wonders briefly if she got the day right, if Alice has been to the parents' evening after all, but decides against mentioning it. Joins her brother in the sitting room instead, watches TV with Joseph until dinner.

If she's staying, Alice will take her coat off and eat with her children. Tonight, she has a cup of tea and makes sure the washing-up is underway before she heads off out to work again. A reminder of bedtimes and a brisk kiss each on her way to the door. This too is normal, so Kim breathes a little easier, dries the plates slowly that Joseph washes fast. Watches the familiar sight of her mother's back receding down the garden path. She can close her eyes and see Alice making her way down the hill to the seafront. Keys gripped in her right hand, left holding her collar together against the wind.

Kim's eyes are sore tonight, scratchy, her lids heavy. She keeps them closed, keeps her mind's eye on her mother a little longer. Imagines the sea flat behind Alice as she opens the salon door, surface skimmed into ripples by the wind. She knows her mother chose the shop for its view across the beach, along the seafront. Has heard her telling the customers, watched her polish the wide glass window clean of rain and salt. Alice plays no music in her salon, she does not talk much. There is calm when she cuts and sets hair. In the summer with the door open and the sea air. In the winter with the hum of the dryers and the wide window misted against the dark afternoons.

Kim opens her eyes again at the kitchen window, her mother long gone, brother back in front of the television. She dries her hands on the damp tea towel, flicks the last crumbs of dinner off the kitchen table. Kim tries to rest her forehead on the cool surface, but can't; her neck stiff, resisting, caught somehow by her shoulders. The days before the parents' evening have been edgy, and she can't relax now, not sure what to do with all the worry.

When Alice is asked about her business, she says she makes a decent living for her family. Margins are tight with debts like hers, but she has no gaps in her appointment book to speak of, few concerns to raise with her accountant.

When Alice thinks about her daughter, as she does this evening, she sees her pale eyes and paler hair, the solid flesh of her face with its closed, impassive expression. Stubby thumbs sucked white and soft and drawn into tight, damp fists.

Alice has long fingers and strong nails: neat ovals without cuticles. She does them last thing before she leaves the salon, after the work is done. Alone with her thoughts and files. Rubbing the cream in, hand over hand over hand.

She didn't argue with what the teacher said this afternoon. *Not an easy child*. Alice has heard those words before now: from different sources, in different disguises, so many times she has come to expect them. Would never say so, but she agrees.

With Joseph it was simple: love arrived with him. Fury when the midwife carried him away from her across the delivery room to be washed and weighed. Kim was early. Only a few weeks after Frank had gone. Gas and air and Alice kept telling the midwife she wasn't ready for the baby, but she came anyway. No tears and not much pain either. And then it took Alice years to get used to her: her rare smiles, her uncooperative arms and legs.

Alice hears the pigeons shuffling in the eaves above the doorway as she locks up. The soft, quivering noise they make in their throats. The water behind her is calm, just a slight breeze coming in across the sands, breaking up the surface a little, touching her cheek as she turns the key in the lock and up the street towards home.

Thursday and Kim is ill.

She vomits once at school. A pile of sawdust and a smell in the corridor. Again when she gets home. Joseph heats the dinner Alice has left in the fridge for them, and when Kim throws up a third time, he phones the shop.

'Can you come home now, Mum?'

'Run her a bath and put her to bed, love. Please. I'll not be late. Make sure she drinks something.'

Joseph does as he is told, and his sister is silent, compliant. When Alice comes home it is dark and Kim is running a fever: dry heat and then sudden sweats which glue her pale hair to her forehead.

Friday morning. Kim can't stand up to walk to the toilet, and so when she needs to throw up again, her mother finds her crawling out into the bright hall.

'No school for you, then.'

An unwieldy dead weight with limbs, Alice carries her daughter to the bathroom.

Cold black tea. Chalky taste of the aspirin mashed into jam and eaten with a teaspoon. Alice is home for fifteen minutes at lunchtime, keeps her coat on. Stands her daughter naked by the radiator, washes her down with a flannel and hot water in a red plastic bowl. Kneeling next to her clammy body, its awkward joints and dimples, soft belly. Kim's eyes are half closed and she sways as Alice works. Hot cloth on face and neck, round ears, down spine, between toes and fingers. Skin turning cool where the flannel has been.

Kim lies in new pyjamas when Alice leaves for work again. Under new sheets and tucked blankets, curtains drawn against the day. The slats of the bunk above her shift and birds' eyes peep from the mattress. Beaks and wings. Kim calls for her mum, but she's gone now, back down the road. The hairspray smell of Alice left with her, and Kim is alone with the birds again. They fly out from between the slats, grey wings beating the hot air against her cheeks.

Alice always hoped it would come. Read about it in the leaflets she got from the midwives and the library. You will not always bond with your baby immediately, but this is normal and no cause for worry.

Kim arrived and Alice had two to care for. Frank gone and only one of her: didn't seem nearly enough. Joseph was four then and she would pick him up from nursery school early. To feel his hand holding her skirt as they walked home along the seafront, to have his arms fold around her neck when she lifted him up.

Alice tried holding Kim after her evening bottle, after Joseph was asleep and they could have some quiet time together, like it said in the leaflets. But it was hard and sometimes it frightened her: sitting with her baby and still feeling so little.

Red-brown spots gather in the afternoon. On the soles of Kim's feet, behind her ears, inside her eyelids. Joseph sees them when the doctor shines his torch in his sister's dark bedroom. He pulls the girl's eyelids down with his thumbs.

'I'll need to use your telephone. Call an ambulance and your mother.'

Joseph tells Kim later that they drove away with the siren on, but Kim remembers silence inside the ambulance. Looking at her mother and then following Alice's gaze to the trees and lamp-posts passing. The strip of world visible through the slit of clear window above the milk-glass in the doors.

Alice Bell's girl had meningitis and nearly died.

The customers in the salon ask concerned questions, and Alice gets a call from the health visitor, too. The woman has a good look at the clean hall, the tidy kitchen Alice leads her to. The grass in the garden is long, falls this way and that, but Alice is sure that everything else is in good order. Thinks she recognizes the health visitor, too: that she has maybe cut her hair before.

Alice gets leaflets from her. Is told about the tumbler test: roll a glass against the rash, she says. Alice thanks the woman, but thinks it's not really any good to her, this information. It's happened now, over; Kim will be home again soon.

The house is quiet after the health visitor leaves. Small. Alice sweeps her leaflets off the kitchen table, dumps them in the bin on the front on her way back to the salon.

Kim has scars. A tiny, round wound in the small of her back, where they tapped the fluid from her spine. And one on the back of her hand from the drip: skin and vein still slightly raised, puncture-mark already healing, fading with the black-turning-yellow bruise. She has fine, white scratch-lines on the soles of her feet, too, but these are more memory than reality. Pin-tip traces to check for sensation, pricks in the tops of her toes that drew blood-drops, which later become blood-spots on the hospital sheets.

The real scar is at her throat. Tracheotomy. Kim can't say the word, but this is where her fingers go at night in her hospital bed, and when she wakes. To feel the way the skin is pulled over, small folds overlapping and grown together. Like melted plastic, the beaker which fell in on itself when Joseph left it on the stove. At first the hairy ends of the stitches are there too. Six black bristles for Kim's fingertips to brush against under the dressing, to investigate in the bathroom mirror when no-one else is there to be looking. One hand on the wheely drip, the other pushing herself up on the sink, closer to the long, clean mirror and the grey-pink pucker of skin in her reflection.

Kim is back at home now, back at school. Weeks have passed already, but Alice still sees the first days in the hospital with her daughter. The pictures come at her from nowhere. When she is doing the books, while she is cutting, shopping, walking, on her way home.

From her bedroom window, Kim watches her mother in the dusk light, coming up the road. She walks with her coat unbuttoned and sometimes she stops, head down, hands deep in her pockets. Stays like that for a minute or two on the pavement before walking on.

They held Kim's body curled and still and Alice watched. Daughter's spine turned towards her, small feet pulled up below her bum. Brown iodine swirled onto her skin, and then her toes splayed as the needle went in: five separate soft pads on each foot, reaching.

They had a bed free for Alice in a room down the hall, but she stayed in the chair by Kim's bed and didn't sleep much. Awake when Kim's temperature rose again and she swallowed her tongue. The doctors drew the curtain round the bed and the fitting girl while they worked. So Alice couldn't see what they were doing any longer but still she didn't move. Stayed put, listening, while they made the hole for the tube in her daughter's neck, and took her temperature down with wet sheets around her legs. No-one asked Alice to leave and she sat in the chair, shoes off, coat on, pulled tight around her chest.

Kim has headaches, too.

Joseph watches while his sister ties the belt round her head. One of Granddad's old ones. Big buckle, cracked leather: round her forehead, over her temples. He pulls it tight for her and then she lies down, head under the blankets, nose showing. Brows pulled into a frown by the belt, jaw clenching, neck held taut against the pain.

Kim's drinks have to be warm because her teeth feel everything, and she is clumsy. Legs bruised from falls and corners, clothes stained colourful by spills. Kim has no sense of edges these days; where a glass can be placed safely, where her body can pass without damage. She creates noise and mess and the mumbling speech that the doctor said should improve quickly takes weeks to go away.

The school calls Alice in again. No parents' evening this time: a meeting with Kim's class teacher and head-mistress this time. Attendance register open on the desk between them.

'When does Kim leave the house, Mrs Bell?'

'Quarter to nine. With her brother.'

'Every morning?'

Alice nods, doesn't tell them that she leaves the house at eight twenty to open the salon. Thinks they are doubtless capable of working that one out. She reminds them.

'My daughter has been very ill.'

'Yes.'

They are writing things down and Alice is remembering again. That Kim couldn't stop herself looking at her tracheotomy wound. That the peeled ends of the dressing curled up off her neck, giving her away, gathering dust like magnets, tacky traces on her skin turning black. Alice visited her at visiting time, whispered: 'It'll get infected.' She smiled when she said it. Didn't want to tell her daughter off; just to tell her. Let her know that she had noticed. That she understood it, her curiosity.

Kim looked at her. Skin under her eyes flushing. Hands moving up to cover the dressing. Alice didn't know what that meant: whether her daughter was surprised or pleased or angry.

'Kim is what we call On Report now, Mrs Bell.'

'She could have died.'

'Yes.'

They blink at her across the desk. Sympathetic, insistent.

'I'm afraid her attendance record has to improve.'

*   *   *

Kim finds different places to spend her days. Sometimes the coast path over the headland where the wind cuts into her legs. Sometimes the burnt stubble of the fields inland, where she flies her kites made out of plastic bags. Most days it is the beach, though, where she lies down under the old pier. On her back on the cracking shingle, waves at her feet, sea wall behind her. Sodden wood, salt, seaweed and litter.

Above her, she can see the gulls' flapping battles through the gappy planks of the old walkway. Lies still, watching the starlings fly their swooping arcs around the splintered columns and rails. Cloud and wind over the water. Storm of black beak and wing reeling above her head.

Alice shuts the salon early and is home before her children. Joseph acts as though it is normal for his mother to open the door for him; Kim steps into the hallway, clutching her school bag as if it were proof of something, tell-tale damp of the day in her clothes and hair. Joseph slips upstairs to his bedroom, Kim stays silent, eyes on the wallpaper while Alice asks her why and where she has been. She watches Kim's face for a reaction but cannot read anything from her daughter's expression.

'Whatever. You'll be leaving the house with me from now on.'

'No.'

Later Alice goes over the scene again. In bed, light out, eyes open. Feels something closing down, tight around her guts. Remembers the screaming battles they had when Kim was three, four, five: doesn't want to repeat those years again. Her daughter smelled of sea and air this afternoon, it filled the corridor. Alice didn't know what to do, what to say, so she said nothing. An almost eight-year-old stranger standing in front of her. Mouth open, breath passing audibly over her small, wet teeth.

Kim doesn't know it, but the school keeps close tabs on her. Her teachers know she comes for registration and then dodges out of the gate behind the playing fields. They don't confront her; instead they call her mother and then Alice hangs up the phone in the back room of the salon, behind the closed curtain, under the noise of the dryers and cries.

Alice doesn't know it, but some mornings her daughter stands outside the salon on the front. The smell leads her there: hot air, warm skin and hair, shampoo. She doesn't go in; instead she watches her mother's face at the salon window. Eyes and cheekbones amongst the reflections. Blank sky, cold sea, ragged palms. Her mother's eyes blinking, face not moving. Lamp-posts with lights strung between, rocking in the breeze.

Another Wednesday, another week or two later, and Kim stands in the salon doorway. Alice has had the phone call already. Knows her daughter hasn't been to school, didn't expect her to show up here.

The rain slides down the windowpane, and, through the open shop door, she can hear it singing in the drains.

Alice takes her daughter's coat from her, sits her down in an empty chair. The salon is quiet and Kim spends the next few minutes watching her mother working in the mirror. She sees that Alice doesn't look at her, only out of the window, or down at her fingers, turning grey hair around the pastel shades of the plastic rollers, pink and yellow and green. Her mother's cheeks are flushed, lips drawn in, and the skin around her eyes pulled taut.

When Alice steps over to her, Kim looks away. Sees the old lady's eyes on them, under the dryer. Alice knows she is watching them, too. Has felt her customers observing her ever since Kim was ill, has grown accustomed to the scrutiny. She stands behind her daughter now. A second or two passes, and she finds herself still there. Not shouting, not angry. Just looking at the slope of her daughter's shoulders, the nape of her neck, her sodden hair.

Alice gets a clean towel from the shelves at the back and then plugs in a dryer, sets to work. At first Kim watches the rain, the gulls fighting on the rail outside, but soon she closes her eyes. Feels the pressure of her mother's fingers, how strong her hands are, how warm the air is, the low noise of the dryer.

Joanna Trollope has written eleven highly acclaimed contemporary novels: *The Choir, A Village Affair, A Passionate Man, The Rector's Wife, The Men and the Girls, A Spanish Lover, The Best of Friends, Next of Kin, Other People's Children, Marrying the Mistress* and *Girl from the South*. *Other People's Children* has recently been shown on BBC television as a major drama serial. Under the name of Caroline Harvey she writes romantic historical novels. She has also written a study of women in the British Empire, *Britannia's Daughters*. Joanna Trollope was born in Gloucestershire, where she still lives. She was appointed OBE in the 1996 Queen's Birthday Honours List for services to literature.

Miss Mackintosh

In human terms, I know I am something of a dinosaur. I know that I belong to one of those extinct categories of the human race, like hunting parsons, or housemaids, or bottle-nosed retired colonels firing off broadsides to national newspapers from genteel towns in West Sussex.

I am, you see, a spinster. Modern society, with its earnest passion for a kind of human caucus race in which none of us turns out to be a loser, would rather I described myself as a single person. This has more style to it, as a description, more dignity, less of the pathetic. To be single implies an element of independent choice in the matter. To be a spinster means that even if someone did once take you down off the shelf and give you a cursory glance, they hastily put you back again, where you have since remained, gathering universal pity and dust.

Looking back, I can see that my spinsterhood was almost destined. I was born – to my parents' undisguised embarrassment – very late in their lives, long after my three brothers, long after the substitution, in my parents' bedroom, of two single beds instead of the meagre double one in which, presumably, the boys had been conceived. They couldn't, my poor respectable parents, ever quite treat me as a *child*, in consequence. I was more of a dear little object, a doll, an ornament, to be handled with a kind of anxious respectfulness, as if I was only on loan to them and must one day be returned, in mint condition.

They started this process by calling me Lucy.

'My Lucy Locket,' my father would say, setting me carefully on a park swing whose seat he had already dusted with his handkerchief, 'my little Lucy Locket.'

I used to sit on the floor of my bedroom – pink, frilled, pristine – and look at the watercolours of little Lucy in my copy of *The Tale of Mrs Tiggywinkle*. I wondered if that was how my father actually saw me in his mind's eye, a long-ago child with a ruffle of curls under her cap, playing decorously in a picture-book farmyard, clad in a goffered white pinafore.

My mother, on the other hand, saw me as her future. She was a small, slight woman, given to nervous headaches and eczema, who I think was perhaps relieved when her three sons took themselves, and their collective maleness, off into the world. In me, however, she saw something that, if she was very careful with it, might be persuaded to stay around long enough to be quite overwhelmed by a sense of obligation. If, my mother reasoned, my childhood could be made serene enough and could be sufficiently prolonged, I might conveniently never see that it needed to be left behind. I might, in short, pass seamlessly from being a doll-child to being a doll-woman, bringing my mother cups of tea and fetching her prescriptions from the chemist.

And so it was. Lucy Mackintosh moved calmly and inconspicuously through her schooldays and then, equally uneventfully, through her college days, reading English and History. My bedroom remained my bedroom, my life at home with my parents remained as seemingly unchanged as the china dogs in their appointed places on the sitting-room mantelpiece, or the checked kettleholder on its particular hook in the kitchen. In modern parlance, I suppose you could say that I was *groomed*, very successfully, to be the daughter at home, the daughter who could, in slow remorseless time, become the parent to the parents. There was no need for me to marry, after all. My brothers had all married and between them had produced seven grandchildren, so what need was there for more? Much better, far better, for little Lucy Locket to stay locked up.

I don't – you must be sure of this – speak with resentment. Even if my parents were acting consciously (which I doubt), I was, after all, perfectly complicit in this process. For a long, long time, even if I didn't actively like my life, I didn't dislike it either. It was all I knew, all I was comfortable with. I moved between being Lucy at home, and Miss Mackintosh at work, at the library in our town, where I rose to be head librarian without either difficulty or opposition. The head of the county library service called me Lucy, but everyone else seemed unable to call me anything but Miss Mackintosh. It seemed to seal my fate, really, to confirm myself, in my own eyes, as the archetypal, unmarried, unmarriageable, daughter at home. Miss Mackintosh, librarian, spinster of this parish. It's almost a parody, isn't it?

Then my mother fell ill. She, who had never smoked, developed first a lump in her breast and then a secondary tumour in her lung. She was ill for five years, five long years dominated by hospital and clinical visits, by radiotherapy and chemotherapy, by her diminishing little figure in a chair by the sitting-room fire, coughing her ceaseless small dry cough into tissues impregnated with balsam. At her funeral I stood in a black-clad group with my father and brothers and sisters-in-law and nephews and nieces and wondered, disrespectfully, how my life would change.

'Will you be all right?' said Alice, my most sympathetic sister-in-law.

I looked at her. She had red hair and big earrings. I said, 'Without Mother, you mean?'

'No,' she said. 'I meant with your father. Will you be all right looking after your father now?'

I looked at my father. He seemed to have grown smaller.

'I don't know,' I said truthfully to Alice. I smiled at her. 'I'll let you know,' I added, untruthfully. When, in all my forty-two years, had I ever let anyone know anything of that kind?

Work was a salvation. It wasn't just that I am good at it, being well-read and patient with the public and competent with information technology, but also that it gave me a wider world. Without my mother, my home life diminished suddenly, dramatically. I could hardly believe the difference her absence made domestically, a difference I rather doubted my father's death could possibly have made. My father moved out of the marital bedroom into a narrow slip of a room which had never been used for anything more than the storing of suitcases and apples, and restricted himself to a diet of soup, and cereals, and bananas mashed with a fork. He also took up an unheralded, uncharacteristic, querulousness with me.

I was, I must admit it, entirely taken aback. I was used to my father's courteous indulgence of me, his almost passive acceptance of life the way his wife and daughter had designed it. I was not at all prepared to be found fault with.

'Well,' my father began saying, rattling his newspaper, 'what about your future?'

I would say something anodyne, something soothing, one of the kinds of things my mother had said to reassure him she was not dying. But I was not my mother and my replies only made my father shake his paper more vehemently.

'I shan't always be here, you know,' he'd say. 'I shan't always be here to give you a home. And then what? Then what, Lucy? Look at you, over forty and still in the house you were born in! What's the matter with you, Lucy? What's the matter?' And then he would give his paper an extra-vigorous flap in my startled direction, and shout, 'It's a woman's *duty* to be married!'

I wish I could say that I was able simply to laugh my father off, turn him aside, confident that I was living the life I had chosen to live, and that he was simply fossilized in values that had no relevance any more. But I couldn't. I couldn't evade him, somehow, I couldn't smile at him serenely, show him how impervious I was to all that he was saying, all that he was implying. I found myself staring at my own reflection in the mirror in my bedroom – the mirror I had had since my fourteenth birthday – and seeing there, rather than a whole, vital person, a kind of shadow instead, a cipher, an echo. I began to look to myself like someone who isn't really there, to think of myself as someone who knows nothing because, in the great scheme of human things, they have experimented with so little. I began to picture myself, with something approaching terror, as little Lucy Locket, trapped in her pinafore, but with grotesquely ageing features.

This frame of mind – or any profoundly unsettling frame of mind, as many of you will know from experience – is not conducive to competence in any area of life. I started forgetting to do things – like turning on the washing machine, or buying my father's bananas (Caribbean only) – and I started to find concentration difficult at work. I made mistakes, I duplicated memos, I failed to follow through. I found myself watching familiar library members – the old men who came in to read the newspapers, the conscientious families, the Catherine Cookson ladies, the local historian – and going off into speculative daydreams about their private lives, their private nightmares. I'd try and imagine sorrow and disappointment, and shabby flats, and money worries, in order to make my own fears the less, in order to persuade myself that nothing in me or my life had changed beyond the physical absence of my mother. I tried to convince myself that if I denied enough for long enough, it would finally give up and go away.

I can't now remember exactly what broke me, but I know it was something trivial, something like failing to follow a computer procedure correctly, or mislaying a report I had laboured long to write. I am not someone who weeps easily, I never have been; not weeping runs in the family, even at funerals. But that day, I found myself crying. I say found myself, because I don't remember starting, I don't recall giving myself *permission* to start, but there I was, in my little cupboard of an office, sobbing my heart out, my forehead against the grey steel top of my old-fashioned filing cabinet.

I sensed someone coming in. I sensed, without turning, that someone came in and hesitated and said something incoherent and went out again. And then two people came in and a man's voice said, 'Miss Mackintosh, I wonder if we can help you?'

I raised my head in a kind of horror. What had I done? How must I seem? I stared ahead, straight across the filing cabinet, my mouth agape.

'As it was the lunch hour,' the voice said, 'Dawn came to find me, there being no colleagues around, and my being such an habitué of the place. We would so much like to help you.'

I turned around slowly. What I must have looked like, I can't imagine, wet and raw and staring. Dawn, my latest little trainee school-leaver, was standing there wearing the expression you might wear after witnessing

269

a traffic accident, shocked and disbelieving. Beside her stood the man I knew to be our local historian, a man known to find working in a public place, like a library, preferable to working in his own home.

'I am Douglas Gilchrist,' he said gravely. 'I think you know me well by sight.'

I nodded. I put my hand up to my terrible face. I had seen him for years, quietly in and out of the library several times a week, and sometimes – there had been much gossip about this – interrupted by a young man; different young men over time, but all of a certain kind, of a certain physical obviousness that contrasted greatly with Douglas Gilchrist's seemly books and files and researches.

Mr Gilchrist looked down at Dawn.

'Could you manage for ten minutes on your own, Dawn, until a colleague returns from lunch? Could you manage if I were to take Miss Mackintosh out for a cup of coffee?'

Dawn nodded vigorously. She looked as if she could manage anything rather than the sight of her boss in floods of uncontrollable tears. She whipped my coat – so neat, so navy blue – off the hook behind the door and held it up for me to put on, with all the eagerness of a puppy.

Mr Gilchrist did not take me for a cup of coffee. He took me instead down an alley off the market place to a pub called the Three Feathers, whose doors I had never darkened in all my years of living in the town, and bought me a double brandy. He didn't ask me what I wanted, he simply bought it. I watched him standing at the bar taking money out of his trouser pocket in that nonchalant way men have, and reflected that no man in all my life, even my father and my brothers, had ever sat me down in a pub at one thirty in the afternoon, and bought me an alcoholic drink.

'And now,' said Mr Gilchrist, putting the brandy down in front of me, 'I think you had better tell me all about it.'

It was as if someone had turned a key, pressed a button. It was as if I had been storing things up in a cupboard all my life, layering them neatly on shelves until the cupboard was so full it would scarcely close, and then Mr Gilchrist, a virtual stranger, came along and opened the doors without warning, so that everything fell out, in an avalanche, at his feet. I don't think it even crossed my mind that to spill every bean I possessed at the first half-kind offer, like some melodramatic teenager, was an outrageous, almost demented way, to conduct myself. I just looked at Mr Gilchrist, sitting there, leaning slightly forward, his spectacles folded in the top pocket of his tweed jacket, and I started talking.

I really couldn't tell you how long I talked. I know it was long enough to drink my brandy, and another, and a cup of black coffee, and to grow so warm in my animation that I needed to take my coat off. I am sure that there was almost nowhere I didn't go, no attic of my heart I didn't rummage in, piling up everything from all those years around Mr Gilchrist's suede-clad feet. I had been brought up to distrust men in suede shoes, but that afternoon I would gladly have knelt on the pub's gaudy, grubby carpet and kissed those shoes.

I might, I'm afraid, have gone on for ever. I might have gone on until the pub closed and a discreetly ordered ambulance came to take me away to whatever well-meaning disastrous scenario is now devised for the insane. But Mr Gilchrist came to my rescue. After listening and listening, he leaned slowly even further forward, and then he said,

'This is such a relief to me.'

I stared at him. My mouth, now loosened by all this talking, hung open.

'A *relief?*'

'Oh yes,' he said. He smiled at me. 'Such a relief, Miss Mackintosh.'

I shook my head. I made a clumsy gesture. He smiled again. He said, 'I have always felt so alone, so very alone, in the potential for humiliation that there seems to be in my life.'

'Humiliation?'

'Humiliation,' he said. 'Solitariness. Isolation. The sense of not really existing because there is no respon-sive sympathy to reassure one to the contrary. Futility. Emptiness. All the things, in short, that you describe.'

'But,' I said eagerly, excited by his reaction, his understanding, 'you have your work! You have your . . .' I faltered a little, and then I said feebly, 'your com-panions.'

He laughed. I wondered if I had said something truly silly, something even sillier than everything that had poured out of me before, like a newborn river leaping out of its mountain cave.

272

'Miss Mackintosh,' he said, '*they* are the trouble. Those companions are often the *source* of all the unhappiness that you describe, that I so recognize. Because I am not attracted to women – not attracted *sexually* to women – I expose myself to precisely the suffering that you have known through having had almost no experience at all. I cannot seem to find companionship in conjunction with my more urgent needs. Where you stand on an empty stage, I stand on one crowded with all the wrong players. We know different forms of precisely the same affliction.'

I did not return to the library until after four. How I must have seemed, flushed with confession and brandy, I cannot imagine, but to my amazement, no-one recoiled from me, and I should hardly have cared if they had. Buoyed up by my astonishing experience, I sailed triumphantly home and watched my father consume a can of chicken soup, two Weetabix and a mashed banana for supper, with something approaching indulgence.

The next morning was another matter, however. The next morning I rose burning with shame, a shame so profound it took all my courage to don my coat and go to work in the library. I could not meet Dawn's eye. I could hardly respond to her kind and clumsy enquiry as to my welfare. I shut myself in my office and wrote Mr Gilchrist a letter. In it, I apologized with dignity for my outburst the previous day. I offered – dignity again – no explanation, but merely hoped he would do me the kindness of acting as if the episode had never happened. I left the note, in a brown envelope with his name typed baldly upon it, above the instruction 'By hand', with the librarian on duty at the desk.

He did not come to the library that day. He did not come the next day. I waited both for him to come, and not to come, and for my composure to return. On the third day – a Thursday – I saw him enter the library and make for his usual corner table. He did not approach the desk. I was in a fever of apprehension and impatience and was about to break every fragile, newly made resolve, when I saw the duty librarian leave the desk with my envelope in her hand, and cross the floor towards him. I waited in my office, my eyes fixed, without comprehension, upon the screen of my computer.

'Absolute nonsense,' said Mr Gilchrist behind me.

I dared not turn.

'I do not accept,' Mr Gilchrist said, 'that we are at the end of anything. We are, rather, at the beginning. I would have telephoned you the next day, had I dared. I have watched you for a long time, in this library, and wondered about you, and now that I have some of the answers to some of my wonderings, I am not about to give up.'

That night, we went together to the cinema. On the following Saturday, he took me to his house, a pleasant small workman's cottage beside the town canal, and cooked me supper.

'I am an accomplished cook,' he said, 'but usually lack an audience.'

The week after, he proposed a concert, a walk in the country and an evening during which he would teach me the rudiments of chess.

'Where are you going?' my father demanded.

'Out.'

'You never go out!'

'I am,' I said, 'now.'

'Who are you going with?'

'A friend.'

'You have no friends!'

'I do,' I said, 'now.'

'You shouldn't be going out,' my father shouted, always now his Parthian shot, 'you should be getting *married*!'

The days of first knowing Douglas lengthened pleasurably into weeks, the weeks unbelievably into months. Occasionally, Douglas would disappear for a few days, on what I privately thought of as his escapades, from which he would return saying, without self-consciousness, how nice it was to be home. These absences did not trouble me. Why should they? Jealousy is only relevant, after all, when it constitutes a threat, and Douglas's absences were no threat to me.

In late spring, almost six months after what I could now see as my great turning point in the Three Feathers, Douglas asked if I could meet him for half an hour after the library closed. He wore an expression of strange solemnity when he made this request, an expression that gave me the uneasy feeling that he had something significant to say, something that might in some way change this new and extraordinary state in which I now found myself. I sat in front of him, at the table I now foolishly regarded as 'ours' in the Three Feathers, and waited for him to tell me that – I had decided upon this – he had now fallen irrevocably in love, and was about to leave our town for London. Or Manchester. Or Hong Kong.

He laid a long envelope on the table.

'Lucy,' he said.

'Yes.'

'Lucy,' he said, 'I have a small speech to make.'

'Of course,' I said politely.

He gave the envelope a little nudge.

'I have been thinking about love, Lucy. I have, since I met you, thought more about the nature of love than I ever have in my life before. And I have come to three conclusions. One is that we are mad to ascribe more value to the more conventional forms of love than to the less conventional. Two, that we are even madder not to seize upon love, so rare and precious is it, wherever we find it. And three, and this is the most important, that there are many, many ways of loving.'

I waited. I looked at the table. I looked, without speculation, at the envelope.

'We have known each other,' Douglas said, 'for almost six months. I would like to celebrate those months, the first months only, I hope, of many. I would like you to come away with me. I would like you to come to Venice.' He gave the envelope another nudge. 'In this envelope, greatly daring, I have put your tickets for Venice.'

I went home that night and opened a can of cream of mushroom soup for my father. He would follow it, I expected, with his current favourite – chocolate-flavoured Ricicles – and a banana. I set the tray on the table beside his chair.

'Daddy,' I said, 'I am going away for a few days.'

'You can't!' my father said. 'You never go anywhere!'

'I am now,' I said. 'I am going to Venice.'

My father looked at his soup. His lip trembled.

'Who will look after me?'

'Alice will,' I said.

'I don't want Alice.'

'I don't expect,' I said, 'that Alice wants you either. But I hope she'll agree, just for a few days.'

My father grasped his soup spoon, and glared at me.

'Who are you going with?'

'A friend.'

'What kind of friend?'

'Just a friend.'

My father raised his spoon at me.

'You shouldn't be going anywhere with a friend!' he shouted. 'You shouldn't be going to Venice! You shouldn't be going anywhere at all! You should be getting *married*!'

I pushed his arm down gently.

'Sorry, Daddy,' I said.

I left him with his soup and his Ricicles and I went up to my bedroom. I went up those stairs – eleven steps, turn, four steps – humming. I went into my bedroom – how small it looked, suddenly, how stale, how redolent of some long journey that was at last over – humming. I turned on the lamps by my dressing table and sat down on the stool.

'There are,' Douglas had said in the Three Feathers less than an hour ago, 'so many, many ways of loving.'

I looked at myself in the mirror, the mirror that had

reflected Lucy Locket in all her stages, the mirror that had reflected the shadow and the echo. But there was someone else there now. I smiled at her. I smiled at Lucy Mackintosh, single woman. Single, *independent* woman.

'*Wrong*, Daddy,' I said.

Salley Vickers was a university teacher of literature and worked for many years as an analytical psychologist. She now writes full-time. She is the author of *Miss Garnet's Angel* and *Instances of the Number Three* (4th Estate). Her latest novel, *Mr Golightly's Holiday* (4th Estate), was published August 2003. She is also writing a non-fiction book on the story of The Book of Common Prayer.

The Dark Wood

'What was it that made him so special?'

When I trained they did not teach us to ask such questions. Instead we were encouraged to enquire closely into the patient's mental state: 'When, exactly, do you hear the voices?' 'Are you aware of anyone else trying to set fire to your property?' 'When did you first begin to experience these suicidal impulses?'

This last was the real killer, if you'll forgive the rather macabre pun. Screw that one up and your patient topped herself. They threw the book at you then – while all the time, of course, covering up to the outside world. But later I learned to do things my own way. Throw out the hook and see what rises to nibble at the bait – then play out the line, a long way if needs be. It takes a while to learn to fish the deep, cold pools of the unconscious; but worth it if you learn to serve those old taskmasters, patience and time.

'He took me to Venice.'

That I understood. It's many years since I first sat in the dim, dark-gold dazzle which is St Mark's and felt my heart dissolve in the liquescent majesty of it. But I have learned, too, that one mustn't impose one's enthusiasms any more than one's prejudices. So I simply asked the question, 'And what is Venice to you?'

She didn't answer immediately but to me that was nothing new. Many times I have sat for the whole fifty minutes and nothing at all has been said – or not openly, for what passes between two people has little enough to do with words. From my chair placed at a discreet angle away – so as not to seem to stare – I watched her. She sat almost opposite me looking at her hands. They were thin-skinned and graceful, the veins the blue of the brocade of the chair, and often she would gaze at them as if seeking some clue to her predicament. On this occasion she got up and went to the window. Each time she did this, maybe once or twice in every three meetings, my heart would beat a stroke faster lest she slip lightly through the window. She was fine-boned but it was not her physique which had made me see her, in my mind's eye, break into a thousand pieces on the paving beneath. She had never suggested she might do such a thing, which was one reason I was sure it must be on her mind. But I never spoke my fear aloud, hoping that reticence would keep her with me more effectively than any lame plea for caution.

'When I was seventeen my father took me to Trieste.' She looked back at me, from her station at the window, to see if the place meant anything to me and I nodded to show it did. I didn't say, 'James Joyce's city,' because that would have been another imposition but I thought it and was not surprised when she followed up with, 'Joyce lived there while he was writing *Ulysses*.'

'Yes,' I said. 'I know.' It seemed this time as if she needed some acknowledgement.

'My father was attending a scientific conference there and I think my mother must have asked him to take me with him. I was getting on her nerves at that time and I expect she needed a break. Anyway, I went off to Trieste to stay in this quite grand hotel with my father and his colleagues, who were mostly there without their wives or families. I spent most days hanging around in my bikini, sunbathing and drinking rum and Coke at the pool bar. I was an embarrassment to my father – he kept trying to get me to go off sightseeing, which, of course, I never wanted to do.'

Again the enquiring look, but this time seeking not so much knowledge as the reassurance that I recognized her adolescent reluctance to do what seemed best to her parents. I nodded again.

'One day his nagging got too much for me and I agreed, pretty unenthusiastically, to go to Venice. My father had explained, in his horribly pompous way, exactly how to get there, what trains et cetera to get and, naturally, I took no notice of him. I was in a state of rebellion against it, hating it for being such a favourite with my father, d'you see?'

I did, and I hoped my eyes let her know so.

'I remember the journey because it was the only time in my life, before or since, that I had my bottom pinched. I could hardly believe it when it happened. The train was very full, and stopped at all these country

283

stations, and at one a man got on, with a vast belly and moustache, just like in a film, and squashed up beside me in the corridor. I didn't know what was happening when I felt this sharp little nip and yelped and he just grinned at me, slightly sheepish, but really rather proud of what he had done.'

'What did you do?' I was genuinely interested.

'Nothing. I was astounded but I was quite tickled, too. Not because I fancied him, or anything (to seventeen-year-old me he seemed utterly grotesque), but for the sheer nerve of it. It cheered me up for the rest of the journey, put me in a better humour about agreeing to the trip at all. But it didn't shift me out of my mood with Venice.'

She paused for a while and looked out of the window. Outside a car backfired and she jumped ever so slightly, and my heart jumped with her; but she settled back down again into her tale.

'I remember getting out at the station. I don't know if you have ever been there but it's not an especially attractive place. And when I got outside and saw the environment was fairly unprepossessing too my heart sort of lifted in defiance because it seemed to me that I was right and all my father's talk about Venice was the usual clichéd stuff I despised. I was determined to dislike it, d'you see?'

Of course I saw and registered this with what I liked to believe was an amused twist of my mouth.

'Well, I walked across the bridge, I forget its name, into the outlying part of Venice and all the time I was saying to myself: See! See! You were right! But I kept walking because I was determined to get to the heart of the place and see the famous St Mark's and jeer at all the trippers I imagined adoring it in a facile sort of way. So I walked nearer and nearer to the Piazza San Marco and all the while I was shutting everything out, because I didn't want to acknowledge what I was seeing, you know, and I turned and twisted about, like someone in a maze, until I arrived at the edge of the Piazza, the far corner from the basilica.

'It was very hot, about noon by the time I got there, and the Piazza was full of that thick, brilliant sunshine you get around midday in Italy. I looked across the space between me and St Mark's and there it was.' She paused again but this time it was as if she was searching for the right words.

'It seemed to me it was a great pearl shimmering in the sun, so extraordinary and so wondrous that without at all knowing what I was doing I fell on my knees, in front of all the trippers I had been so despising. I didn't know then whether it was in praise for the amazing beauty or humility for my equally amazing arrogance but I think now it was both and that then, for the first time, I really understood the meaning of prayer. I don't remember how long I stayed on my knees, or what the people around me thought, but I have the impression that they were all quite understanding and certainly no-one asked me whether I was OK or if I wanted a drink of water or anything, as they would do here.' She unleashed a savage gesture at the London outside my window and I found myself feeling ashamed of my cold-seeming Englishness.

'When I got back inside myself I went into the cathedral and just sat and looked and looked at the gold and the green and the red and the blue, feeling as if I was on the floor of heaven. That's why they made it that way, you know, so's you'd have advance warning of the life to come.'

For a moment her eyes levelled with mine and the Englishness found itself unequal to their unabashed fervour.

'Afterwards I went to all sorts of churches and men kept looking at me and calling me "Madonna". I didn't then know it was a general Italian term for "lady"; I really thought that something divine had happened to me and that they had, somehow, recognized that and were likening me to Our Lady.'

She laughed, but I was pleased to note that she was not disparaging of her naive, younger self. So I risked, 'It sounds as if something pretty miraculous had happened to you.'

'Maybe. It was, as you say, for me a kind of miracle. I don't recall what else I exactly saw because I was in a kind of daze all the rest of the day and when evening came I wanted so much to stay and eat my dinner there and look out over the water at the extraordinary light.'

'And did you?' I really wanted to know.

'No. I was too much still in my father's thrall to cope with that kind of showdown with him. As it was, I was much later back than he had expected and I had to pretend it was because of a cancelled train. I remember I hated having to lie about that; me who lied about everything in those days. I didn't want anything to taint what had happened, you see.'

In her eyes I thought I could see the seventeen-year-old who had compromised her own struggle towards truth.

'And you went back to Venice? You returned?' It had become important to me that she had.

'Not for years. Not until Josh and I went there.'

'And the basilica, was it as remarkable as before?' The almost pun on Mark, the saint who gave his name to the place, was unintended; it's like that in my business – words carry connections we don't immediately perceive.

'Even more remarkable.' Unconsciously she echoed the pun. 'It was tricky having Josh there. Luckily, he mainly wanted to sit about in cafés drinking Amaretto and smoking. I saw masses of other churches by myself. He hated churches. Poor Josh.'

My withers were unwrung; to my mind her first husband sounded a barbarian and this did nothing to disabuse me of the diagnosis.

'And then?'

'Then I went again with Thomas.'

Thomas was her second husband. It was with Thomas – or, I should say, over Thomas – that she had first come to my attention. He had brought her, catatonically depressed, to the hospital where I work as a consultant. She had remained with us a while as an in-patient, principally because I considered it unwise to return her too soon to an environment which seemed to have brought her to us in the first place. But there are limits to a doctor's influence and I had reluctantly returned her to her husband's care on the understanding she would come to the hospital as a day patient. After a while I had offered her an appointment at my rooms in Wimpole Street and she had seemed grateful for the opportunity to escape the hospital waiting room. From that time on we met every Wednesday at 4 p.m. I found I came to look forward to our sessions.

'And how did Thomas like Venice?' I spoke carefully because Thomas was not so straightforward a matter between us as Josh. Josh was the result of trying to please her father; this much we had established. But her reasons for marrying Thomas, her second husband, were more mysterious. I had met him a few times; once when he brought her in to hospital and again when he had visited the ward or collected her from my out-patient clinic. He was a tall, good-looking man with a face I found oddly cruel, although, of course, I never said so. I suspected him of sexual arrogance; to be sure he was far from faithful.

'Oh, he liked it all right. He loves old buildings, you know . . .' Thomas was an architect who lectured at the Institute of Architecture in London.

'So you were happy there with him?'

It was an unfair question because we both knew she had never been happy with Thomas but the subject of her second marriage always made me want to be slightly sadistic to her. She lost some colour at my comment and I felt, as I had done before, a heel.

'Not happy, no.' As usual, tension made her diction overprecise. 'But he was interested and very informative. We did everything together.'

There was an appeal in her tone as though begging me not to find her too pathetic. I relented and tried to redeem myself by saying, 'Thomas would make a knowledgeable partner to see Venice with.' But we both knew this was barren praise.

Silence awhile. We were each of us pensive. I was experiencing remorse for my hidden jibe but wondering afresh what it was in her that made one want to wound her. She was an attractive, accomplished woman, youthful for her years, but it seemed to me somewhere along her life she had betrayed her own gifts. She had intended, she told me, to become an academic, and had drifted into adult education while writing a thesis and got stuck there. She might have amounted to someone considerable and it annoyed me that she had given in to comparative mediocrity.

'Yes, he was knowledgeable but I was always lonely with him.'

Ah, there now was her merit. She might flinch if you lashed her but she took her punishment. Relief made me charitable.

'It must have been a special kind of hell to be lonely in a place that meant so much to you.'

'Yes, yes it was, although I didn't know I was lonely at the time. It was only later . . .' A pause; it seemed she wanted help.

'Later?'

'Later, when I went there again. I went there again – but I have never told anyone.'

There are moments when I understand why I do the job I do, when I know I am about to be vouchsafed some precious and fragile hidden truth and I almost shake in anticipatory awe.

'Would it help to tell me?' The well-worn formula but with its own reassurance: not everything is cured by 'telling'.

'I am telling you, aren't I? That's why I'm here.'

'Forgive me,' I said, meaning it.

'He came to one of my Adult Education classes. I was teaching a course on Dante's *Inferno* and he joined it. I didn't like him at all at first.' She sounded spirited.

'Why not?'

'He seemed opinionated. Overeager to impress. I thought he thought he was God's gift to women, if you want to know, and I wasn't having any of it.'

'And was he?'

'Was he what?'

'Was he God's gift to women, as you put it?'

'Depends what you mean.' She sounded sulky. I had a flash of sympathy for her father long ago in Trieste. Then she recovered her humour. 'No, he wasn't, not in the way you mean, although he'd had more women, it turned out, than you and I have had hot dinners. He told me all about them.'

'It's not an entirely unknown device to make a woman interested.' There was something in my tone I knew I wouldn't like when I had time to reflect upon it.

'Oh, it wasn't at all like that.' She was scornful now. Disapproval is one of the many things prohibited in my profession – if 'disapproval' is what it was . . .

'No, he told me because he told me everything about himself, I mean really everything – not just the things

290

which put him in a good light as people usually do, even in subtle ways. He told me when he fell in love with me.' She brought that out proudly, a clarion.

'And how did you take that?' I wanted to hold on to some reserve but I was strangely excited by her declaration. A kind of thrill was tracing a fingernail down my backbone.

'Very gracelessly at first. I didn't believe him, thought he was out to dupe me, although I had, by this time, grown fond of him. I used to miss him when he didn't attend a class, though he was rarely absent. He was a most diligent student.'

For a second I saw her as she must once have been as a teacher – authoritative, benign. 'What did he do?'

'He was a journalist, quite a well-known one – hadn't gone to university. He seemed to me about the brightest man I had ever met. Far brighter than Thomas.'

'And Thomas,' I said, seizing my opportunity, 'did you tell him about your admirer?'

'Oh no. Thomas would have scoffed and I liked Jack too much for that!' It was the first time she had named the other man and, for the second time, I felt that weird trill down my spine. 'I let him take me out for lunch. It was a fantastic lunch and I couldn't eat a thing.'

She had resumed her objectless stare out of my window and I found myself noticing the way her jacket fitted on her waistline. It was of a fine wool material but the colour didn't suit her.

'He took me home afterwards and on the way he stopped in a lay-by and said, "I don't think you know how much I want to look after you." Just that. I didn't know what to say, and we just drove on with him telling me funny stories and me sitting there like a lemon saying next to nothing and feeling sick as a dog.'

She smoothed the jacket over her waist with her hands although she couldn't have seen me staring at it; it's like that with some patients.

'Why sick?' I asked; I didn't like the dog reference – it made me think of spaniels.

'Because of Thomas. I loved Thomas, or believed I did.' It was the first I had heard of any doubt on the matter of her love for Thomas and I felt a rush of optimism. This Jack sounded like a good thing.

'Anyway, I went on seeing him and not telling Thomas. We didn't sleep together, in case you're wondering, and being a shrink you will be, but not because either of us didn't want it. I couldn't because of Thomas, d'you see?'

'I think I see.'

'We drifted into a kind of agreement. I would sort things out with Thomas and we'd run away together. I wasn't quite myself in those days.' She laughed. 'I suppose that must sound mad to you. I'm hardly "myself" now.'

'At this moment I would guess you are more like yourself than you've been since I've known you,' was my answer to that.

'Well, I got into more and more of a state, about the secrecy, you know. One day I lost it. I said if he was going to hold me to leaving Thomas and running away with him I couldn't see him any more. The guilt was too much for me.'

'And how did he take that?'

'Very badly. I've never seen anyone so upset. I was terrified because I felt I had done him some monstrous wrong and I could hardly bear it because, well, because I loved him too, although I didn't know then how much.'

'And . . . ?'

'After a bit he calmed down. He rang me and asked me to come to supper at his flat. And when I got there, in a state of high anxiety, he said, "Look, I love you too much not to be in your life so I will be in your life in whatever way you'll have me. But there is just one more thing I would like you to do for me. I'd like you to come with me to Venice." You know, I'd never even mentioned Venice to him,' she said by way of explanation.

And, to me, it was explanation enough. For her, so hidden, so hard to read, to have a man pluck this secret from her must have touched some dangerous trigger, enough to shatter the closest marriage ties. I glanced at my watch and saw it was time. One of those occasions when one longs to send professional etiquette packing. But my next patient was an obsessional who I knew from experience would already be waiting agitatedly below in the waiting room. Even so, I lingered, allowing time to seep beyond the usual limit.

'Would you like me to give you a space tomorrow?'

She didn't even thank me but simply assented and left the room without a backward look.

I was awaiting her arrival, avidly, next day but she didn't show up and I didn't see her until the following week when she arrived, without comment, at her usual time. I never asked her why she did not keep our extra appointment but although I never billed her for it she included the missed hour in her cheque when she settled the monthly bill. Afterwards, I felt she was paying me in compensation for my disappointment.

'So did you go to Venice with him?' Training not withstanding, I couldn't suppress my eagerness to find out.

'Oh yes, I went to Venice with him.' There was a kind of desperation in her voice which made me catch my breath as if at my own pain. 'We stayed a fortnight. It was, quite simply, doctor' – she had never before given me my title – 'the most extraordinary fortnight of my life. He took a small apartment for us by the bust of Dante on the walls of the Arsenale, and the lions which stand outside and guard it. He pretended he had set them there to guard me. I became very attached to one of those lions. We walked everywhere and everywhere we walked he talked to me all the time, all the time, not rubbish, you understand, but proper conversation. He had a great gift for nonsense – I can't explain it . . .'

She was angry today. I tried tact.

'This must be difficult for you. Take your time.'

Mistake.

'Of course it's difficult – I loved him, don't you see – I loved him passionately, passionately!' She almost accused me.

'Where is he now?'

That stopped her. Be direct, is my advice to my

294

training students. Avoid the bogus. Don't try to be kind. But this is easier said than done.

'I don't know.'

Of course I knew she didn't. I had known since the last session all I needed to know about what was wrong with this woman. I knew now what had puzzled and vexed me, why she allowed her husband to philander with other women till her collapsing self-esteem reached breaking point. I knew now she had done the one thing for which, I suspect, we are never forgiven – the sin against the Holy Ghost: she had looked true love in the face and then turned her back on it. There exists no cure in the psychiatric textbooks for that. My blood ran cold for the pity and the terror of it.

She finished the tale for me over the next few sessions. How she had returned from Venice and had gone home to deliver the news to her husband. Quite what had assailed her lion-hearted resolution between the journey from her beloved St Mark's to the London suburb where she and Thomas lived I could not get her to pin down. Nor could I, in so dire a matter, pin it for her. We all have our own crosses on which we nail ourselves.

Since then I have wondered if, perhaps, a sudden access of happiness is too much for those who have been starved of it, who may, like the victims of torture or prisoners of war, need to be fed on small portions of unfamiliar sustenance lest the digestion become overwhelmed and fail. I knew that what I felt for her could not be adequately defined by compassion. I felt for her, and for her Venice lover, the affront to fate which is one effect of tragedy: a noble promise made void.

Not long after concluding her tale she stopped coming to see me altogether. I was not much surprised but that did not prevent my wishing to see some more of her. I even conceived a half-plan that I might run away with her myself – I had no ties, having said goodbye to my only wife long since. But I knew too much about her and, besides, I felt too much for the wrong done to her lost beloved.

She told me that after her second dereliction he had resigned his position on a good London newspaper and gone suddenly abroad. I pictured him roaming the world, seeking solace with other women but never again trusting to any other human being. I quite hated Thomas, which was paltry of me, for he was merely the victim of his own limitations. We all are, in the end.

I did hear once more from my former patient. It was some years after I last saw her when I had almost given up my practice. I came into work one fine January morning to find a card postmarked *Venezia*. On it was a picture which stirred a memory but which I could not immediately place. The inscription read 'Arsenale, Venice', and on it I could make out two of the three lions which, she had told me, all that time ago, guard the old naval fortification by the bronze bust of the exiled poet who wrote the *Divine Comedy*.

I knew, already, who it was from, and I looked with some eagerness at the writing on the back:

Ne mezzo del cammin di nostra vita
mi reitrovai per una selva oscura
che la diritta via era smarrita.

'In the midway of my life I came to myself in a dark wood where the straight way was lost to me . . .'

The opening lines of Dante's 'Inferno'. But I never heard if the lost soul that was my patient recovered her Paradise.

Jane Yardley was brought up in an Essex village and went to university in London, where she has lived ever since. She has a Ph.D from Charing Cross Hospital Medical School and works on medical projects around the globe. Much of her life is therefore spent on aeroplanes and in hotel rooms, and this prompted her to get to work on her first novel, *Painting Ruby Tuesday*. Her second novel, *Rainy Day Women*, is published in June 2004. Both are published by Doubleday and Black Swan. Jane has synaesthesia, a condition that mixes the senses – so that she has, for example, the gift of hearing music and seeing numbers in colour.

Hot House

'It says here . . .' Richard peered against the sun to check what it said here. The Falcon of the Plantagenets, all hooky beak and knuckled claws, glared threateningly back at him from under mad eyebrows. 'It says Edward the Third used it as a badge.'

Even the lion and the unicorn managed to be pigeon-chested, he thought to himself, like someone had been at them with a bicycle pump. And that heraldic bull looked as though he'd been brained and was about to topple backwards off his Portland stone pedestal to shatter across the tarmac.

'Badge?' repeated Margaret.

'That's what it says. So did his mum sew it on his blazer, or what?'

Margaret had had the foresight to leave her own blazer in the coach, but Richard hadn't, and his was flagging, she now made the effort to notice. The boys would have used the word 'knackered' – his jacket was crinkled and kinked like a cauliflower leaf. Earlier today, Margaret had endured from her friend Lynn a diatribe, straight out of the 'cloud cuckoo land' school of criticism, about failing to spot what was under her nose. She realized now that the only thing she had previously spotted about Richard Elphick was that in exams he came top more often than she did. Now, pressed, she thought she remembered that he had free school dinners. It was June 1967, and they were twelve.

'And *this* one,' she read when they reached the other end of the line-up, '"The Yale of Beaufort", Heaven preserve us, could apparently swivel both horns independently. I've heard everything now,' she added, which made a total of two of her father's pet expressions in one short declaration.

'It says somebody donated all ten of them to the Queen,' said Richard.

'And the Queen re-donated them here, pronto.'

'Well, you would do, wouldn't you?'

'And the donor kept himself anonymous,' finished Margaret.

'Well, you would do, wouldn't you?' said Richard again.

They were together because earlier in the day they had both, though independently, melted away from the school party, a patrol from which had no doubt been drag-netting Kew Gardens ever since. Pity that the uniform was so conspicuous, particularly Margaret's dress in blazing lime like a traffic light. Against its visual violence her face looked sallow and her sun-streaked hair was traduced to the appearance of straw up at the riding school – muddy, rained on and peed on.

* * *

Midday. Picnickers sprawled across the grass in a spangle of kipper ties and twinkling ring-zips. Their transistor radios broadcast news bulletins between plays of 'A Whiter Shade of Pale' and tracks from the Beatles' *Sergeant Pepper* album. Then more bulletins, more Beatles, and 'A Whiter Shade of Pale' again. All day. All night.

'I mean, they're just garden gnomes, aren't they?' said Margaret, examining the lolling tongue of the Scottish unicorn.

Richard was thinking about the Plantagenets. Those were the days; no nuclear capability, no mutually assured destruction. His heavy-hearted imagination pictured comic-strip yokels ploughing this alluvial soil unclouded by the distinct possibility that the world would have wiped itself out by next Wednesday.

'Hey, I've found a dead ringer for Mr Shawcross!' he said. 'Same squint, same dodgy smile like he's plugged himself into the mains. What do you think of this war, then?' He directed his non sequitur at a nearby griffin. The question echoed a while before Margaret caught on and responded.

'You mean, who do I want to win?'

No, that wasn't what he meant. Win, lose or draw, it was all the same to Richard; he was fishing for entirely different information. 'Yeah,' he said.

But Margaret had no idea whether Richard thought it was Egypt's fault or Israel's, and she didn't want to start an auxiliary war. 'I just hope not many people die.'

'Yeah,' said Richard again. 'Only, my dad says . . . He says it's World War III round the corner. Mankind on the brink,' he added in self-conscious parody. Actually, it wasn't even a parody, it was *precisely* what his father had said on Saturday night when they'd got home from Granddad's, though he'd said it to the telly. It was the same phrase he'd used when Richard was seven and American spy planes detected missiles on Cuba. 'That what *your* dad says?' he probed.

'Oh, yes,' said Margaret, not to be outdone, though her father was relentlessly cheerful these days and hadn't so much as mentioned the Middle East since his limerick about camels. 'My father's most awfully worried.'

'Yeah.' Richard's spirits trickled downwards like mud in a drain, and he wished he hadn't asked. On the coach this morning, very adult and off-hand, he had broached the subject with one of the teachers, who told Richard not to be so silly – the conflict was local and confined to the armed forces; it wouldn't involve significant civilian casualties even over there, let alone wipe out the human race. A second, confirmatory comment would have relieved Richard no end. But apparently Margaret Lindsay's father was worried sick.

There wasn't a lot more mileage to be had from the Queen's Beasts, so the pair of them wandered up the steps and started a long circuit of the Palm House. They had agreed earlier to keep away from any space with an open vista, and had spent the past couple of hours skulking around Latin trees, including a couple of weeping beeches big enough to move in with the furniture. But it was lunchtime now, and the rest of the first years would be herded into the café, queuing for sandwiches and pop; no teacher was going to risk leaving that rabble short-staffed in order to search for a mere two of them.

'D'you ever think,' Richard asked her, 'about what it was like back then? Plantagenets, I mean. Tudors. All them lot.'

'I think they must have been really smelly and itchy, actually,' Magaret told him. 'They had bugs and lice.'

'Yeah,' said Richard.

'There weren't proper lavatories, even. Ladies in crinolines used to slip out into the garden saying they were going to pluck a rose, and then do it behind one of the trees!'

'Yeah,' said Richard, who suspected that crinolines were a bit later, and that not everybody's garden had had trees. 'No nuclear wars, though,' he pointed out. 'Only piddly battles.'

'But they had the Black Death,' Margaret reminded him. 'Bubonic plague. And smallpox.'

'Yeah.'

'So their faces were all pus and scars. And when the Tudors arrived, so did syphilis.'

'Yeah?'

'Henry the Eighth got it and spread it about. And all the sailors had it and slept with everybody so *they* got it. And people who didn't catch it inherited it. So basically, they *all* had it.'

'Yeah,' said Richard, thinking that all that facial pus probably protected a few of them. But he wasn't terribly interested in syphilis, which was not among the immediate threats to his welfare. Being on the edge of

London now that the war had actually started was terrible to Richard. Although it was a defining feature of the international situation that nowhere was safe, at least Basildon was unlikely to be the *direct* target of an intercontinental ballistic missile; and Richard had decided on Sunday night, over a bleak tea with the BBC's most funereal newsreaders, that if his choice of scenarios was either to watch a mushroom cloud billow in terrifying symmetry from beyond Ilford or to see nothing because he was underneath it and already dead, he would go for the former. Below them in the rose garden, a transistor tuned to Radio London was playing 'A Whiter Shade of Pale', followed, owing to some kind of mix-up, by Petula Clark. When she faded, Big L promised on-the-hour news. Enough was enough.

'Let's go inside,' Richard decided, striding towards the lofty, bulbous atria of the Palm House. Margaret caught the note of urgency.

'Why? Have you seen a teacher?'

'Yeah,' said Richard.

Green heat – that was their first impression. Amid the Victorian fancywork of soaring white cast-iron, in the milky light filtered through glass opalescent with dirty steam, pots of architectural palms, floppy ferns and piping bamboos slowly sweated and dripped. Chandeliers of green baby-fists turned out to be bananas. Furiously coloured fruits dangled over notices warning that they blistered and burned. Everywhere were voices and feet.

'This is super, isn't it?' said Margaret. 'Exotic.'

'Yeah,' agreed Richard. The humid vegetable smell reminded him of the greenhouse in his granddad's back yard. They had trekked up there last week by a series of jolting buses and trains for the Whitsun holiday. There was a girl, Suzanne; Richard had sat with her on the kitchen step Tuesday evening and listened to Radio Caroline play the whole of *Sergeant Pepper* out of a neighbour's window. Today, this was like a memory from early childhood, magical and remote. He tried to imagine Suzanne in the fizzing rubble of a nuclear holocaust but his feelings for her didn't transcend this weight of worry. Instead he wondered about the Palm House when the bomb went off – would it shatter or would it vaporize? Behind a giant palm, someone dropped their picnic basket onto the metal grating and Richard jumped a foot in the air.

'*Ylang ylang.*' Margaret had turned tactfully away and was reading one of the plants at random. '*Cananga odorata. The perfume tree.*'

'Eelang eelang?' repeated Richard, recovering. 'Sounds like backing vocals for a Phil Spector number.'

'*Its jasmine-like oil has medicinal properties,*' read Margaret. 'Probably means it's an aphrodisiac,' she scoffed.

'Yeah, probably,' said Richard, with a dim sense of yet another loss from dying so young. 'Fancy some lunch?' he asked. 'I've brought my own sandwiches, and my mum always packs for an army.'

'Oh,' said Margaret. If Richard's family was poor, and it did seem, on reflection, that they must be, it wouldn't be right to gobble his sandwiches. For all Margaret knew, there was a ravenous pack of siblings at home waiting to feed off the leftovers.

'I'll only chuck 'em if you don't,' continued Richard, helpfully.

'Then yes, please.' She couldn't say she was actually hungry; there was a dull nausea beneath the wretchedness that had driven Margaret away from her classmates. But logic suggested that this hole in her stomach would feel better if it were filled.

They perched on a stone ledge in the marbled shade of a lot of cycads – survivors from the Jurassic period; dinosaur trees. Richard tugged from his regulation satchel a lumpy cube of greaseproof paper and a bottle of pop.

'Once we've shifted this lot' – the paper crackled in his hands – 'I'll have room to stuff my blazer back in. I should've done like you and dumped it in the coach.'

'If I'd realized, I could have carried it around in *my* bag,' Margaret told him. Hers was new and ultra-fashionable, a glossy carrier bag decorated with one huge sunflower. Girls in the sixth form had them. Lynn had one. But Margaret wouldn't think of Lynn. Her eyes filled.

'*You're* worried and all, aren't you?' Richard asked gently, with his mouth full.

Margaret helped herself to a sandwich. Tendrils of grated cheese sprouted extravagantly from the sides and showered her frock. She never got these at home. Worried? Of course, it was this war! *That's* what was the matter with him. Lynn's critical brickbats thudded in her head. Well, even Margaret hadn't failed to spot

Richard's simmering misery; it was exactly this that had soothed her and kept her with him all morning. Yet she hadn't managed to put two and two together when he'd started harping on about nuclear war. They had trundled through the Royal Botanic Gardens side by side, these two with their grown-up names and children's powerlessness, cracking jokes, the cool, derogatory quips glittering above their respective pre-occupations, which they hauled behind them like yoked oxen.

'Yes,' she answered him now, 'I'm worried to death, Richard,' the words themselves being true, isolated from the context.

'D'you remember Cuba?' he asked. 'You know – the Cuban Missile football match, October 1962. Kennedy versus Khrushchev, away game. Scheduled for a replay with new managers,' he added, flogging the metaphor.

'I *know* about it but I don't remember. We were only little, weren't we? My father's very protective. He would keep anything like that from upsetting me.' Margaret said it without thinking; her own words now fired themselves into the flesh of her mind, barbed.

Protective, thought Richard. A protective father who kept his worries from upsetting the children. Now there was a thought.

'It's probably because I don't have a mother,' continued Margaret. 'She's dead.'

Richard mumbled embarrassment into his Cheddar.

'It's all right, I don't miss her, I never knew her. She died having me. We've never needed a mother!' Margaret said forcefully.

'I'd miss my mum,' said Richard. 'Does your dad work?'

'He's an architect.'

'That's nice. My dad used to have a job but then he got this bad heart.'

'Oh.'

'Mum does a bit of cleaning sometimes, but it's difficult with all the kids. I'm the oldest of six.'

'Are your parents Roman Catholic, then?' It had come up in Biology.

'No, just accident prone,' said Richard. 'Another cheese and pickle, or Marmite?'

But neither of them had any appetite for more food, now the initial pangs were dulled.

'Fancy some pop?'

'Yes. Thanks.'

'And my mum had triplets. It was in the papers.'

'Oh, how sweet!'

Margaret finished drinking and they sat in silence amid all the pungent pampered vegetation, the peeling vaulted arches. Above them, steam hissed suddenly from elderly pipes, in pumped jets. Rivulets trickled over the algae and rust of the ribbed roof and plopped onto the flagstones; shoes and voices textured the green air.

'Have you got brothers and sisters? I mean, before your mum . . . ?'

'No, only me and Daddy, and our housekeeper Gwyneth.'

'Do you . . . ?' Another fractured enquiry.

'Carry on if you want to,' said Margaret, guessing that

this was something else about nuclear attack. She wouldn't shy from any discussion of the end of the world; she'd welcome it.

'Do you think about them being . . . ? You know. Killed. If.'

'Yes.' She improvised so that he wouldn't be alone. 'My head is haunted by terrible images of broken, dismembered bodies scattered across the orchard. Impaled by falling masonry.'

'Orchard,' repeated Richard, who lived in a council house and until he was seven had lived in a caravan.

'And shards of glass,' added Margaret. 'Do you want to give me your blazer? In my carrier bag it won't get so crumpled.'

Richard thought for a moment and acquiesced, vaguely registering the memory of a hundred crumpled-blazer rows with his mum. Margaret swept from her skirt the yellow worm-casts of fallen cheese, and carefully folded his tormented jacket into her most fashionable of accessories. As she did so, the thought hit her like a deep, hard punch just how unlikely it was that her father had chosen this present himself. He wouldn't know that girls wanted flowery carrier bags, and neither would the elderly Gywneth. Only a girly sort of woman would know. A Jeanette sort of woman. It was another terrible smidgen of evidence to support Lynn's devastating assertion. At the thought of her father and this Jeanette conspiring about little presents for her, misery blotted out the sounds and scent of the Palm House. Margaret wished Richard's bomb would go off and kill the lot of them.

She fiddled with the bag, wearing an expression weighty with nonchalance. Richard recognized and respected her distress; he waited for Margaret to straighten up before saying, 'I couldn't half do with a cigarette. Do you ever?'

'Every week at riding school,' she told him surprisingly. 'But no marijuana, and I don't drop acid or anything.'

Drop acid! thought Richard, scandalized.

But I could do with some now, decided Margaret, remembering the LSD tales of older girls. Flight from reality sounded good to her. 'Know what I hate most?' she said.

'What?'

'Everyone else being happy. No, not *happy*,' she amended. 'Just not bothered. I mean, here's me feeling like . . . like . . .'

'Like shit.'

Margaret conceded the point. 'And people all around just getting on with what they're doing.'

'Yeah.'

Richard, who was introduced to this phenomenon back in his caravan days, in fact, October 1962, had recently seen it written down in a poem in their school library: suffering takes place 'while someone else is eating or opening a window or just walking dully along.' Accustomed only to poetry that was either frilly or muscular, he had been astounded that anybody considered this a fit subject to write about.

*   *   *

After a while they moved on. The temperature having risen further with the sun, the atmosphere had now been ratcheted up to the level of febrile jungle. Margaret and Richard wandered idly among the massed pots: thick Tarzan ropes and sugar cane, snaking creepers and serpentine hoses. *Elaphoglossum. Psychotria ankasensis. Chamaedorea metallica.* The spicy tang of wet earth; small, running children like twittering, brilliantly coloured birds.

'Let's go up, shall we?'

'Yeah.'

They climbed the twisting staircase and bounced along the mezzanine walkway with its soupy air and splintered light.

'Know what those are called?'

'Those what?' asked Richard.

'Decorations.' With an index finger Margaret traced the outline of the white ironwork in front of them. 'That's acanthus, and that's lotus. They're classical motifs used a lot in architecture.'

'Right,' said Richard. He had been thinking of the Palm House as engineering rather than architecture. Clever how such thin struts held all that glass; the weight must be directed outwards, like with buttresses. 'Does your dad teach you a lot, then?'

'It doesn't feel like teaching,' she said. 'We just go to places together. Historic houses. Abroad, too. We've driven through Italy.'

And until now this family life had been so routine as hardly to be worth talking about. Until Lynn had started on at her, in the coach: 'Of *course*

Jeanette's his girlfriend, you spastic!'

'Jeanette's just a *friend* friend!' Margaret had kept objecting, shocked and frightened.

'Pull the other one, Maggie! Comes to your house for dinner, tags along when you go shopping, evenings they go up to London.' Lynn had piled up her indictment in gloating tones of *schadenfreude*. So what? her sneer implied. Lynn's own security had been rocked last year when her mother had an affair with their neighbour. 'You can't expect the man to live alone for ever.'

'He doesn't live alone!' Margaret had shouted, and been silenced by a teacher.

'And I bet they *do it*, too. I bet you anything!'

Jeanette did come to dinner sometimes, yes, on several occasions had driven up in her little sports car and joined them for a meal cooked and served by Gwyneth. She was really young, decided Margaret with distaste; big-eyed and miniskirted, and she talked to Margaret about flower power. Other images tumbled across Margaret's inner vision: her father's buoyancy; quiet phone calls; more evenings out than usual while Gwyneth babysat. An unusually edgy and irascible Gwyneth, Margaret recognized with terrified hindsight. Had Daddy told her . . . ? Was her place about to be taken by . . . ?

Until now, jealousy had meant nothing more to Margaret than the trivial rivalries of the playground. There was no precedent in her life for this drenching black wash of humiliation, this wringing of her viscera. She wanted to howl like a dog under the wheels of a car.

Forced now to think of her father as a *man* with a *girlfriend*, she saw someone slim and strong and quick. A forehead high beneath receding hair; dark eyes; a sardonic humour.

'If only the Ancients had built shopping centres,' he would say across the plans of yet another one, 'they could have used up all that sand for concrete and solved their desert problem!'

'There was a young man from Madrid . . .' he would begin. Or Madras. Or Mustique. Or Milan. Or Bognor. 'If the town is called Bognor Regis because George the Fifth went there for his health, why didn't they rename it when he died?'

Yet on *this* subject – not one jocular word. Margaret's mind seethed with imagined secrets. 'Let's keep it from her, Jeanette, darling, until we have to.' 'Yes, you're right, darling.' 'I think so, darling.'

'I need to go to the lavatory!' Margaret announced to Richard in far too loud a voice. 'I've got my map. See you back here!'

She clattered, panic-stricken, down the iron staircase in a whirl of livid lime. Richard watched her frock flash along the aisle below, another exoticism among the bird-of-paradise plants and passion flowers. He thought again of Suzanne. She had not only listened to the Beatles with him; she had also agreed to take her knickers off.

Monday. Breakfast. 'It's started!' his father had shouted across the house. 'Israel's launched a pre-emptive strike on Nasser's airforce. Arab tanks are rolling as I speak – what did I tell you?'

'Now then, Ron,' Richard's mother had shouted back in routine remonstrance from above a fuming nappy, 'you'll only make yourself bad!'

'Just how is Eshkol going to fight a war on four fronts? Answer me that! There's 465,000 troops and nearly 3,000 tanks – and that's just *Egypt*! That's not even Jordan and Syria!'

'Ron!'

'And how's Kosygin going to take this humiliation? Those planes and tanks are Russian! So what does America do? Talks about sending an *armada*! Armageddon, more like! Did you hear me?'

'Half Basildon heard you, Ron Elphick!' his mother had yelled. 'You know what the doctors said!'

Richard had just taken a mouthful of bacon and eggs; he'd chewed and chewed but couldn't swallow. He'd waited for his sister to come out of the toilet and then spat it into the bowl. That was yesterday. Today he'd had no breakfast at all, hiding in his bedroom until the last minute and running out of the house shouting 'I'll have a sandwich on the coach!' as he scooted past his mother, who was battling at the cooker in a sea of wriggling toddlers.

Margaret wended her way back from Brentford Gate. Her eyes, raking the surroundings with a terror that had prompted a couple of mothers to look behind them, hadn't spotted any teachers. But what would happen when eventually she and Richard were forced to give themselves up in order to go home on the coach? Would their delinquency be reported to her father?

316

Margaret's imagination clicked through images like a kaleidoscope, half of them variants on a haughty, grown-up Margaret announcing that since *he* clearly deemed it all right to do what *he* liked without reference to *her*, then *she* had carte blanche to do likewise, the other half playing out the disorganized tantrums of a thwarted two-year-old.

Entering the Palm House again by the north door, Margaret shambled between teak tubs and savagely serrated fronds. The twittering children had gone, and the place felt sluggish, like a vast becalmed tank. Looking up, she found Richard exactly where she'd left him, leaning on the iron balustrade. She waved but he didn't; he wasn't looking. Margaret was about to turn back to the spiral stairs *when she noticed something* – it blazed through her own pain like a torch. Richard couldn't see her because he couldn't see anything; the boy stared sightless across Decimus Burton's triumphant dome, the vivid canopy, the giant attalea palm, looking with unutterable dread beyond every living thing to the blood-boltered permafrost of a nuclear winter. As Margaret watched, the pearly glass dribbled its brew into Richard's hair. He flinched, a gesture as unthinking as the protective flexing of a threatened mollusc. His intelligence had congealed.

Could he be right? wondered Margaret. Certainly the radio and television had been chanting the same inescapable litany for days: Golan Heights, Gaza, Sinai, Suez, Nasser, Moshe Dayan, Security Council, Kosygin, Johnson, *crisis, troops, Tanks*, MOBILIZATION, **AIR STRIKE! WAR!** So could Richard be right that this conflict would catapult them headlong into World War III?

Margaret decided that she didn't believe it. Otherwise, surely her own father wouldn't be quite so bloody bouncy, Jeanette or no Jeanette. For some time now she had understood why her eighth birthday party was marred by so much crying and hiding – her friends' responses to pasty-faced grown-ups snapping at everyone and whispering together, on 27 October 1962. No, Richard's father was probably just enjoying a rant; although her own world had been thrown off its axis, it wasn't about to be incinerated. Life would go on.

Margaret looked up again at the blind eyes of her classmate, as good as dead amid all that vitality, the vigorous, burgeoning, green-bud-thrusting proliferation, the sheer dogged, inveterate, enduring, millennia-resistant survival. She took a moment to get her story straight, and then trotted up the steps to tell Richard that she'd just heard people talking, a woman who said her brother was in Mr Wilson's government, and the world leaders secretly believed that the worst of the danger was over.